"When we get to [...] to let me know if [...] right or feel right[...]"

Her gut was telling her that it had been a mistake to think that she could be with Royce 24/7 and not relive the memories of that summer. The best summer of her life.

"Okay," Jules said.

He opened the door, checked the hallway, then motioned for her to come. At the stairway entrance, he quietly said that he'd go first.

He's just being careful, she told herself. *No need to start seeing shadows in the corners.*

They got to the third floor and he smiled at her reassuringly, as if he'd sensed her nervousness. "So far so good."

She swallowed hard. "Really good."

Royce reached out his hand, wrapped it gently around her arm. His skin was very warm and she could feel the transfer of heat. "It's going to be fine," he said. "I will not let anything happen to you."

* * *

Don't miss the next romance in Beverly Long's exciting new miniseries, Wingman Security!

* * *

If you're on Twitter, tell us what you think of Harlequin Romantic Suspense! #harlequinromsuspense

Dear Reader,

While I've been a part of the Harlequin family for many years, this is my first Romantic Suspense. I'm excited to be joining all the very talented Romantic Suspense authors that I have enjoyed reading for so many years.

Bodyguard Reunion is book one in the four-book Wingman Security series. Wingman Security is an elite security firm, specializing in both personal and property security. The four partners are all former air force. Wingman Security is headquartered in Vegas, and that's the setting for the first book.

In *Bodyguard Reunion*, Royce Morgan unexpectedly has the opportunity to provide personal security for pharmaceutical CEO Juliana Cambridge, who is visiting Vegas on business. It should be a routine job. But given that Jules is the woman who broke his heart eight years earlier when she married another, it's anything but routine. Especially when it becomes clear that someone is trying to kill her.

JC, as she's known in the corporate world, can't run from her troubles or from Royce. She needs to be in Vegas for a reason that has nothing to do with business and everything to do with unraveling secrets that her mother took to her grave more than fifteen years earlier. Secrets that could destroy her father, a man Royce Morgan has good reason to hate.

I love reunion stories, love the idea that sometimes you really can have a second chance, a do over if you will, to beat the odds and finally get that happy ending with the one you loved and lost. I'm hoping that you'll be rooting for Royce and Jules!

All my best,

Beverly

BODYGUARD
REUNION

Beverly Long

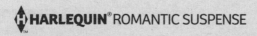
HARLEQUIN® ROMANTIC SUSPENSE

Recycling programs
for this product may
not exist in your area.

ISBN-13: 978-0-373-40219-9

Bodyguard Reunion

Copyright © 2017 by Beverly R. Long

Printed in U.S.A.

Beverly Long enjoys the opportunity to write her own stories. She has both a bachelor's and a master's degree in business and more than twenty years of experience as a human resources director. She considers her books to be a great success if they compel the reader to stay up way past their bedtime. Beverly loves to hear from readers. Visit beverlylong.com, or like her at Facebook.com/beverlylong.romance.

Books by Beverly Long

Harlequin Romantic Suspense

Wingman Security
Bodyguard Reunion

Harlequin Intrigue

Return to Ravesville
Hidden Witness
Agent Bride
Urgent Pursuit
Deep Secrets

The Men from Crow Hollow
Hunted
Stalked
Trapped

The Detectives
Deadly Force
Secure Location

Visit the Author Profile page at Harlequin.com for more titles.

To all the readers that have sustained my career. Twenty years and twenty-plus books later, I want you to know that it's been a privilege and a joy to write stories for you.

Chapter 1

Royce Morgan stood under the hot water and let his tired muscles simply enjoy. He'd spent the last six days providing security for people who had too much money and too few manners, on a mountain in Wyoming, wearing skis, with daydreams of a warm fire and bourbon the only thing keeping him sane.

He was grateful to be back in Vegas where a brutal February day was forty-five degrees.

He dumped some shampoo in his hand, scrubbed his very short hair and stuck his head under the spray to wash it out. When he was done, he realized his cell phone was ringing. Reluctantly he shut off the shower, shoved the sliding door open, and grabbed for a towel and the phone in one swipe.

"I am not late," he answered, looking at the number.

"Not yet," Trey said.

His business partner believed that arriving any later

than an hour early was the height of slothfulness. "Listen," Royce said. "I almost froze my ass off out there."

"Lose any fingers or other important appendages?" Trey asked.

Royce looked down at his naked self. "Everything seems to be attached."

"Good to know. Be an interesting worker's comp claim."

"Don't I know it." In addition to a full caseload, Royce handled the finance and risk management for Wingman Security. Made sure everybody got paid, that the bills didn't stack up and that their assets were protected.

He put the phone on speaker and set it down so that he could dry himself off.

"Look," Trey said, "we got an inquiry on the voice mail. Some guy who needs protection for a company executive. He wants a callback first thing this morning."

Royce wasn't usually responsible for contracting new business. That was Rico's domain, but since Rico and Seth, the third and fourth men of the four-man partnership, were currently enjoying themselves on a beach in Mexico, that left him and Trey to pinch hit. Trey had evidently decided it was Royce's turn at bat. "What's the number?"

Trey rattled it off and Royce used his finger to write it on the fogged-up mirror. "Got it."

"Remember that I'm tied up with the Anderson project for another two weeks," Trey said.

"Understood," Royce said. Trey was part of a team watching the private airfield of Billy-Bob Anderson, an eccentric billionaire from Maine who spent the winter in Vegas. He flew his own experimental aircraft and worried incessantly that everyone from Russia to Elvis's ghost was intent upon copying his design. His plane was under twenty-four-hour guard.

That was probably the only reason that Trey hadn't taken the call himself. "I'll let you know once I talk to the guy." He clicked off and took a second to enter the number into his phone.

Wingman didn't take every job that came their way. It was probably what had allowed them in four years to build a very successful niche security business. However, executive protection was in their wheelhouse, so Royce was hopeful.

He walked naked into his kitchen and poured a cup of freshly made coffee that he'd had the good sense to start before getting in the shower. He stood at the counter, sipping gratefully.

Then he pushed Send on his phone and listened to it ring. He figured it was just about to go to voice mail when it was answered. "Hello," a man said.

"This is Royce Morgan. I'm returning the message you left at Wingman Security."

"Oh, thank God," the man said.

Whatever the issue, this guy was rattled. Royce straightened up and set down his coffee cup. "How can I help you?" he asked.

"I'm Barry Wood, the chairman of the board of Miatroth. We're a pharmaceutical firm and the CEO of our company needs security."

Drug companies. Lots of people hated them. Thought they were screwing the consumer with inflated prices. "Where are you located?" Royce asked. They primarily worked in the western portion of the United States.

"New York City," the man said.

Royce felt a pang in his middle. He took a quick sip of coffee. He hadn't set foot east of the Mississippi River for over eight years. He didn't even like to fly over the Atlantic coast. Too many memories. Too many regrets.

"I'm not sure why you've contacted Wingman Security," Royce said. "We're located in Vegas."

"Our CEO is attending a conference there."

"When?"

"Right now. And last night, there was some trouble. Can you meet us at the Periwinkle Hotel?"

Swanky place that stood out in a world of lavishness. "I can be there in a half hour."

"Excellent. Suite 1402. We'll be expecting you."

Royce finished getting dressed, pulling on dark slacks, a blue button-down long-sleeved shirt and a sport coat. Then it was into his BMW. Reluctantly, he kept the top up, hoping that by noon it would be plenty warm enough to drive around with it down.

The Periwinkle was a mammoth structure of stone and glass with a few thousand tons of iron thrown in. At least forty stories, with a corner location, it had a presence on the Vegas Strip. They had staff parking cars, opening doors, offering water and dark chocolate, and pushing elevator buttons. That was all before he reached the main lobby on the third floor. Once there, he switched elevators and pushed the button for the fourteenth floor.

The carpet was thick and quiet as he walked down the hall. He rapped on the door and waited. And waited. He knocked again. He pulled his phone, looked at his recently called numbers and was just about to press Send when the door swung open.

A thin man, maybe early sixties, stood on the other side. He wore a dark suit, and with his pasty complexion, almost screamed "Undertaker." He was wringing his hands.

"Mr. Wood?" Royce asked. "I'm Royce Morgan."

"Thank you for coming," the man said.

"I thought for a minute that you might have changed your mind when the door didn't get answered."

"I...I was talking with JC," Barry Wood said. "To be perfectly honest, she's being a good sport about this but I'm confident that she's not overly enthusiastic about us arranging for security."

She. Royce looked over the man's shoulder. The suite was big, probably over two thousand square feet if the bedrooms, which he couldn't see, were in proportion to the living room and dining area that he could. There was leather furniture the color of butternut squash and a glass-topped table that had a massive iron base. Two of the six chairs at the table were pulled out, as if they'd recently been sat in. On the table was a manila folder with papers inside.

Had his knock sent the client scurrying off to her bedroom? "Define *not overly enthusiastic.*"

"Resigned to the inevitable." He led Royce into the suite. "She had to make a quick phone call. It will just be a minute. Have a seat," he added, waving toward the leather couch.

Royce sat.

"Can I get you some coffee?" Barry asked.

Royce shook his head. It was likely that he wasn't going to be here long enough to drink it. In addition to turning down jobs that weren't right for them, they generally declined to offer security to those not really wanting it. It just never worked out well. A good security plan required cooperation between the person providing it and the person benefiting from it. "Can you tell me what has happened?" he asked.

"Yesterday was the first day of the conference. We got

in around noon. JC took a few people out to dinner. It was just four blocks so they walked. They were returning to the hotel, and were very close, when she was almost struck by a car."

"How'd that happen?"

"They were on the sidewalk and the car careened toward them before suddenly straightening out and speeding off."

"She wasn't hurt?"

"Well, one leg is scraped and bruised. She had to leap out of the way and unfortunately encountered a piece of rough stone that decorates the corners of this hotel. But other than that, she's fine. Lucky."

"What did the police say?"

"Nothing. We made a report once she was back inside but the only description we have is that the car was a black sedan. There's probably thousands of them in Vegas."

"How do you know that it was JC that the vehicle was aiming for? You said that she was with several others."

"We can't know for sure. But since she has been getting death threats in the mail, it's our best guess."

"Death threat, Barry," a voice said from the hallway. "Let's not exaggerate the…"

Royce didn't hear the end of the sentence because his damn ears were ringing. He knew that voice. He'd heard that voice in his dreams for years.

He turned fast. And there she was. Juliana Cambridge.

The woman he'd loved. And lost.

Because he wasn't good enough.

She was still very beautiful. Fine, delicate features. Dark shiny hair, worn short. Very blue eyes that had sometimes appeared violet in the morning light.

"Hello, Jules," he said. "It's been a long time."

* * *

JC hated looking stupid. But knew, caught midstep, one foot in the air, with her mouth open, it was hard to look anything but.

"Royce," she said, her voice too high. She swallowed hard, managed to get both feet solidly planted and pressed her lips together.

He looked good. Wonderful, really. Broad shoulders, trim waist, long legs that had eaten up city blocks. His dark hair was shorter now, not even skimming his collar. His hazel eyes had a few lines at the corners but it simply made him look more handsome.

"You're JC?" he said, his tone incredulous.

In many boardrooms across the country, it was still a man's world. The good news was that it was changing. But there was still a benefit to someone not immediately knowing that Miatroth Pharmaceuticals was led by a woman. "Yes," she said.

For someone known for her attention to detail, she hadn't even thought to ask Barry the name of the security specialist who was en route. He'd been going on and on about the credentials of Wingman Security, how he'd verified that they were the best in the region. She, quite frankly, hadn't wanted to hear anything more.

"You worked at Geneseel," Royce said, his voice even. Too even.

"I changed jobs about three years ago," she said. He'd have known that if he'd bothered to keep tabs on her. But then again, she'd stopped typing his name into the search field after the first year.

Too painful.

Barry stepped forward. "I didn't realize the two of you knew each other."

"Yes, uh, Royce lived in New York a long time ago. We…we had common friends."

That was true. There was no need for Barry to know more.

Barry frowned. "Well, maybe that's good," he said. "Addresses your concern of having a stranger with access to the intimate details of your life."

Royce would be much worse than any stranger. She looked at her shoes. "So, how have you been?" she asked, like an idiot.

"Fine," he said.

This was so awkward. She slowly walked around the couch and sat in a chair opposite it, trying to give herself some recovery time. She tried never to think of Royce. To have him here in her living room was startling at best.

"I'm sorry," she said. "But there's been a mistake. I'm not interested in additional security."

"But…" Barry said.

She'd known Barry for her entire life. And she knew she was throwing him a curveball. "Perhaps we can discuss offline."

"It would be negligent of the board if I didn't insist. It would be negligent of you not to accept," Barry said, his voice stronger than before.

"Perhaps I should *step out*," Royce said.

She felt a pain near her heart. The emphasis was intentional. It had to be. It settled the question of whether he remembered their last meeting, eight years ago. The one where she'd ask him to *step out* for just a moment.

So that she could have a conversation with her father.

Which had ultimately led to her staying in New York and Royce returning to Texas.

What the hell was he doing in Vegas?

Chapter 2

"That's...not necessary," she said.

Her delivery was clipped. He'd hit a nerve.

It should have felt better. "Tell me about the death threat," he said.

She tucked a wayward piece of hair behind her delicate ear, a gesture so familiar that it was as if he'd seen it yesterday rather than eight years ago. She looked tired. And when she'd rounded the corner of the couch, he'd seen the slightest hint of a limp, as if her scraped leg might be sore.

All of that pulled at his gut and he reminded himself of all the reasons that he had to be mad at her.

"There have been three letters," she said.

"Three," he repeated. "I thought you said threat. Singular."

She waved a hand dismissively and he noticed that she wasn't wearing any rings. Eight years ago, she'd told him she was marrying another. And like some idiot, he'd set up an alert on his computer, so that when it happened, he could rub his own damn nose in the happy news. And sure enough, four months after he'd stormed out of her father's house, his computer had practically blown up with news media reporting on the marriage of Juliana Cambridge to Bryson Wagoner.

After that night, he'd stopped looking, stopped hoping that she was going to magically wake up one day and decide that she'd been a fool.

He'd been the fool.

"Three letters," she said, bringing him back. "I think they're all from the same person."

"Is that what the police say?" he asked, looking over at Barry, who was back to wringing his hands together.

"They can't say conclusively," Barry said. "But there is a similarity in tone between the documents. But they were postmarked in different cities."

"What cities?"

"Boston, New York and Vegas," Barry said. "In that order. All arriving within the last month."

"Yet you still decided that attending a conference in Vegas was a good idea?" he asked, unable to keep the sarcasm out of his tone. This was probably why contracting new business was generally up to Rico. Diplomacy came naturally to him. Royce had to work very hard at it.

Jules—he could not think of her as JC—sat up straighter on the couch. She was wearing a light blue sweater and a matching blue-and-black-checked skirt with black tights. She looked very much like the pretty young girl he'd taken to dinner that first night, except then she'd been animated and now she was controlled, her somewhat pointed chin almost rigid.

"The last one arrived in our New York office just yesterday, after we'd already arrived here."

"Yet you stayed."

"We're a major sponsor of the conference. I'm part of a panel presentation tomorrow and then speaking at the awards dinner two days from now."

That would be Thursday. "How big of an event?"

"Couple hundred."

Lots of people to watch. Lots of potential threats. "Do you have any of the letters with you?" he asked.

She shook her head. Barry stood up. "I have copies," he said. The man picked up a briefcase that had been on the floor, leaning against a wall. He opened it and pulled out papers.

"This is the first one. Like I said, from Boston."

Royce took it. One sheet. It appeared the sender had cut letters or portions of words out of a magazine and strung them together in a simple poem.

Pills and potions
A witch's brew.
Danger comes to those
Who lay claim to the stew.

He took the second sheet. Same look, a different four-line verse.

Those who cause death
Must be made to pay.
I will have justice
And ensure He has his say.

Was *H* capped in the fourth line for a reason? Or had the sender simply not been able to locate a lowercase *H*?

A cap suggested importance. Or respect. *Ensure He has his say.* Ensure *who* had their say? A tightness settled in his shoulders. Revenge was a powerful motivation.

He picked up the third. The one that had come most recently, from Vegas.

You will beg for mercy
I will enjoy witnessing your pain.
The world will know the truth
That your greed was a runaway train.

He read it a second time and then tossed it aside. The idea that these letters had been directed at Jules made him sick. "You have no idea who sent these?"

She shook her head no. "The police are investigating. As you probably know, they can test paper and ink and even trace it back to the original publication. All we know is that whoever sent this has access to twenty-weight copy paper sold in almost every big-box store in America, and *People* magazine. Miatroth products are distributed across the United States and in many other countries. Millions take a Miatroth drug every day. It's like looking for a needle in a haystack."

"But they upped the ante last night when somebody took a swipe at you?" he said.

"Somebody maybe took a swipe at me," she said. "I have my doubts. I think it's very possible that it was somebody who was texting and suddenly realized they'd veered off course. Fortunately, they corrected. Or it was somebody who'd been drinking and wasn't their best at driving in a straight line."

She could be right. People were idiots in their cars, seemingly forgetting that they were in control of several tons of moving equipment. "But they didn't stop."

"They didn't hit anyone. No reason to stop."

"There are very few coincidences in real life," Royce said. She could have been badly injured. Somebody should have been there to protect her. Why wasn't Bryson Wagoner with his wife after she'd received the first two threats? "Is your…husband traveling with you?" he asked, finding it hard, even after all these years, to say the word.

Jules licked her lips. "No husband. I'm divorced."

He felt almost light-headed. Divorced. He shouldn't be shocked. Lots of people were divorced. But for some reason, it wasn't what he'd expected from Jules.

He had a thousand questions.

Most of them inappropriate. "Recently?" he asked. An enraged former spouse was always a security concern.

She shook her head. "Six years ago."

He worked really hard to keep his expression neutral. His head was spinning. That meant…hell, she'd been married for less than eighteen months. "What's your relationship with…him?" He knew his name. Bryson Wagoner. Appropriate since the man had needed a damn wagon to carry all his family money.

"Fine," Jules said.

Fine. What the hell did that mean? The silence in the room stretched out.

"Well, what do you think?" Barry Wood asked.

He *thought* that very little surprised him anymore, but Jules had knocked his socks off. He *thought* his heart was beating too fast. He *thought* she was still the most beautiful woman that he'd ever met. "I think you're right to be concerned," Royce said.

"We appreciate your opinion." If possible, Jules's jaw was even tighter, and her lips barely moved when she spoke.

"It's what I do," he said, suddenly defensive. He and

his partners were damn good at providing security. They had celebrities, politicians—hell, even some royalty— on their client list. A pharmaceutical CEO was nothing.

But that wasn't true. Jules Cambridge had never been nothing. Royalty in her own right, she'd been her father's little princess.

And in contrast, he'd been the commoner, who should have been content to stay outside the walls of the Fifth Avenue fortress, admiring from afar.

He'd been so damn stupid.

"Will you help us?" Barry asked.

There was no way.

Jules stood up, her movement jerky. "Barry, we need to discuss this. I can assure you that Royce is not going to be interested in providing the service."

That was exactly what he'd been thinking. She had no right to take away his opportunity to turn *her* down. And it irritated the hell out of him to hear her say it so matter-of-fact.

She could take her business down the street. There were other security agencies in Vegas. A couple that were very decent. Not as good as Wingman Security, that was true. If only one of his other partners was available, he could refer her internally, but that wasn't the case.

Jules was in trouble. *You will beg for mercy. I will enjoy witnessing your pain.* "Actually, it's your lucky day," he said, his gaze steady on her.

She opened her mouth.

"What you two need to do," he said, switching his eyes to Barry, "is lock the door behind me. Don't open it to anyone but me. Can you manage that?"

Barry nodded.

"Good. Then I'll be back within the hour with my clothes and a contract."

Chapter 3

"I'm sorry, JC," Barry said, just seconds after the door closed behind Royce. "But I'm confused. You look very upset. I thought we'd agreed."

She managed to smile at the man. She understood that he was worried. "I suspect you're thinking that one hell of a slam is coming."

Barry settled back against the cushions. "That was quite a night. You stalked off to your bedroom, your nose in the air. And it was a ferocious slam. Knocked the trim right off the frame."

"All because I couldn't go to a Metallica concert. I was fifteen."

"Your father hated to disappoint you but he hated the idea of you getting hurt even more," Barry said.

She was eighteen years older now. And while she hadn't been able to understand her father's motivations at the time, she did understand Barry's now. She also understood the very real business reasons behind them. There was a twenty-million-dollar insurance policy on her life. As a result, they'd had to report the threats to the insurance company and they were insisting on added security.

So she had quietly acquiesced. Never dreaming that Royce would walk through the door.

Barry would have had no way of knowing about the relationship. After all, by almost anyone's standards, it had been rather short-lived. And her father, if he had deemed it necessary to discuss Royce with Barry, would have only referred to him as Juliana's *summer indulgence*. As best she could remember, he had never called Royce by name.

But he'd known his name and he would remember his name. It was the one way that she could very easily get Royce kicked off the job. If she mentioned it to her father, the man would immediately demand that Royce be replaced. He'd call his good friend Barry and that would be that.

And she'd be responsible, again, for causing trouble for Royce.

It was a few days. If they were indeed the best, that's what she wanted, right?

She did not believe that the car last night had deliberately tried to kill her. If so, why back off? But the letters were not so easily dismissed. In a world where crazy things seemed to happen more and more often, the idea that somebody had come unhinged and was intent upon causing trouble for the CEO of a drug company was not a comfortable one. She'd been all for reporting them to the police.

She was all for staying safe.

She certainly didn't want anybody on her team to get injured because she couldn't get past history.

Plus, she had a very good reason for staying in Vegas. Family. She hadn't told Barry, didn't intend to. Knew it would get back to her father, and there was no way she was ready to have that conversation yet.

"It's fine, Barry. We'll make the best of it."

Royce had said he was coming back with clothes. Which meant that he intended to stay with her.

There were two bedrooms in the suite. Plenty of space.

Right. When he'd run back to Texas and she'd stayed in New York, *that* had barely been a comfortable distance.

"I'm going to get some work done," she said, "before Royce comes back."

"I'll stay," Barry said.

She shook her head. "It's not necessary. Go back to your own room and get some rest. I don't think either one of us got much sleep last night."

"You heard Royce."

"I know, I know. I won't open the door to strangers. I promise."

Barry stood up. "I appreciate you going along with this. I really do."

"I appreciate that you haven't said anything to my dad about the threats." She'd asked him not to and he'd reluctantly agreed. Of course, he had no way of knowing how strained her current relationship was with her father. For so many reasons, some known only to her.

"I won't as long as we're doing everything in our power to keep you safe. I'm not underestimating how uncomfortable it might be to have a shadow 24/7. But you know your safety is important to me. For a lot of reasons."

She reached for his age-spotted hand. Squeezed it. "I

know that it might be highly improper for the CEO to say this to the chairman of the board, but I love you."

He smiled. "You've always been like a daughter to Eileen and me."

"I know." She walked him to the door and locked it securely after he left. Then she stood with her spine against the door, feeling the wood press against every one of her vertebrae.

Eight years ago, she'd made a bad decision for what she thought were all the right reasons.

And after he'd stormed out of her father's house, she'd tried to forget about the hurt in Royce Morgan's eyes. The hurt she'd caused.

It hadn't been easy. Even though she'd thrown herself into her work, into planning her wedding.

And then into her marriage.

Her short, disastrous marriage.

Royce had looked shocked when she'd said she was divorced. He hadn't known. But now that he did, would he demand an explanation? Would he think he was still entitled to one? Or would he not care enough to even ask? She wasn't sure which question scared her more.

The only answer was to keep it strictly professional between the two of them, to not even venture into conversations that could take on a personal bent. To avoid a trip down a memory lane that was blighted by deep potholes full of deceit and regret.

She walked over to the table and picked up the folder that Barry had tried to show her earlier. Skimmed the executive summary that had likely been prepared by Barry's assistant. It hit the high points of three different Vegas agencies and ended up with a paragraph that supported the recommendation of Wingman Security.

Elite security team. Top-notch references. Impressive clientele. Professional demeanor.

There was a handwritten note. "A little more expensive than the others, but consensus is, they're worth it." She didn't recognize the writing.

That's probably what had swayed Barry. He was nicer about it but came from the same school of thought as her father. If it cost more, it must be better.

Royce had clearly made a success of himself. And security made sense. She remembered him telling her that's what he'd done in the military.

He'd been a decent and principled young man, although there were times when those qualities had been overshadowed by his beat-up leather jacket and motorcycle boots, his hair that was long enough to pull back in a ponytail and his language that was likely appropriate for the battlefield but not the boardroom.

He'd been different than anyone she'd ever met.

Now he was wearing silk pants, shirts with monogrammed cuffs and Italian shoes.

Time had changed them both. Things had been said. Actions taken. There was no going back.

Only forward. And the best thing she could do was try to get a few things done before Royce returned. Her laptop was still in her bedroom. She pulled herself away from the door.

As she crossed the threshold of her bedroom, she heard a buzz from the cell phone that she'd left on her bed. She glanced at the number and let out a sigh of relief. Charity was finally calling back.

"Hi," she said, trying to sound casual. "How's it going?" Their relationship was too new, too fragile, for her to chastise the young woman about taking a full day to return the call.

"Not so good," Charity said, her voice barely a whisper.

"What's wrong?" JC asked, picking up her pen. She always thought more clearly when she had something to write with.

"Nothing."

Charity sounded...bad. Not that JC had that much experience talking to her. This was only their second conversation in two months. "I was hoping we could meet for lunch," JC said.

"That's probably not a good idea," Charity said.

No way. She was not going to let Charity blow off the meeting. She'd told Royce that she'd come because Miatroth was a major sponsor and she was presenting. That was true, of course. But the real reason she'd agreed to attend was that it gave her a reason to be in Vegas, an opportunity to get to know Charity better.

A woman should know her sister.

"I won't take no for an answer," she said, still keeping her tone light.

There was silence on the other end. Then a sigh. "Listen," Charity said. "I'm in trouble."

"What kind of trouble?" JC asked, clenching her pen.

"The kind I don't want to talk about on a cell phone. Can you come here?"

Royce had been very specific—she was not to leave the hotel. And she'd promised him. "I don't know," she hedged. "It's complicated."

"Isn't everything?" Charity said, sounding resigned. "Never mind. I'll figure something out. I'll call you—"

"Where are you?" JC interrupted. She just knew that if she failed Charity this one time, the woman might never call her again. She could not risk that.

Charity rattled off an address. JC scribbled it down, then read it back.

Since the day she'd discovered her dead mother's diary and realized that everything she'd believed to be true might not be, she'd had so many questions.

And Charity might be the only one with the answers. "I'm on my way," JC said. "We'll talk when I get there."

Royce called Trey from the car and got him started on the contract. Then he swung by his apartment and packed enough dress shirts and slacks to get him through a couple days. He added a few more casual things and his toiletries. Before zipping up the bag, he added boxes of ammunition for the Glock he carried. He hoped like hell he wouldn't need it, but he believed in being prepared.

Then he was out the door a second time. When he got to Wingman Security, the paperwork was ready.

"Rico is going to be impressed," Trey said. "You wrapped this one up fast."

Royce debated telling Trey that he had known the client years before. The partners didn't keep secrets from one another.

But he just wasn't ready to talk about it. Wasn't ready to admit that seeing Jules had been a blow, almost taking his breath away. He folded the papers and stuffed them in his jacket pocket. "I'll be at the Periwinkle for the next few days. Suite 1402."

"Nice digs," Trey said. "Have you had a chance to check out the hotel?"

"Some." He'd looked on his way out. "Main entrance is on ground level. Both an elevator and an escalator gets you to the lobby, which is on the third floor. Elevator from there goes to floors four through forty. No key-card access required for any floor." That meant that anybody could access any floor, which was not good. "On the fourteenth floor, there are six suites—three on each side of the elevator bay, which is in the middle of the hotel. Stairs at both ends of the hotel. Those do require a key card to open the door on any floor, including the first." That was better news. That meant that people couldn't simply wander in off the street, find the stairs and get anywhere in the hotel. "Hotel connects via overhead walkway to a separate three-story conference center."

"Sounds good," Trey said. "Stay in touch."

"I will," Royce said, and walked out the door.

When he got back to the Periwinkle, he pointed at the spot where he wanted his car parked and gave the valet an extra hundred bucks to convince him. Nothing impeded a quick getaway like having to wait for a car to be brought around. That was a beginner mistake.

He hadn't even been a beginner when he'd started the agency four years ago. Not with his military experience.

He liked to think that he always had a plan, a backup plan and an it's-going-to-hell-fast plan.

Twenty feet inside, remembering Jules's love for dark chocolate, he extended his arm toward the sterling silver tray, only to draw it back fast. His job wasn't to bring her candy. His job was to ensure that the CEO of Miatroth stayed safe while in Las Vegas.

He got to the fourteenth floor, walked down the hallway and rapped on the door. And waited. Just like before. This was getting old.

He knocked sharply, loud enough to make most everybody on the floor take a look out their peephole to see if it was their door getting assaulted.

When that didn't get a response, he yanked his phone out of his pocket, jabbed his index finger on Barry Wood's telephone number and took a deep breath.

"Hello, Royce," Barry said.

"Are you going to open the damn door?"

"What?"

"I'm standing in the hallway. I've been standing in the hallway for five minutes."

"Royce, I'm back in my room on the twelfth floor. JC had some work to do. I made sure she locked the door behind me when I left."

A chill spread across the back of his neck, as if someone had slapped an ice bag on it. "Call the front desk. Get somebody up here with a key. But text me her cell number first."

Royce hung up and waited for the text. It came and he dialed. He heard it ring, then switch to voice mail. He swallowed. "This is Royce," he said fast. "Call me. Please, just call me."

He called twice more before Barry and somebody in a navy blue suit wearing an assistant manager name tag showed up. He waited impatiently while the man used his key to open the door. Then he was into the suite, moving swiftly through the rooms.

She wasn't there.

Her clothes were still in the closet. Her sundry items still on the bathroom counter. Her stupid phone on the bedside table.

No signs of struggle.

He turned to the manager. "I need to know if Ms. Cambridge left this hotel and I need to know it five minutes ago."

"Can you describe her?"

Right down to the heart-shaped tattoo on her left inside thigh. "Five-six. A hundred and twenty pounds. Dark hair, above the collar. Fair complexion. Very dark blue eyes. She's…beautiful."

The man relayed the information to whoever he'd dialed on his cell phone. From what Royce could tell, the

call got transferred a couple times. Finally, the man nodded. "She got into a cab about twenty minutes ago. By
herself. Seemed fine. Gave the valet a five-dollar tip."

At these kind of places, the valet gave the cab driver
the instructions. "Does he remember the address?"

Royce waited impatiently while the question was
asked again and answered. The manager nodded. "Bell
Street and Howard Avenue."

Royce knew Vegas like the back of his hand. There
could be absolutely no good reason for Jules to be in that
part of town. Drugs were sold there. But not the kind you
bought with your prescription card.

Add in the guns and the human trafficking and you
had all the things that tarnished Sin City's sparkle.

He was running for the elevator when he heard Barry
call from behind.

"What are you going to do?"

"Whatever it takes," he said.

Chapter 4

Sweat was running down the back of JC's neck by the time the cab came to a complete stop. She'd wanted to ask the driver to turn down his heater, but for the last fifteen minutes she'd listened to the man, who was probably fifty in a world where fifty didn't look like thirty, quietly beg the person on the other end of the phone to please let his mother keep her dog. He'd promised repeatedly to replace the carpet that said dog must have ripped up.

Her own mom had loved her little Yorkie. And after she'd died, the dog had never been the same, even though JC had watched her father try to woo the dog over. Instead, the animal had seemed to mope around her parents' home for months until one night the little guy had fallen asleep and never woken up.

She'd figured he'd died of a broken heart. She'd understood the feeling. The loss of Lara Cambridge had been sudden and very horrible.

"Twenty-six fifty," he said.

She gave him a hundred and got out of the cab.

He rolled down his window. "I don't have change, lady."

"I don't want any," she said.

It was enough that for a brief second, the man's tense posture, the stiff way he held his head, it all seemed to relax. He rolled his window up. Stopped halfway.

"Best be careful in this neighborhood," he said. Then he pulled away, leaving her alone. Cars, mostly old, were parked on both sides of the street. There was little grass and only a few trees to soften the rough appearance of the small wood-framed houses that lined the road. A big dog running behind a chain-link fence barked, startling her. She saw a swing set in one yard with a rusty slide that couldn't possibly be safe for a child.

Across the street, several houses up, she saw an old woman wearing a housedress, her back to the street, sweeping her sidewalk. She glanced again at the scrap of paper where she'd written down the address and Charity's brief directions. *Apartments on the corner.* Had to be the three five-story brick buildings that were bunched together as if there might be safety in numbers.

She'd been so distracted after talking to Charity that she'd run out of the hotel without her phone. Hadn't realized it until she was already blocks from there. If she had it, a quick call to Charity would have made it easier. Instead, it took her several minutes to identify that apartment 302 was in the middle building. She walked across the yard that was more weeds than grass, grateful that she'd pulled on her flat-heeled boots before leaving the hotel. She was almost at the door when she saw a police car cruise by.

It was the kind of neighborhood that likely required

regular patrol. There were two officers but neither seemed to glance her direction. Eyes were focused straight ahead.

She reached for the handle of the glass door that looked as if someone had thrown a slice of pizza at it, hadn't been happy with their aim and tried it again. That or it was dried vomit.

She was sticking with pizza.

Inside, there was a very small lobby, maybe five feet by five feet. Mailboxes, thirty of them, lined one wall. Directly across was the elevator that looked a hundred years old, which she thought was likely not possible, since the building had probably been built in the seventies or eighties. But the painted doors were scratched and dented and when they opened, the smell of urine was oppressive. She got in and pressed the three with her elbow.

The idea that Charity was living in the place made her sick. And the knowledge that if circumstances had been different it might have been her instead made her arms feel heavy as the elevator slowly climbed to the third floor.

When the doors opened, the heat hit her. How could it feel as if it was eighty-five in the hallway when it was fifty degrees outside? She quickly glanced both directions. All five doors were closed.

She found apartment 302 at the end of the hall. Stood outside the door, her fist raised to knock.

She had some idea what to expect. Charity had no social media accounts, at least that she'd been able to find. But the private investigator she'd hired had unearthed a senior class picture of the girl taken six years ago.

She'd stared at that photo for weeks that had turned into months, working up her nerve. The idea that she was opening a door that might never be fully shut again was a bit terrifying. She could be inviting trouble into her life, into her father's life. Maybe unnecessarily.

She'd almost managed to convince herself that it was too great a risk, that it didn't matter. But in the end, she'd realized that she had to know. She had to know if what her mom had believed to be true was indeed fact.

Had to know the extent of her father's betrayal.

She pressed a hand flat against her stomach, which was rumbling with nerves. What was Charity going to think of her? If she'd done any searching, she'd have seen plenty of JC. Miatroth's recent clinical trials in the war against pancreatic cancer had gone amazingly well, and in the last month, JC had been interviewed many times.

She'd have preferred to orchestrate a meeting, to set it up just so to give her and Charity the optimal opportunity to get to know each other. But Charity's admission that she was in trouble had changed all that.

Her plan was to meet Charity, find a solution to whatever trouble she was in and get back to the hotel before Royce returned so that he never had to know she'd left in the first place.

Otherwise, he was going to have one more reason to believe that she couldn't be trusted.

JC knocked sharply on the door.

It swung open. And there she was.

Charity had big dark eyes that seemed to fill her narrow face. Her straight hair was almost black, much darker than it had been in her senior class picture, and hung down past her shoulders. There was a silver ring at the edge of her right eyebrow and her nose was pierced. Those were also new in the last six years. She was wearing a shapeless olive green cotton dress with a drawstring waist and flip-flops.

Too thin, almost waiflike, and JC's first impulse was

to feed her. "Hello," said JC. Should she hug her? Nothing about Charity's body language told her that would be the right move. She settled for extending her hand. "It's nice to finally meet you. I'm JC…uh…Juliana, but I go by JC."

Charity didn't move. Instead, she glanced at JC's extended arm, then settled her gaze back on JC's face. The silence stretched on.

And JC silently lectured herself not to fill it. She sometimes did that when she was nervous.

"I guess I wasn't sure you would come," Charity finally said.

JC tried not to take it personally. Trust had to be earned. Basic tenet of doing business. "I was concerned," JC said. "May…I come in?" she asked.

Charity shook her head. "We've got to get out of here before Bobby comes back."

"Who's Bobby?" JC asked, already knowing the answer. The investigator that she'd hired had uncarthed the name of the man she was living with. But she couldn't let Charity know that. She looked over the girl's shoulder. She was at least three inches shorter than JC's own five foot six.

Charity tossed her hair. "Just this guy. He can be a real jerk sometimes."

She turned and that's when JC saw the open suitcase on the couch. Wadded-up clothes were hanging over the edges of the inexpensive luggage. Two pairs of gladiator sandals, one black, one brown, seemed to be taking up most of the room.

"You said you were in trouble," JC said. "The kind of trouble where you need to leave?"

"The kind of trouble where I think it's possible that I'm going to be *that poor girl* on the ten o'clock news,"

Charity said, her voice low. "Bobby's got some anger issues and I don't feel safe. It was probably a mistake for me to move in here."

In the information that had been gathered about Charity, there'd been no mention of violence involving her and Bobby. "How long have the two of you been together?"

Charity ran a hand through her long hair. "Not that long. A few months."

"Where were you planning to go?"

Charity shrugged. "I don't know. I've got a couple hundred bucks. Should get me a place to stay for a week or so until I figure things out."

Not a nice place. But they could have that discussion once she was safely out of the apartment. "Maybe you better finish packing," JC said. She looked around. The apartment was very sparsely furnished with just a couch and two folding chairs. A flat-screen television was perched on top of two stacked red plastic crates. A counter separated the kitchen from the living room and it was loaded with dirty dishes, potato chip bags and empty ice-cream-sandwich boxes. There was a big orange cat lying on the far end, its head lifted, perhaps interested in the visitor but not quite enough to be concerned.

Charity wasn't moving. Just standing there, watching JC.

"Can I...help you with anything?" JC asked.

It took Charity a minute to answer. "I guess I'll need Hogi's food," she said finally, her head moving in the cat's direction. She walked toward her suitcase.

JC had no idea whether or not the Periwinkle allowed cats. But if not, she suspected that a special damage deposit might take care of the problem. "Do you have a cage for him?"

Charity looked at her as if she might be stupid and used her elbow to point at the top of the fridge.

Well, of course. JC set her teeth. Now wasn't the time to get into an argument. She wanted to get out of there before Bobby decided to come back.

She found the cat's food in a bag near a filthy litter box that caused her to breathe through her mouth. She grabbed the small bag of food and backed away. Then she reached for the cat cage on top of the refrigerator.

The cat turned his head, saw what she was doing and, showing more energy than she'd expected, bolted off the counter and down the hallway.

"Oh, my God," Charity screamed. "Don't let Hogi see that. He'll think he's going to the vet."

"I'll get him," JC said.

Charity held up her hand. "Just wait here. He'll be under the bed. You're a stranger. He'll never come to you." She picked up a photo album that had been wedged behind the suitcase. "I had these pictures. I thought you might want to see them. Since my mom is in them, you know."

"Thank you," she said. She took the album.

Charity ran down the hall, leaving JC alone in the squalid little living room. The cover of the photo album was a brown padded vinyl. JC flipped it open. Inside were ten or twelve plastic sheets, most of the four-by-six slots filled.

Baby pictures. They had to be of Charity. The eyes gave it away. Unable to resist, she flipped a couple pages, looking for the woman who had been Charity's mother.

There. Holding Charity.

Pretty, with long blond hair. Not as thin as Charity but still slender. She was slumped in a chair, like she might be exhausted.

Had she already realized by that time that she'd be raising Charity alone? Or had she known that from the minute she'd gotten pregnant?

So many questions.

But maybe now she was finally close to getting answers. She could hear Charity calling to the cat. "Come on, Hogi. Come out right now."

Her sister had a hint of the South in her voice. JC was so intent upon listening to it that it surprised the heck out of her when the apartment door suddenly swung open.

A man, his gut hanging over his belt, wearing a black tank top and gray cargo shorts, stared at her. His hair, long and pulled back into a ponytail, was a dirty blond. He was maybe thirty. "Who the hell are you?" he asked.

When she didn't answer immediately, he looked beyond her. "Charity," he yelled.

JC stepped forward. "You must be Bobby. I'm JC." Instinctively, she extended her hand.

He ignored it. He was staring at the suitcase and she could see red spread up his neck. He turned.

JC moved fast and got in front of him, blocking his way to the hallway. "Hey," she said, "let's talk—"

He pushed her and she stumbled backward. But years of staying upright on a soccer field had her quickly back in his face. She kicked his shin, right above the ankle joint, right where she knew it would hurt most.

"You little bitch," he said, punctuating his remarks with a right hook.

JC managed to duck the first punch. "Help," she screamed. "Somebody help us."

But help wasn't coming. And when he grabbed her and shoved her back, knocking her head against the cheap drywall, she knew she was in terrible trouble.

She kicked and twisted but he was strong enough to

fight off her attempts with one hand and keep his other hand around her neck, anchoring her to the wall. And his hand was squeezing, closing her airway.

And she knew that she was going to die.

Far away, she heard Charity yelling. "Stop it. Stop it, Bobby. You're going to kill her."

She was right.

"Run," JC managed.

But Charity didn't. Instead, she pounded on the man's back, yanking at his hair, scratching his skin.

But still he hung on.

Until suddenly, his hands were gone. And she sank to the floor, gasping in air. There was a terrific buzzing in her ears and it took her seconds to realize that the sound she heard was someone's fist pounding into flesh.

If she wasn't mistaken, Royce intended to beat Bobby to death. "Royce," she said weakly. She staggered to her feet. Another punch. She lurched toward Royce. "Stop," she said.

But he didn't until she fell into him. He turned and caught her before her face hit the floor. Which was good because if not, both she and Bobby would have been out cold.

"Jules," Royce said, his eyes wild. "Damn, honey. Are you—"

"Las Vegas Police Department. Open up."

Before they could do that, however, two Vegas cops burst through the door, guns drawn.

Royce kept one arm around her and raised his other. "I'm Royce Morgan of Wingman Security. This is my client Juliana Cambridge, and that—" he looked at Bobby, who was just coming to on the floor "—is the piece of crap that attempted to kill her."

As far as introductions went, it was one of the most

concise that she'd ever heard. She looked around for Charity and realized she'd disappeared back into the bedroom.

"Ma'am, are you okay?"

She was confident the responding officers were the same ones she'd seen cruising by. She nodded, not sure her voice was steady yet.

"She needs an ambulance," Royce said.

She shook her head. "Maybe later," she said softly.

Royce didn't look satisfied, but he pressed his lips together.

"Who are you?" the shorter officer asked, pointing at Charity, who was now slowly walking down the hall, holding her cell phone. JC assumed that she'd been the one to call the police.

Even being in the neighborhood, they would have arrived too late. If Royce hadn't come, she'd be dead. How had he found her?

"I'm Charity. Charity White."

"Do you know this man?" the same officer asked.

Charity nodded. "Bobby. Bobby Boyd. This is his apartment. I've been…living here."

The cop began writing in the small notepad he'd pulled from his breast pocket.

"And what's the relationship between you and Ms. Cambridge?" the taller Hispanic officer asked.

"We don't have a relationship," Charity said. "This is the first time I ever met her. Her mom was friends with my mom."

That wasn't exactly what JC had told Charity. *My mother knew your mother.* That had been her explanation as to why she'd sought out Charity.

But JC kept her mouth shut. It certainly wasn't the time to blurt out that she and Charity might be half sisters.

From there, things moved pretty quickly. The cops talked quietly to Bobby, who was coming around. An ambulance arrived. Bobby looked small and nonthreatening on the gurney. His eyes were filled with anger but he stayed quiet, as if he'd maybe been in this situation before and understood the importance of keeping his mouth shut.

After he was gone, Royce guided her over to the couch and made sure she was sitting before talking quietly to the cops in the kitchen.

Then it was Charity's turn. The heavier, younger cop motioned for Charity to join him in the kitchen. JC twisted her neck, watching, but the cop stood in front of Charity, blocking JC's view.

The Hispanic officer pulled up a folding chair in front of her, forcing her to turn her back to Charity. It dawned on her that it was not by chance they were doing their best to question them separately in the small apartment. No doubt they wanted to see if their stories matched.

Royce stood behind her, his hands flat on the back of the couch. He did not interrupt or ask any questions, which was probably why the cop let him stay. The questions were easy at first. Full name. Address. Phone where she could be reached.

"Walk me through what happened once you arrived here," the cop said.

"Charity was in the bedroom, trying to get her cat, when Mr. Boyd arrived home. I tried to engage him in conversation. But he appeared angry and I was concerned for Charity's safety. She'd already confided in me on the telephone and in person that she was afraid of the man. He pushed me, I kicked him in self-defense and then he took a swing at me. I ducked but then he started choking me." She kept her voice steady, dispassionate, as if she was reporting revenue figures at a board meeting.

The cop looked up from his report. She could almost see the message that passed from the cop to Royce as the two locked eyes. *She's damn lucky you got here.*

Nobody needed to point that out to her.

The officer stood up. "I think I've got this."

It was just a few minutes more before Charity and the other officer completed their quiet conversation in the kitchen. Then the two cops left almost as quickly as they'd arrived.

JC stood in the living room. The space was strangely quiet. She looked at Royce. "This will be inadequate, but thank you."

Chapter 5

Thank you. She'd probably been less than a minute away from being choked to death and now she was calmly thanking him. "I don't know what the hell you were thinking," he said. Better that than tell her she'd taken ten years off his damn life. "I told you to lock the door. I assumed it was understood that you needed to stay behind it, stay locked in, protected."

He was practically spitting his words. He took a breath, reaching for calm. Charity was watching them closely, obviously listening. The woman looked to be early twenties and she might be very pretty with a little more meat on her bones and those stupid piercings removed.

So their moms had been friends. That was nice, but given that Jules had never actually met Charity, wasn't it a bit much that she'd immediately dropped everything to come to the woman's rescue?

Of course it was. If it had been anybody else. But Jules

was…a good person. Truly decent. Despite everything, he believed that. Once she'd realized that Charity was in trouble, she'd have wanted to help.

He could easily imagine the convoluted reasoning. Their mothers had been friends. Ergo, Jules's mom would have wanted her to help Charity.

He knew, from the many conversations they'd had eight years ago, that the summer Jules was fourteen, she and her mother had been in a car accident. Jules had suffered a serious leg injury but survived. Her mother had died. It had been a devastating loss and Jules had confessed that most everything she'd done or accomplished after that had been because it would have made her mom proud.

Graduate at the top of her high school class. Proud mom.

Finish college in three years. Proud mom.

Go to graduate school and get a great job afterward. Proud mom.

So he wasn't second-guessing her motivation to help Charity. None of that, however, made him any less angry that she hadn't thought twice about the promise she'd given him to stay at the hotel.

She could have died. He'd blown every red light and totally disregarded any speed limit. But still, he'd almost been too late. She needed to understand that she'd been both foolish and very, very lucky.

So that she never did anything like it again until he could figure out where this threat was coming from and neutralize it.

"How did you know where I was?" she asked.

"Valet remembered the intersection. Once I got here, there was an old woman sweeping her sidewalk."

"I didn't think she saw me."

"Old people watch what's going on in their neighborhoods. She saw you come into this building. Otherwise, I'd have had no idea where to search." He'd yelled at the old lady, asking if she'd seen a dark-haired woman in a blue sweater, and she'd pointed at the middle building. He'd wasted precious minutes on the second floor before he'd gotten to the third and heard Jules yelling for help.

He'd come through the door, knowing that he was going to kill whoever was harming her. He supposed he was lucky that he'd had to stop to keep her from dropping like a stone to the floor.

Otherwise, it would likely have gone very differently with the cops.

"Are you sure you don't want to see a doctor?" he asked. Her neck was still red and he knew the bruising was coming. He'd feel a lot better if she was checked out.

"No," she said. She looked at Charity. "Get your cat and let's go."

"But Bobby's going to jail," the young woman said. She reached for one of the half-full chip bags on the counter, as if the last fifteen minutes had solved all her problems.

"If charges are pressed, which I hope they are, he'll still likely get bail," Jules said. "He won't be behind bars for long. I don't think it's in your best interest to be here when he comes back."

"She's right," Royce said. He tried to ignore the heat that spread from his gut to his neck when Jules shot him a grateful look. He was mad at her. For so many things. Gratitude wasn't going to sucker him in, make him forget.

"Who are you again?" Charity asked, likely irritated that it suddenly seemed as if it was two against one.

He glanced at Jules, wondering what she'd shared with Charity. Before he could speak, Jules jumped in.

"His name is Royce Morgan."

"Okay," she said dismissively. "But what's with the two of you?"

Royce realized that the girl had not heard his introduction to the cops. From the corner of his eye, he'd seen her beat feet back to the bedroom and had considered that she was fleeing down the fire escape before she'd reappeared a minute later. He just bet that the girl had some drugs or other illegal contraband in the bedroom that she hadn't wanted the cops to stumble upon.

"We can get into that later," Jules said.

Charity shrugged, as if she really didn't give a damn.

"You said earlier that you would need to find a place to stay," JC said.

"Yeah, that's right."

"I was wondering if you'd consider staying with me," Jules said.

Charity chewed on the nail on her right index finger. "Why would I do that?"

"It will give you a chance to think about alternatives. I'm in town for just a few days, so it wouldn't be for long, but it might save you a few bucks."

Royce wasn't happy. He'd known Charity for about ten minutes, but the impressions were forming fast. She didn't choose her friends well and she had terrible manners. She'd not offered one bit of thanks to Jules for trying to save her ass.

He didn't relish the idea of her being around. But if the alternative was that Charity would be staying in some dive and Jules would feel the need to visit, that was even more unacceptable.

Charity shoveled in a big handful of chips. "I don't know. There shouldn't be any more danger," she said, talking with her mouth full. "And it's not like we're friends."

"We could be friends," Jules said. "Please, I'd really like to do this for you."

Charity shrugged. "Okay, I guess."

As far as rocking endorsements, it fell a little flat. But there was something not quite right. Charity's words and tone were mildly accepting but her eyes seemed brighter, as if she might really be excited about the offer.

Maybe the kid was more scared than he'd given her credit for.

Jules smiled at Charity. "Go get your cat. I'll feel better when we're out of here."

When Charity was back in the bedroom, he spoke quickly. "I don't know if this is a good idea."

"I'm grateful for your discretion," Jules said, her voice low. "I'll tell her what's going on but not just yet. But, Royce," she said, her voice a little sharper, "please understand that while I respect your opinion, I make my own decisions."

He shook his head. "You might be the CEO, but right now, I'm in charge of your safety. You need to keep your head in the game. This just seems a little hasty."

"I have the ability to offer her some temporary shelter, to give her a chance to get her act together. I think my mom would have wanted me to do that."

Bingo. It was always going to come back to that.

"Fine," he said.

"But for now, I don't want her to know what's going on. That I need protection."

Great. She not only wanted to tie his hands, she wanted to put a bag over them. "That won't work. If she's staying with you, she's going to have to understand the rules."

She drew in a deep breath. "I'll tell her that you're

providing security. That's it. Nothing about the letters, nothing about the car that may or may not have been aiming for me. I don't want her getting frightened and running away."

"You seem to be really concerned about a girl you just met. I understand that your mom was friends with her mom, but—"

"Please, can we talk about this later? I just want to get out of here."

The plea pulled at his gut. Jules looked tired, and he realized that while she had dismissed her need for medical care, the attack had still taken a toll on her. "Fine. Let's make tracks."

Make tracks. That took her back. Way back. To eight years ago. She'd been working and living in Manhattan.

It had been crazy busy at work, where she was already a senior director at Geneseel Drugs after just three years on the job. For weeks, she'd been working day and half the night, too, tying up the loose ends of yet another acquisition of a smaller, less profitable competitor. When friends planned the inevitable Memorial Day get-together, she'd declined. They'd been relentless.

"It's the first summer holiday," they'd said. "You have to come."

She'd finally agreed and walked the six blocks through the financial district. She didn't need directions. She was as familiar with that part of the city as her own neighborhood. She'd gone to a private high school close by and every day after school, she'd walked to her father's office, where he'd been an executive vice president at one of the largest banks in the city.

He made a good salary. That was obvious. Maybe not when she'd been a young child, but once she'd gotten into middle school and high school, she'd always known that her dad probably made more money than the dads of her friends.

Music lessons. Dance lessons. Club soccer. European vacations. Whatever she'd needed or wanted, he'd worked hard to provide it for her.

Because he hadn't wanted her to miss her mother. She had, of course. But she'd tried to never let him know how much. Hadn't wanted to add to his pain.

By the time she'd arrived at the rooftop bar that warm windy spring night, the party was in full swing. She'd chatted and mingled and downed two glasses of wine on an empty stomach. Almost burped it back up when she caught a glimpse of Royce across the room and he smiled at her.

He was simply the most handsome guy she'd seen in a long time. He had presence. That was the only way to put it. Tall, certainly over six foot, and solid with wide shoulders and a broad chest. He was casually dressed in a gray T-shirt, faded blue jeans and scuffed motorcycle boots. She could see the edge of a tattoo on his right bicep, all swirly lines and irregular shapes. He was drinking a beer.

He totally looked as if he could kick some butt.

And the immediate attraction she felt was hard to ignore. But she did, giving him just a brief smile in return before turning her attention back to the woman she was chatting with. The woman had noticed her interest, however, and confided that he was recently back from serving overseas, and a friend of a friend.

And she'd had a crazy desire to talk to him. But she didn't. Her breakup with Bryson was too fresh. She wasn't ready. Intellectually she knew that.

Even though her body was practically humming at his blatant sex appeal.

Forty minutes after arriving, she was on the curb, waiting for a cab to take her back to the office, when the storm broke and pouring rain hit.

Out of nowhere, a big umbrella appeared, held by the man from the party. Up close, he was even better looking. "Tough night to be making tracks," he said with a wickedly sexy smile as the wind threatened to rip the umbrella out of his grasp.

"You don't look like the type to carry an umbrella." It was a stupid thing to say but the only thing she could think of.

He laughed and a shiver of heat had run up her spine. "Belongs to the bar."

"Don't you need to give it back?"

"I will. Tomorrow."

They shared a cab and when he asked her to have dinner with him, she said yes. Maybe it had been the wine, maybe it was the storm. She didn't know. All she knew was that she didn't want to go back to her office, she didn't want to go home to her empty apartment, and she rather desperately wanted to have dinner with him.

A relative stranger. Friend of a friend. Not likely a serial killer.

The thoughts had tumbled upon one another until she'd been nodding yes. She thought dinner might be awkward but it wasn't. He spoke proudly of his years in the air force and made it seem as if it really wasn't a huge deal to have served in both Afghanistan and Iraq. He talked of the people he'd served with, the people they'd helped, even the enemy. And she ate her pasta and felt like a Lee Greenwood song, simply proud to be an American.

She talked of her work, the intricacies of acquisitions, the theatre she'd seen the previous week, and showed him pictures on her cell phone of her best friend's little girl, who at eighteen months had her very first tutu.

She told him about Bryson Wagoner. Not much because she figured it bad form to talk to one man about another. But he'd asked if she was currently seeing anyone and she'd confessed to breaking off the relationship after Valentine's Day, when he'd tried to propose.

They lingered over coffee and dessert, and like a crazy person, she thought about inviting him back to her apartment. But finally, when the restaurant was shutting down, he hailed down a cab and carefully put her inside, with just a casual peck on the cheek.

And she realized that she might have just had the best night of her life and it wasn't going to happen again. At the last minute, she pressed her business card into his hand.

It had taken him two days to call, two frantic days of jumping every time her office phone rang only to be disappointed. She didn't tell anyone about him. Didn't want to admit to her esteemed colleagues that she'd been duped by some guy or that it simply hadn't been as special as she'd built it up in her mind. At least not for him.

She'd been practically shaking when his call had finally come in. She'd—

"I'm ready," Charity said, interrupting her memories. She was holding the cat cage and it was swinging as Hogi turned circles in the small space.

"Great," JC said. What was important now was that Charity was coming home with her. They would get a chance to know one another, to become friends.

A chance to find the truth.

She reached for the doorknob but Royce beat her to it. "I'll go first," he said. "Keep close behind me. Do exactly what I say when I say it."

"Fine," she said. She made a deliberate attempt to relax her jaw. Her poor teeth did not deserve to be mashed together. She managed to smile at Charity. "Doing okay?" she asked.

"I guess," the young woman said. "Are you some kind of cop?" she asked Royce.

"No," he said.

"Royce is part of my security detail. Goes with the territory of being a CEO," JC said, making her tone light.

"Cool," Charity said. "I'm kind of hungry."

"We can get lunch at my hotel," JC said, happy that the young woman didn't have more questions.

"Is there a pool?" Charity asked, her eyes big, looking more like a little girl than a woman old enough to be living with an abusive boyfriend. JC thought longingly of what it might have been like to have Charity live with her, like a real little sister.

"Of course," JC said.

"Not going to be any damn swimming," Royce said. "Let's go."

Chapter 6

Her red dress had gotten his attention. He'd been nursing a beer, thinking about leaving, when he'd seen her across the rooftop patio. The wind had been playing with her skirt, making it swirl around her legs, and he'd had to tighten his grip on his bottle because his damn hands were simply itching to know if her skin was as soft as it looked.

She'd given him a dismissive smile and he'd been just reckless enough to think *the hell with that*. The rain had been fortuitous and he'd been ready to insist upon dinner when she'd graciously agreed.

And he'd had a great three hours. Still, when the night had ended, he'd been prepared to let her go. Had told himself to be content, to simply enjoy the serendipity of their meeting. She was out of his league.

But damn her, she'd pressed her business card into his hand and he'd gone home and slept with the damn thing under his pillow. For two nights. And when he wasn't sleeping, he'd been staring at it. Until finally he'd called.

Yes, the red dress had made an impression. But it was a strapless white bikini that had been his Achilles' heel. Two weeks into their relationship, he'd met Jules at the pool that was on the roof of her condo building. She'd been all long legs and sweet curves in a bit of nothing that had him instantly breaking into a sweat.

And she'd been a damn fish once she got into the water. But he was a good swimmer, too, and he caught her. And when her warm body brushed up against him, he cursed the few other guests lounging around the pool.

He somehow managed to let her go, to let her swim away. Had managed to lie next to her on the beach chair, like a reasonable person, pretending to read a damn book. Had managed not to touch her.

It had almost killed him.

It was their sixth date in two weeks and he desperately wanted her in his bed. But he was waiting for a sign that she was equally needy, equally ready.

Jules was different. Jules was important.

They shared a bottle of chilled white wine that she had in her bag. And hours later, after the summer sun had finally slipped beneath the horizon, and they were the only two left at the pool, he didn't protest when she led him toward one of the curtained cabanas. And when she confidently stepped out of her suit, he wondered how much more wonderful he could stand.

They made love. And afterward, he realized as he held her still-quaking body close, that it had been a terrible mistake.

It was going to be so hard to let her go.

Ten weeks later, at the end of summer, he'd found out just how god-awful it could be.

And now, eight years later, he was helping her herd a belligerent teenager and a mangy cat into a dirty elevator. Really hadn't seen this one coming.

"Nice car," Charity said when they got there.

He didn't answer. He was busy looking up and down the street, trying to spot anything unusual. He wanted Jules back inside her hotel.

The back seat of his BMW was barely big enough for Charity, her suitcase and the cat carrier. But once she got wedged in, and Jules had taken the passenger seat, he didn't waste any time getting the car started and driving.

The only sound inside the car was the damn cat, making some kind of squealing noise that wasn't a purr, or a meow, or anything faintly resembling any noise a cat should make.

When they got back to the hotel, he saw two of the doormen look at the cat carrier and exchange glances, but nobody tried to stop them as they proceeded up to the fourteenth floor. Thankfully, the cat had stopped squealing now that it was out of the car.

Once inside the hotel room, he had Jules and Charity wait near the door while he did a quick inspection of the rooms. When he was confident the space was clear, he motioned them forward. Charity, still holding the cat cage, turned in circles.

"Wow. I've never stayed in a hotel like this before," she said.

"There's your bedroom and bath," Jules said, pointing off to the left.

Charity nodded, still looking awestruck. "I guess I should let Hogi out. He really liked it when we stayed at the Super 8."

Well, then, the cat should be ecstatic at the Periwinkle. Calling up all his cat friends, inviting them over for tuna.

The vision in Royce's head made him think that he might really have lost his mind. But then again, it was easier to think of stupid things than remember what it had felt like to see Jules's body up against the wall, her air supply being shut off.

Her, being there in that squalid little apartment, in that kind of danger, it made him crazy.

Once Charity and her cat had gone off to her bedroom, he turned to Jules. "All of this was unnecessary," he said. "All you had to do was stay here. Like I asked."

Jules sighed. "I'm sorry, Royce. I really am. But in retrospect, I'd do it again. If that man had come home and seen Charity all packed up and ready to go, well, like she said, she might be one of the horrible news stories that we hear about and shake our heads. I couldn't have lived with myself if that had happened."

And I couldn't have lived with something happening to you. He thought it, but he didn't say it. They'd ended their relationship eight years ago; there was no reason for her to know that the old feelings that he'd long believed buried had sprung up from the dead and were now a waving red flag. And he was the sorry-ass bull that couldn't keep from charging.

"So you two have been corresponding back and forth for some time?"

"Today was our second conversation and our first face-to-face meeting. But what does it matter?" she asked, her tone suggesting that he was pushing some buttons.

"Because my job is to provide security for you. And you've just introduced a new person into the mix. So now my job is to figure out who this new person is and identify any risks that she may pose to you. It's what you're paying me for."

"Fine," she said, her mouth barely moving.

"What's her mother's name?"

"Linette White."

"And how did your mom and Linette become friends?"

"She came to the house to wash windows," she said.

He supposed odder things had happened. But not much odder. "There had to be more than that."

"Of course."

Royce had trained himself to hear even the slightest nuance in a person's delivery, to note a change in tone, pace or inflection. And that's what he heard now. Was she lying to him? Why?

"And that was…?" he prompted.

"I think my mom was impressed by her work. She must have thought that Linette could do more. Ultimately, she recommended Linette for a position at the bank where my father worked."

"So your dad was friends with Linette, also?"

She shook her head. "I'm not sure about that. I just know that my mother kept in contact with Linette for several years after she stopped coming to our house to wash windows."

"When's the last time your mom saw Linette?" he asked.

She shrugged. "I'm not sure," she said. She looked him squarely in the eye. "Linette died eight months ago. I guess that takes her off the list of suspects who may or may not be trying to harm me."

He didn't take the bait. "I'm sorry to hear that," he said.

She didn't acknowledge his half-baked consolation. "Is there anything else?"

"How is it that you and Charity found each other?"

"Recently I remembered that Linette had a daughter and I hired someone to find her."

"You just remembered this? And felt compelled to find someone that you'd had no contact with?"

"Yes."

Now he was fairly confident that she was lying. But he didn't think she was about to tell him the truth.

He wanted to know more. But since his gut was telling him that it was unlikely Charity had written threatening letters and postmarked them from three different cities, he decided it could wait. He opened the leather briefcase that he'd pulled from the car. "I have the contract," he said.

She took it, glanced at it and tossed it on the coffee table. "I'll give it to Barry."

"Tell me about Barry," he said.

"I thought we'd covered that. He's the chairman of the Miatroth board."

"And..."

"How do you know there's an and?"

He glanced at his watch. "We could probably get through this more quickly if you were more forthcoming with the answers."

She sighed. "I've known Barry since I was a kid. He's my dad's friend."

He did not want to talk about Jules's father. "And that's how he got to be the chairman of the board of Miatroth?"

"Of course not. Barry was an executive at Geneseel. That's where we met. He later retired. It's not unusual that former industry executives become board chairmen somewhere else."

He had sensed that Barry cared deeply about Jules. He was confident the man was not a threat to her.

"Tell me about your schedule," he said. "We need to start planning."

She nodded, as if she'd accepted the inevitable. "Fine. But I'm going to order some lunch first. Charity said she was hungry. What would you like?"

To hear the truth. "Anything is fine."

"Still like burgers?" she asked, already picking up the receiver of the phone.

"Still like turkey clubs?" he asked.

The air in the room seemed to still. They had a history. Brief, perhaps. But significant. They knew things about one another. Simple things. And very intimate things.

She put down the phone. "Is this going to work?" she asked.

"It might be best if we stop making assumptions about the other," he said, talking as if he had a stiff board up his butt. He was rattled and hated the feeling.

"It's hard," she admitted. "In some ways, it doesn't seem as if eight years have gone by. Maybe that sounds silly to you."

No, it didn't. But he couldn't admit that.

She was staring at his left hand. "You aren't wearing a wedding ring, Royce. Did you ever marry?"

Had barely dated. Had told himself, and the others who were brave enough to ask, that he was too busy working and going to school. Hadn't been a monk, that was for sure. But the relationships were brief, unencumbered.

He hadn't been stupid enough to think he was waiting for Jules. Just hadn't been willing to accept something that was so much less than what he'd known that summer in New York.

"No," he said. "Appears you weren't married for long."

"No," she whispered. "Bryson deserved better."

He could not have a conversation about the man. Eight years ago, she'd told him it was over. He'd believed her.

Had never guessed that she'd lie about something so important. Had never guessed that a few short months later, she'd hurt him so badly.

Chapter 7

JC ordered lunch and then handed Royce a paper copy of her electronic calendar. It was color coded. "My assistant does that," she said, a little embarrassed to be caught being so anal retentive. But he didn't appear to care how she kept track of her life.

He pointed at the first entry, a two-hour block this afternoon, that she'd labeled "Financial Review/Cole Hager/Wallington Hotel."

"Cole Hager. Who is that?" he asked.

"He's the senior analyst for a large mutual fund. Our board is hoping that he'll come out strong in support for us."

"Isn't it the CFO's job to talk to investors about financial results?"

"Yes. And he'll probably do that. But I've met Cole once before and it's not that strange that he'd want to talk to me, too."

"He can't come here?"

"I don't want to ask him to do that. At this point, it would look like a power play on my part and that's not in my best interest."

He made no response to that. Simply settled his index finger on the *X* that she'd used to block out 10:00 a.m. to noon the next day with *Sparrow* next to it. "What's this?" he asked.

She'd written the information on the sheet after she'd printed her electronic calendar. Her assistant would be upset that it wasn't appropriately color coded. "Sparrow is the room name," she said. "Evidently, all their meeting rooms are named after birds."

"What's happening there?" he asked.

"That's the panel presentation I mentioned this morning. I wasn't originally scheduled to do it but evidently one of the original presenters had a conflict. Wayne Isman contacted me and asked if I'd fill in."

"Wayne Isman. Your old boss at Geneseel?"

She was surprised that he'd remembered. "Yeah. We've kept in touch over the years. We do some humanitarian work in Africa together. This particular presentation is on new pathways to fighting drug-resistant bacteria. Wayne knows that's a topic near and dear to my heart and he figured I wouldn't need much prep time."

"Who else is on the panel?" he asked.

"Besides Wayne and me, there's a physician from Mass General."

"Name?"

She knew where this was going. "Really, Royce? You think my two fellow panelists are hit men in disguise?"

"I think that they'll be the two closest to you during the event. That automatically puts them on my watch list."

"Fine." She reached into her bag that was at the end

of the couch and pulled out a sheet of paper. "This is hot off the press. Wayne is getting enough printed that we can give one to every attendee."

He stared at the paper and she regretted the impulse to show it to him. Not only were there biographies for Wayne Isman and Dr. Lilah Moorhead, there was also one for her. He knew her educational background and her work history. But would he be surprised to learn that she'd served on a presidential committee? Or that she authored a white paper that had gotten her an appearance on the *Today* show?

"I remember you thinking a lot of Wayne Isman," he said, pointing at the man's picture.

She was grateful that he didn't want to talk about her. "He was a wonderful boss. I learned so much from him. Very bright and, of course, he's got that killer accent, too," she added.

"Australian, right?" he asked.

She nodded. "I could listen to him read the phone book and be totally entertained."

"The phone book, huh? I haven't run across one of those, but there's a manual that describes how the dishwasher works in that cupboard." He pointed across the room.

It was a spark of the old Royce, the one who made easy jokes and found pleasure in silly things.

"I'm sure that would be lovely, too. Wayne is one of the most respected people in the industry," JC said. "The project we've been collaborating on is making children's vaccines more readily available in underdeveloped countries." She paused. "Of course, I let him do most of the talking in the meetings."

"The accent thing," he said. "I got it."

He was staring at the paper. Wayne was a good-looking

man. Was it possible that Royce thought they were collaborating on more than the vaccine project?

"Wayne Isman has been married for many years. He talks about his wife all the time. I met her once and thought she was lovely. And he's crazy about his three daughters."

"How nice for him," he said, as if he couldn't care less.

Maybe she'd read him wrong. Or maybe she'd been hoping that he was just a teensy bit jealous.

She was pathetic.

"Do attendees preregister for these sessions?" he asked.

"No. This is like most conferences. There are concurrent sessions and attendees are free to choose whatever sparks their interest at the time. There are probably seven or eight different sessions in each time slot. Presenters have been advised to plan for 150 to 200 attendees."

"I wish you wouldn't do this," he said.

"We're not confident that it's even a real threat."

"We're not confident that it isn't."

She sighed. "Look, I don't want it to be obvious that I've got security."

"I'll do the best I can," he said. "But no promises. If I feel that the situation warrants it, I'm going to shut it down."

"The session?" she said incredulously.

"At least your participation in it."

He was serious. "Royce, I have a professional reputation to maintain."

"My job is to keep you safe. That's the priority."

Of course that was what she wanted, too. "All I'm asking is that if it's possible, I'd like the two goals not to be mutually exclusive."

He shifted his attention back to the calendar. Six to ten

on Thursday night was colored green and labeled Ballroom. "Is that the awards dinner?" he asked.

"Yes. It may not last that long, but I wanted to plan on the careful side."

She was not the type to arrive three minutes before going onstage—after anyone remotely responsible for the event had had a mild stroke for fear that she wasn't going to show—and then leave as soon as the applause had ended.

She would arrive on time, mingle with other attendees, participate in dinner conversation, hopefully give a great speech and then hang around to answer questions afterward.

He leaned back in his chair. "Who else has access to your schedule?"

"Glory, my administrative assistant, and I are the only one who can see the details. Others, many others, of course, can look at my calendar and know if I'm busy or out of the office. Makes it easier to schedule things."

"We need to change that. Immediately."

"But—"

Royce shook his head. "Can Glory do that on your behalf?"

She nodded. This was a small hill. Certainly not one she intended to die upon. "Yes."

"Good. And I need Glory's information. Full name, address, social."

"Miatroth has a rigid background screening process, I assure you."

"I don't care. How long has she worked for you?"

"Five years."

"No recent issues? Strange behaviors? Odd conversations?"

She shook her head. "She's amazing." She wanted

to implore Royce not to do anything that might upset Glory. The woman was already a little irritated with JC because she hadn't gotten to come to Vegas, one of her very favorite places. "A good assistant is worth his or her weight in gold."

"Noted," he said.

A knock on the door made her jerk. Royce motioned for her to stay where she was. He looked through the peephole. "Room service," he whispered, turning to look back at her. "Fast."

"Bet the orders from the suites get priority."

This from Charity who'd again emerged from her bedroom. She was carrying Hogi. The cat seemed calmer and when Charity put him down, he promptly jumped into one of the deep windowsills and pressed his nose up against the pane.

Royce opened the door and motioned the young man outside to come in. Then he watched him like a hawk, as if confident that he was intent upon doing them harm versus getting the tray delivered and returning to the kitchen for the next one.

She signed the room charge slip and added a generous tip, not only because of Royce's scrutiny but partially in pity for the checkered bow tie and cummerbund the poor man had to wear. She'd always thought periwinkle blue was sort of a pretty color before this, but the combination of it and olive green just wasn't nice.

Once he was gone, the three of them sat down at the glass-topped table. For a few minutes, the only sounds in the room was silverware softly clicking against the plates.

Royce was almost half-done with his burger before he spoke again. "So, Charity, are you a student?"

"Like in college?" Charity said, her upper lip raised in a sneer.

Royce nodded.

"Not for me," Charity said.

Royce put down his fork. "So you're working?"

"I would," Charity said. "But nobody seems inclined to help me have the American dream."

If Charity had come across as snippy in the interviews as she was acting now, JC understood why she was unemployed. But based on what the private detective had been able to dig up, the kid had had some hard knocks and she suspected some of Charity's bravado was more for show. "I have a few contacts," JC said. "I'd be happy to make some calls."

"We'll see," Charity said.

JC snuck a look at the clock in the kitchen. She did not live in a world where one wasted a whole morning. Not that meeting Charity had been a waste. No, that was totally worth it. But to miss a whole morning of work was going to set her back substantially. "I have to be at the Wallington in an hour," she said, looking at Royce.

He nodded. "That hotel is fairly new, at the far end of the strip. Will take about fifteen minutes to get there."

JC pushed back her chair. "I'm going to get ready," she said.

Charity stood up, too. "I'm going down to the pool."

She smiled at the young woman. "Great. Have a good afternoon. Let's plan to eat dinner together at seven."

He knew there really was no reason that Charity couldn't use the hotel services. While they'd arrived back at the hotel together, it was still unlikely that anyone would readily connect her to Jules. And, even if scumbag Bobby had somehow already wrangled a way out of jail, he wouldn't know to come to the Periwinkle.

Besides, it wasn't his job to protect Charity.

But for whatever reason, it seemed as if Charity was important to Jules, and that quite frankly made her important to Royce. Even if she was uneducated, unemployed and not terribly concerned about either.

Not in school, not working. Not impressive. If she intended to shake down Jules for money, he hoped Jules was smarter than that.

While Jules got ready for her meeting and Charity got ready for the pool, Royce made phone calls. The first one was to a trusted contact within the Vegas police department. After their brief conversation, Royce was satisfied that he'd know about Bobby's release before Bobby would.

The man had had his hands around Jules's neck. That vision was going to linger in Royce's brain for a while and it put Bobby on the list of people to watch.

Next he started a background search on Charity. Jules seemed satisfied that their mothers had been friends, so that automatically made Charity a friend. Royce wasn't so easily convinced. He suspected Jules would be irritated that he'd initiated the background search, but that wasn't his concern right now.

He was focused on keeping her alive.

When Jules came out of her bedroom, she'd changed out of her casual sweater, skirt and boots to a sapphire-blue suit with a white blouse. She looked crisp and professional, and he knew that when she walked into a room, both the women and the men there would take notice. The women would be a little jealous, secretly wishing they could pull off the same look.

The men—well, that was simple. They'd all want to have her in their beds.

It had gotten him in trouble once before.

Chapter 8

They'd been three weeks into their relationship, a week past the mind-blowing experience in the pool cabana, when Jules had invited him to attend a work thing. It was a banquet and she was on the short list for something called the President's Award of Distinction.

The thing was black tie and he spent two hundred bucks he didn't have renting a tuxedo. The shirt was too tight around the collar and the pants loose enough that Jules had joked, on the way to the event in the cab, that she could easily slip a hand inside.

The thought of that kept a smile on his face even as they walked into a cloud of heavy perfume and forced laughter. The event was on the top floor of the Waldorf Astoria in New York City, and the room had been full of vice presidents, senior vice presidents and all kinds of other self-important titles. Then there were the up-and-comers, the saps a few corporate layers down who had aspirations of rising to the top.

Jules was technically one of the saps, but he knew she was different. For one thing, she was the most beautiful woman in the room. She'd worn a gold gown, and her skin had fairly shimmered in the dim lighting. He saw the men in the room looking her direction, and somehow, his brain cells evaporated and he morphed into a monosyllabic grunter who had difficulty matching nouns with verbs.

He was not just a fish out of water; he was more like a fish washed up and rotting on the shore.

He knew his deficiencies. There was no prep school or Ivy League university on his résumé. No internship with one of the big six consulting firms. He'd been an unengaged student who'd graduated from high school and then spent a good portion of the next decade in countries the people in that ballroom didn't want to think about, let alone talk about.

Jules had tried to include him in the dinner conversation, but after the third or fourth knowing look from someone else that made him realize he hadn't said exactly the right thing in the right way, he'd pretty much stopped talking altogether.

There was a pompous ass at the table happy to step in and monopolize Jules's attention. And when the awards had been announced, and Jules named the winner, his hug and congratulatory kiss on the cheek had lasted seconds too long for Royce.

And like a damn caveman, he'd grabbed the back of the guy's tux and yanked him a foot off the ground. It had been Jules's pinched white face that had finally cleared his head.

He'd set the man back on his feet, knowing he'd embarrassed Jules on her big night and that it wasn't going to be possible to redeem himself.

The cab ride home had been absolutely silent. They reached her apartment and he expected that she'd tell him not to bother getting out.

But Jules had held out her hand, looked into his eyes and said, "Come up. We can talk where it's private."

And the short story was that she'd forgiven him. That's what she'd said and what he believed. At least until that fateful day in her father's apartment. After that, he'd had lots of time to wonder if that night hadn't been the beginning of the end.

Had that been the night when she'd realized he was never going to fit into her world?

"Are you ready?" she asked as she slung her leather bag over her shoulder.

He held up his keys. "Are you nervous about leaving Charity alone in your suite?" He spoke softly. She had not yet left for the pool and he didn't want her to hear him.

She shook her head. "No."

"If your clothes, jewelry and other valuables are gone when we come back, don't blame me."

She looked him in the eye. "I have my wallet, my computer and all my extra jewelry in this bag. If she's so determined to rob me that she wants to go to the trouble of hawking some clothes, well, so be it. I'm not an idiot, Royce."

"I have never thought you were an idiot, Jules," he said, his teeth almost gnashing together.

"Never?" she challenged.

What was she looking for? An affirmation that she'd been smart to kick him to the curb? A declaration that she obviously didn't make great decisions because look how well her marriage had turned out?

Not a lot to be gained by staring into the rearview mirror. Distortion and regret were a bad combination.

He opened the door a crack to check the hallway. Then he motioned for her. "If we're going, let's get to it."

Traffic on the strip was heavy, and the sidewalks were filled with people strolling around in light jackets on the pleasant winter day. She'd seen the New York weather this morning on the news, and it was snowing there.

"I suppose putting the top down is out of the question," she said.

He nodded. "Probably not in your best interest."

She didn't argue. Couldn't fault Royce for taking his job seriously. Couldn't fault him, either, for questioning her judgment in befriending Charity and giving her the run of the suite.

But she needed to trust Charity so that, in turn, Charity would trust her. They were going to have to bond together to find the truth. At this point, JC wasn't settling for anything else.

She and Royce did not talk again for the fifteen minutes it took to reach the Wallington Hotel. Once they arrived, she saw him give the valet parking attendant a hundred dollars to park his car just so. It dawned on her that he easily handled the transaction, and she had the feeling that he had come a long way from the young man who'd gone a bit pale when he'd seen the menu prices at the restaurant that first night they'd dined together.

She'd wanted to pick up the check but had refrained from insisting. He'd been thoroughly charming in a most refreshing way, but she'd worried that he might be a traditionalist and be offended if she offered to pay.

And she hadn't wanted to risk that because she'd had such a good time talking.

Here they were, eight years later, all the words evidently having been said. She stepped into the revolving door and he crowded in behind her. They were so close they were almost touching. She caught his scent of sandalwood and took another quick breath so that she could draw it deep into her lungs.

Her body felt instantly warm. Memories. So many memories.

In bed. Him behind her. Pounding flesh. Hot skin.

So much pleasure.

As soon as the path was clear, she moved fast, desperate for some distance, some perspective.

"Stay close," he whispered, his hand clamping down on her upper arm.

"Fine," she said, shaking him off. Inside the lavish hotel, she wasn't surprised to see slot machines just off the large lobby. Almost every place in Vegas had gaming. She knew it was available at the Periwinkle as well, just not quite this close to the registration desk. She wasn't averse to pulling the handle of a slot machine a time or two. But she hated the idea that people were losing money they didn't have on the foolishness.

She headed toward the bar, looking for Cole Hager. The first time she'd met him, she'd thought he was smart and asked good questions. She saw him at the back booth. He had a drink in front of him and he was reading something on his phone.

She motioned to Royce and he gave her a short nod in response.

She stopped in front of the booth. "Mr. Hager. JC Cambridge. So good to see you again."

He slid out of the booth and extended his hand. "Please, just Cole. Very nice to see you as well, JC." He glanced at Royce.

"This is Royce. He's…a friend. You don't mind if he joins us, do you?"

Cole smiled. "As long as he's not bored by return on investment and equity growth charts."

"I'm sure he's not," JC said easily and slid into the booth.

She undoubtedly thought he *would* be bored because the discussion would be above his head. Had no way of knowing that after New York he'd gone to college and gotten not only an undergraduate degree but also an MBA with an emphasis in finance. He could definitely keep up. Still, he pretended to ignore them, not willing to let them know that he was tracking with everything being said. Instead, he sat at an angle in the booth, where he could watch the front door. He couldn't see the back exit of the bar, just a swinging door that led to the kitchen. The only people coming through it were servers carrying trays of food.

A young woman wearing a very short black skirt and white shirt approached the table to take their drink orders.

"I can speak for their whiskey," Cole said. "Want one?"

Jules shook her head and ordered an iced tea. Royce did the same. Cole ordered a refill.

As he pretended not to listen, he grew more and more impressed with Jules. She clearly knew her business, knew the details of their financial performance and was very effectively making her argument that investing in Miatroth was smart.

Cole Hager looked convinced. Although Royce suspected that Jules could be spouting pork statistics and asking him to invest in hot dog stands and he'd have lapped it up, because he quite frankly seemed pretty focused on the way her jacket hugged her breasts.

Finally the man, who had looked at his watch at least a half-dozen times during the interview, said that he was late for another meeting and needed to run. He stood and hung on to Jules's hand just a second too long before walking quickly out of the bar.

Royce waited as Jules gathered up her papers, and then they also left. As they crossed the hotel lobby, Royce said, "Well, that's an hour of my life that I'm never getting back."

Jules turned, giving him a look that had probably encouraged junior executives to polish up their résumés.

He was in the wrong. He was being paid to provide a service, and quite frankly, meeting in an air-conditioned bar with Jimmy Buffet tunes playing in the background didn't warrant combat pay. And he wouldn't have made the comment to any other client. He'd have kept his damn mouth shut.

But he'd wanted to make some kind of point with Jules.

Which spoke volumes about his maturity level.

"I'm sorry," he said.

She waved aside his apology. "I'm worried about him. I don't recall him having a drinking problem, but two whiskeys before cocktail hour begins is hitting it pretty hard."

"He seemed a little enamored with you," Royce said. They walked outside and the parking attendant hurried over to get their claim ticket.

"I don't know about—"

Royce tackled her just as the window behind them exploded in a shower of glass. He shifted, pulled his weapon with his right hand and used his left to grab the back of Jules's jacket.

"Stay low," he said.

And then he propelled them both back inside the hotel, away from the windows. "Call 911," he ordered the wide-eyed desk clerk.

Then he turned his attention to Jules. She was pale and her breaths were coming fast and there was, oh, God no, blood running down her face. Had she been hit?

"You're bleeding," he said. "Get me a damn ambulance," he roared.

Then, with one eye still on the door, he grabbed her hand. "Sit," he said, pulling her into a nearby armchair. He took a closer look at her injury. She had a horizontal slice at the edge of her hairline, and blood was trickling down the right side of her face. The cut was a half-inch long and he had no way of telling how deep.

It was not a bullet hole.

"I think you caught a glass fragment. You'll be fine," he added, reassuring himself more than her.

"Okay," she said, sounding dazed.

He saw two middle-aged men, both in blue suits similar to what the assistant manager at the Periwinkle wore, quickly exit an elevator. The desk clerk pointed their direction. The men split—one headed toward him and Jules while the other tried to calm a group of women travelers who were screaming.

Jules wasn't screaming and the good news was that she looked a little less dazed. "What the hell just happened?" she asked, her voice still weak.

"My guess is a high-powered rifle from about a thousand yards out. Just sit tight. Help is on the way."

Blue Suit stopped in front of them. He had a name badge. Kent Meartz—Manager. He stared at Jules, at the blood that was trickling down her face.

"We've called an ambulance," he said. He wiped away the sweat on his upper lip.

Royce could hear it coming. The siren was getting louder.

But he realized it wasn't going to get there fast enough when he saw two things that made him unhappy. The first was Cole Hager. He was across the lobby, statue-still, looking right at Jules.

But before he could make eye contact with the man and let him know to keep his damn distance, the man turned and left, practically running.

Now, wasn't that interesting.

But Royce didn't have time to think too much about it because the second thing that had made him unhappy was gaining ground. Two men and a woman were running across the lobby, toward the shattered window. He recognized the woman as a local news anchor. One of the men with her had a camera around his neck.

"How the hell did they get here so quickly?" he muttered.

The manager turned to look. Then looked back at Royce, looking even more miserable. "The staff from *News 7* uses one of our meeting rooms every other week. Team building."

Royce looked at Jules, and she had enough spirit to roll her eyes.

He stepped in front of her just as the trio spotted them and veered to the left. Like dogs looking for meat, they trotted over.

"I'm Sky Barker from Channel 7," she said. "What happened here?"

"No comment," Royce said.

The guy with the camera took the lens cap off.

The siren noise was now blaringly loud. The paramedics had to be right outside the door. "You're impeding medical care," Royce said. He knew he couldn't keep them from covering a legitimate news story, but he was going to give it the old college try. "Please move out of the way," Royce said, pointing across the lobby.

Thankfully, the manager seemed to have his head in the game and he motioned for the trio to follow him. "Our general manager will provide a statement for the press."

Royce remained stationed in front of Jules until they were across the lobby.

"Hey," she said, "how do you know it was a high-powered rifle from about a thousand yards out?"

Royce turned to smile at her. "Not going to let that go, huh?"

"No."

"I saw a glint of something."

"And you knew, just from that?"

"I managed to stay alive in countries where there were plenty of people hoping for a different outcome. You learn not to waste a lot of time when you see something that doesn't look just right."

"Do you…" She swallowed hard. "Do you think someone was shooting at me?"

"Given what else has occurred since you arrived in Vegas, I don't think we can make any other assumption," he said.

She let her head drop. "I really wish I'd said yes when Cole Hager encouraged me to have a whiskey."

He didn't mention that he'd seen the man staring at Jules. But that didn't mean he'd forgotten it. As far as he was concerned, Cole Hager had some explaining to do.

Chapter 9

Royce had saved her life. Again.

Because he'd seen a glint of something.

Amazing.

She simply had no words. But there was no time for them anyway because the paramedics had entered the lobby and were moving quickly in her direction.

A young man who looked barely legal to drive slapped a blood-pressure cuff on her and looked satisfied when it was 115 over 72. Then he used a penlight to temporarily blind her as he checked her pupils. Finally, he examined the cut on her head. After a little poking, he ripped open some antiseptic pads to clean it. He said, "I'm pretty sure there's no glass in it, but I think it's deep enough that you're going to want to get it stitched up."

That was enough that when the police arrived a few minutes later and wanted to talk to her, Royce interceded. He gave the officer both their names and his business card. Then he said she'd been advised to seek medical treatment and asked if she could please provide a statement later.

The words were a request but it seemed rather like a forgone conclusion the way he said it.

Luckily the cop didn't take offense. If she had to guess, he was mostly relieved that nobody had taken a bullet at the scene and nodded that they could go.

Before she knew it, they were in his car, on the way to an urgent care center that he looked up on his smartphone. As he drove, he was constantly checking his mirrors. "Are we being followed?" she asked.

"Nope. I'm making sure of that."

"That's good then, right?"

He nodded. "Yeah, but I have some bad news. As we were exiting the hotel, I saw the photographer. I think he might have gotten a picture."

She waved a hand. "Nobody watches network news anymore."

"I'm more worried about how you'll trend on social media."

"Ugh." That made her head hurt more than any chunk of glass ever could. They drove for another minute. "I'm going to have to tell Charity. And Barry so that he can handle the board. And—" she stopped and slid a sideways glance his direction "—if the story gets any traction, probably my father."

To Royce's credit, he didn't crash the car.

"Give him my best," he said as they pulled into the medical facility.

He stayed close while she gave the receptionist her insurance information. When they called her name, he stood up.

"You don't have to come back with me," she said.

"I do," was all he said.

Once they were in a treatment room, a nurse came in, took her blood pressure again, looked at her eyes again and took her temperature. She keyed everything into a laptop computer and then advised them that a doctor would be right in. Fifteen minutes later, she was proved right.

"A couple stitches should do it," Dr. Michele Snider, a middle-aged woman who needed her roots tidied up, pronounced after looking at her cut for about five seconds. "I don't think you'll even have a scar," she added.

"There go my bragging rights," JC said. She smiled at Royce but he didn't smile back.

Once the stitches were in and covered with a small bandage, she finally pulled a mirror out of her purse to look. She studied her reflection for a minute.

It wasn't great, but if she parted her hair just a little differently and swept her bangs to the side, it was possible that nobody would even know.

"I should give the police a statement," she said as they walked back to the car.

"Do you feel up to that? Maybe you should go home and rest."

"I think I'd prefer to get it over with."

Royce nodded and scanned through the contacts on his smartphone. In just minutes, he'd connected with the Las Vegas Police Department.

When Royce ended the call, he said, "We got lucky. Mark Mannis is the detective on the case. I met him a few years ago and he's solid. He's going to meet us at your hotel in twenty minutes."

The drive to the hotel took ten minutes. While they were in the car, JC called Barry. He was upset to hear that she'd been injured and really not happy that the news might have snapped a picture. She played it down. Finally, he said he would inform the executive committee of the board but not the full board, unless the story got more play than she anticipated.

Once inside the hotel, she was relieved to see that the suite was empty. She wanted to get the next part over with before she had to talk to Charity.

Ten minutes later, the detective showed up. JC could immediately tell why Royce had been satisfied with Mark Mannis. He was early fifties, had a confident handshake and a professional demeanor.

"Can you tell me what happened?" he asked, addressing the question to her.

"I was a couple seconds behind the action," she admitted, "but I'll do my best. We had just exited the hotel and Royce was handing our parking voucher to the attendant. The next thing I know, I'm on the ground and a bullet has hit the window behind me."

Detective Mannis turned to Royce. "What did you see?"

"Glint of light, about thirty degrees off the horizon."

"Good eye," Detective Mannis said. "I'm sorry, Ms. Cambridge, that you had the bad luck to be standing next to Ramone Jakarati when his brother's war followed him to work."

Huh? What the heck was he talking about? She looked at Royce but he was frowning at the detective. "I don't understand," she said.

"Ramone Jakarati's older brother has known gang affiliations. We believe he was responsible for a couple murders of rival gang members that occurred this past month but we don't have quite enough yet to arrest him. Today, the rival gang tried to exact their own justice by killing Ramone, which is a damn shame because Ramone mostly keeps his nose clean. He has parked cars at the Wallington since it opened."

Royce stood up. "So you think that we got in the middle of a gang war?"

"It's the most reasonable explanation," the detective said.

Royce shook his head. "You might not think that once you hear Jules's story."

The detective looked between the two of them. "I'm listening."

Royce motioned for her to tell it. She tried to be concise as she told him about the three letters and the car almost striking her. When she finished, he didn't say anything for a minute.

Finally, he shifted in his chair. "I want to congratulate you on your decision to hire Royce. Wingman Security is very good at what they do."

She had not told him about her history with Royce and did not intend to.

"I guess we're not going to know for sure whether this attack was directed at you or at Ramone until we catch the shooter," he added.

"What are the chances of that?" she asked.

He shrugged. "Based on where the bullet hit the glass and ultimately landed, we've identified a likely origination point. Now that we've gotten this additional information, we'll go back and take another look."

She'd complicated their open-and-shut case, making them question what they believed to be true.

Well, that was fair. She, too, was feeling rather undone by the last hour. She'd gone from denial, thinking the letters were simply ugly stupid threats, to accepting that someone really wanted to hurt her. It had been a painful transition. Now she was back to thinking that there was a chance that it had been much ado about nothing.

"In the meantime, I think you're going to want to be careful, Ms. Cambridge," Detective Mannis said.

Royce would probably want to put her in bubble wrap. She'd be lucky if she could stub her toe. "Of course," she said. She stood up. Both men did, as well.

The detective shook hands with both of them and then Royce walked him to the door. When he came back into the room, he looked tired. She suspected she looked the same. It had been quite a day. At eight o'clock this morning, neither of them had realized the other was in Vegas. Late morning, it had been the altercation at Charity's apartment. Midafternoon had them ducking bullets. And now, with dinner on the horizon, confusion was the theme of the moment.

"What do you think?" she asked.

"I don't know. About all I'm certain of is that the shooter was a bad shot. Regardless of whether he was aiming for Ramone or for you, he missed you both." He looked up from his folded hands. "Not that I'm sorry about that," he added, with the sleepy smile that she'd always loved.

She felt her heart lurch in her chest. For the moment, she'd felt as if the last eight years had slipped away. That smile was the one she would often see early mornings, after she and Royce had awakened from the night and made love as the sun had risen.

"What?" he asked.

She felt the heat all the way up to her ears. She sure as hell wasn't telling him the truth. "I was thinking that I should put a couple dollars into one of the machines. I think this might be my lucky day."

He didn't answer because both of them heard the door

of the suite opening. In walked Charity, wearing shorts and a bikini top with a beach towel draped over her shoulders. She was really way too thin. She carried a book.

"Hi," Charity said, looking at them. "What's going on?"

"We were discussing dinner," JC said easily. She willed Royce to go along. "What's your pleasure?"

"Can we go out?" Charity said.

"We're eating in," Royce said immediately. He leaned forward, toward the coffee table, and pushed the hotel restaurant menu in her direction. "Here's your choices."

She looked for a few minutes and then tossed the menu down. "I'll take the shrimp scampi," she said. "I'm going to shower first."

JC waited until she heard the bedroom door open and shut before she spoke. "Thank you. I'll let her get cleaned up and then tell her. I'm going to give her just enough that if she sees something, she's not totally surprised but not so much that she gets nervous."

"I hope *you're* nervous," Royce said. "It might give you the edge you need." He handed her the menu. "What would you like?"

Her appetite had been lost somewhere between getting shot at and getting stitches at the urgent care center. But she knew that she needed to eat. "Crab cakes," she said after quickly glancing.

He picked up the phone and rattled off Charity's order, then JC's, and finally ordered a steak for himself. After he finished, he hung up. Then, seeming a little ill at ease, he picked up the wine list.

"They've got a nice pinot noir," he said. "Maybe I should have gotten you a glass of that."

Had he remembered that was her favorite wine? She reached for the drink menu. He was right. It was a small

Oregon vineyard with a great reputation for their pinots. Not everyone would know that. "You didn't used to drink wine," she said.

He stared at her, his eyes unreadable. "I suppose we're both pretty different than we were eight years ago," he said.

Was she? A better leader, she hoped. Broader knowledge of the pharmaceutical industry, for sure. Her butt a little less firm? Ick.

He was even more handsome. She liked his short hair. It showed off the high cheekbones, the wide jaw. He'd been very tan eight years ago and that was still the same. Back then, she'd thought the tan came from his time in the service. He'd said it was from his trip from Texas to New York. "Do you still have a motorcycle?" she asked.

He looked surprised at the question. "No. I sold it. Needed the money for school."

"School?"

He nodded. "Texas A&M. Bachelor's in business, master's in finance."

"Wow. I had no idea."

He frowned at her. "Didn't think I had it in me?"

"Of course not. You were always incredibly bright. You just never talked about going to school."

There was a long silence. "Maybe we should have talked more," he said finally. "Maybe I'd have realized that it wasn't over between you and Bryson."

She felt a pain in her chest, as if a knife had gone deep. It had been over. But by admitting that, she would be opening a door that she wasn't ready for. She put down the wine list. "I'll be in my room. I've got a lot of work to do." She moved to grab her briefcase but then heard Charity's door open.

The girl came down the hall, wearing the green dress

she'd worn earlier. Her wet hair hung down to the middle of her back. She was carrying her cat.

JC only wanted to escape to her room, where she might have a good cry, but she knew that she needed to have this conversation first. "Do you have a minute?" she asked her.

"Sure." The girl sank down on the couch and put her bare feet on the edge of the glass coffee table. Hogi took a spot on the chair, lying on the beach towel that Charity had left there earlier.

"I have something that I want to tell you. I don't want it to scare you but forewarned is forearmed."

"Okay," Charity said.

"Royce and I had some excitement today. After my meeting at the hotel, as we were leaving, we were almost hit by stray bullets."

Charity's dark eyes got even bigger. "A drive-by?"

JC didn't correct her. "I got a little cut. Nothing serious," she said, lifting up her bangs.

"You think you'll have a scar?"

"Hope not. Anyway, it is possible that a news reporter may have gotten a picture. If they discover that I'm the CEO of Miatroth, it's also possible the picture could get some play. If you saw it, I didn't want you to be surprised."

"Did they get the shooter?" Charity asked.

"Not that I know of," JC said. "Listen, I just wanted to tell you about this before you heard the information somewhere else. I wanted you to get the facts from me."

Charity pointed at Royce. "Where were you when this happened? I thought you were security," she accused.

"Royce pushed me down," JC said quickly, automatically defending him. "He saved my life."

"Wow. Just like that old movie, the one my mom always watched." She snapped her thin fingers. "I know. *The Bodyguard*. The one with Whitney Houston and Kevin Costner."

As she recalled, Kevin Costner had loved Whitney Houston. "Trust me on this, not exactly that. I can't sing," JC added.

"My mom thought Kevin Costner was so hot," she said.

She was happy that Charity didn't seem to be freaking out. Had Linette White also thought Joel Cambridge was hot? The idea made JC's empty stomach cramp up. But it was the opening she'd hoped for. She didn't necessarily want to have the conversation in front of Royce, but this was a natural segue.

"I think my mom thought he was hot, too," JC said. "Our moms probably had a lot in common. Did your mom like to read?"

"I guess. She worked part-time in a bookstore. Checking people out."

That information had been in the report that she'd requested. It was a minimum-wage-type job. How had Linette White supported herself and her daughter? During their first conversation, after JC had expressed sympathy over Charity's mom's death, she'd asked about Charity's father and the girl had shared that she'd never known him.

With that information, a thousand other questions had popped up in JC's mind and she'd known that nothing short of meeting Charity in person was going to make her happy.

The private investigator she'd hired had confirmed that Linette White had never married. It had not answered the question of how the woman had managed to support herself and her daughter on a part-time salary.

Was it possible that Linette White had gotten financial help from Joel Cambridge? Was it possible that her father knew about Charity but had never acknowledged her? How could he have done that?

But then, JC had never expected her own mother would send a message from her grave. Well, not exactly. As best as JC could tell, the message had been written just weeks before her death. Unfortunately, it hadn't been found for another nineteen years.

Old secrets.

Charity remembered that her mom worked at a bookstore. But she'd also worked as a secretary at the bank. What did Charity know about that? "My mom had really good organizational skills," JC said. "Really good at remembering details. I have a great assistant and I know how wonderful it is to have someone like that in my office."

"My mom was more of a hot mess," Charity said. "I was the kid who never got her school supplies bought on time and I don't think I ever turned in a permission slip when I was supposed to."

JC forced a smile. Linette White had moved from Brooklyn, New York, to Charleston, South Carolina, when Charity was two. That had been easy to discover. She'd received public assistance for a short time in Charleston but it had stopped by the time Charity was four.

"Lucky you," JC said. "I played piano and my mom was excellent at keeping track of whether I'd practiced my hour every night."

Her father had been a patron of the arts, especially the symphony. He had been the one who insisted on her musical training.

Had he wanted the same for Charity?

Charity yawned, her mouth wide-open. "I don't play any instruments. I guess my mom—"

She was interrupted by a sharp knock on the front door.

Chapter 10

"Room service." Royce heard.

Hogi, proving to be not much of an attack cat, jumped off the couch and ran back to Charity's bedroom.

"Oh, good. Dinner," Charity said, apparently happy enough to change conversations. "I'm starving."

Royce let the hotel employee in. Nobody said a word while the young woman set the table with rolled silverware in cloth napkins, crystal water glasses, and individual salt and pepper shakers. She carefully set down the sterling silver serving dishes and removed all three covers with a flourish.

By the time Royce closed the door after her and returned to the table, Charity was already eating. Jules had waited for him.

He sat, wishing he'd had the good sense to order a drink. Something strong. Or at least the pinot noir they'd discussed.

Learning about wine had been one of the more enjoyable things he'd done these past eight years. Certainly more fun than the statistics classes he'd endured.

Conversation during dinner was pretty limited. Jules didn't say anything directly to him. He realized that she was probably mad at him. He shouldn't have made the remark about Wagoner and that they maybe should have talked more.

Jules had had the right to change her mind.

She'd no doubt made the right choice. That's what he believed at the time. Would probably still be thinking that, but now that he knew the marriage had lasted only eighteen months, his strong conviction had taken a hit.

Who had initiated the divorce? How did she feel about it? And damn him, since he'd promised to never give one more thought to the arrogant Joel Cambridge, he really wanted to know what her father had thought about Jules's marriage ending.

So he put up with her ignoring him. She did talk to Charity. About the pool, the book that Charity had been reading, even the cat who was back in the window.

Charity answered but seemed more focused on her food. She ate as if she hadn't eaten in months, attacking her dinner.

Once Jules finished maybe half of her dinner, she pushed her chair back from the table. "If you'll excuse me," she said, "I've got a lot of work to do. I'll be in my room."

Charity gave her a nod. He wanted to say that he was sorry, that he hadn't meant to make her angry. But he kept his mouth shut. Jules would not appreciate him giving Charity any reason to question that he was more than a hired security guard.

And really, was he? The past was the past.

He and Charity ate in silence and after she took her last bite, she pushed her plate away, got up and settled on the couch to watch television.

He finished his steak and opened his laptop. Tomorrow, Jules had her panel presentation. And even though she'd been quick to dismiss the idea that her fellow panelists could be any danger to her, he still intended to do a quick background search on both. He pulled out the speaker biographies he'd stuffed into his briefcase earlier.

Wayne Isman was listed first. He typed in his name, hit Search, and his laptop screen was immediately filled with information. Lifelong resident of New York. Married. Three daughters. Recently his name had been circulated as a possible replacement for the cabinet post for the retiring secretary of health and human services. Jules hadn't mentioned that last piece.

Lilah Moorhead was listed last. He keyed in her name. Distinguished career, most recently appointed to the medical staff at Mass General. Nothing popped out as unusual to him.

Then he allowed himself to settle in on the middle portion of the paper. He read about Jules. Presidential committee? The *Today* show? He wasn't surprised. He'd realized early on that she was destined for big things.

And he hadn't wanted to hold her back.

With his fingers poised above the keys, he fought the impulse to type in her name. In seconds, he could have information about her marriage, her subsequent divorce, her financial situation.

It wasn't unusual that they would do a background check on a client. Neither he nor his three partners ever wanted to be surprised by anybody.

But he knew Jules. Knew that she could not be a threat to him or anyone else. He closed his laptop and picked up his cell phone. He needed to check in with Trey. "I'm stepping out," he said to Charity. "I'll be right outside the door."

She didn't bother to answer.

The hallway was empty and he dialed his partner. "Hey," he said.

"What's going on?" Trey asked.

"Just hanging out. Watching *Dancing with the Stars*."

"And I thought my assignment was bad," Trey drawled. "At least I get to *look* at the stars," his partner added, "when I'm on nights."

"My client got shot at today."

"Damn. Injuries for either of you?" Trey asked, his tone all business now.

"Jules…the client caught a glass fragment at her hairline. Got a couple stiches." Four, to be exact. Every pinch of the needle into her delicate skin had felt like an arrow into his heart. She'd taken the treatment in stride, not making a big deal of anything. He'd been a hair away from demanding to see the doctor's diploma and getting a sworn statement from the clinic that she was competent to provide care.

"Did they arrest the shooter?" Trey asked.

"No. It's possible that the bullet wasn't meant for my client. Could have been meant for the parking attendant, some sort of gang-related retribution."

"Stay sharp," Trey said. "I heard from Rico and Seth. They're flying back on Friday."

Jules was scheduled to fly out on Friday. His life would pick up where he'd left it before he'd taken this assignment.

He knew that was a lie. Seeing her again, it had changed everything. Made him realize how much he'd given up. Made him realize that all he'd been doing these last eight years was keeping busy.

"I'll check in tomorrow," he said, and ended the call. He opened the suite door. Charity didn't even look up.

That was fine with him. He sat back down at the table, ignoring both her and the television. It wasn't as if he didn't appreciate the dancing. He knew it was harder than it looked. Four years ago, thirty-six sessions had taught him that. The tango had almost broken him but he'd endured, and if the teacher had been the type to give out stars, his might not have been gold but it would have been a solid silver.

He heard Jules's door open. Within a minute, she was in the living room, holding a pillow and blankets.

"For the couch," she said, before beating it back to her room.

"Thank you," he called after her. He'd accepted the fact that he was going to be bunking on the couch ever since Jules had uttered the invitation for Charity to crash at the hotel.

Charity scowled at him. "You spend the *night*?" she asked, her tone incredulous.

You want *your hair to look like you dipped it in black ink?* Took everything he had not to say it out loud, in the same manner. "Yes."

"Wow. Round-the-clock security. I guess JC is something."

He didn't answer. He went back to work on his computer. He'd not yet had a chance to look up information on Cole Hager. He was confident that the man had to have known that it was Jules sitting in the chair, bleeding. Why hadn't he crossed the room, offered his help?

Afraid of blood? Maybe. Had he seen the damaged

window and suspected that the shooting wasn't over? Possibly.

All Royce knew for sure was that Cole Hager's actions seemed odd. And anything odd or unusual needed to be looked at. It took him just a few minutes to pull up the information. There was nothing that he didn't expect. Hager had the right education—both an undergraduate and a graduate degree from Ohio State—and the work experience—almost ten years on Wall Street—to be doing exactly what he'd done today with Jules. Royce flipped some screens. Now here was something interesting. A DUI three years ago and one seven months ago. He'd lost his license with the second offense and done ten days in jail.

But he'd kept his job. Probably told his employer some lie about needing to suddenly take a vacation, maybe a sick relative or something. He'd done the time, gone back to work and the boss was none the wiser.

Functioning alcoholics managed to hold down jobs all the time.

But jail, even short sentences, changed a person. It was a scary place. And he suspected Cole Hager might have taken a few licks or worse while he was there. He no doubt wanted to keep his nose clean and avoid other complications with the law. That might be a reason why he'd run today.

Or maybe he'd had something to do with the attack? He'd picked the location of the meeting. He'd been looking at his watch repeatedly during the conversation. Maybe his excuse that he had to meet someone else had been bogus. Had he been timing the ending of the meeting for another reason?

None of it made sense. Hager lived in New York. The same place where Jules lived. Why come to Vegas to orchestrate a hit on someone when he could have more easily done it on his own turf?

I'm watching for you, Royce thought as he looked at the man's photo on the screen. Cole Hager wasn't going to get anywhere near Jules.

When the show ended, Charity stood up, stretched and walked back to her bedroom. She did not say goodnight. She took her cat, which had at some point during the evening left the window and taken a spot on the back of the couch.

Royce assumed she was going to spend the rest of the evening in her room until her door opened fifteen minutes later. When she entered the living room area of the suite, it was readily apparent that she was going out.

She wore a short black dress and black sandals that crisscrossed halfway up her calf. Her eyes were lined with black makeup and her lips were a slash of red.

She was too thin but he had no doubt that she'd catch a few eyes wherever she went.

"What's going on?" he asked.

"I'm meeting some friends," she said.

He was confident that Bobby hadn't yet made bail—otherwise, he'd have been notified. "I thought you were new in Vegas. Not a lot of opportunity yet to meet people."

"I make friends quickly," she said.

"Where are you going?"

She stared at him. "I can't imagine why you think that's any of your business," she said, her tone icy.

"You're a guest here. Jules is going to care if something happens to you. I'm going to care that she's upset."

"You like her, don't you?" Charity said. "I can tell."

"She's a client," Royce said. He owed this woman no

explanations. "I happen to think that my clients appreciate me having their best interests at heart."

Charity shook her head. "That's not what this is. But I don't really care." She took another couple steps toward the door. "Don't wait up."

"I don't get you," he said. "You're not in school, yet you don't work. Aren't you interested in doing something with your life?"

"I am doing something," she said.

"What?"

"None of your business." She opened the door, walked out and didn't bother to close it behind her.

He got up to shut the door and watched her until she got to the middle of the hallway, where she disappeared from view as she stepped into the elevator banks.

She was up to something. He just wished he knew what the hell it was.

Chapter 11

It took Charity twenty-two minutes to walk to the bar. Eight of those minutes were on the strip, another ten minutes in a decent off-strip neighborhood, and the last four minutes she spent traipsing past people sleeping in doorways and thin dogs barking in weed-filled alleys.

She should have taken a cab but she was a little short on cash right now.

Not for long. Not if she had her way.

She entered the Gold Pot Bar and scanned the dark interior. Every time she came here, the green garland hanging from the dingy white drop ceiling looked more ridiculous. Not as tacky as the naked ceramic leprechaun next to the cash register, but close.

But Lou liked the place.

She saw her friend halfway down the wood bar, leaning in toward the man next to her, her head cocked, as if the guy she was talking to was the most interesting man on the planet.

Lou was good at working people for free drinks.

Charity took the empty stool on the other side, being careful to avoid scratching her leg on the cracked leather seat. When Lou turned her head, Charity mouthed, "See if he'll buy me a drink, too."

And Lou, who had no shame, turned back to the mope and did exactly that. Within minutes, Charity had a Guinness sitting in front of her. Then she leaned forward, made eye contact with the guy and said, "I need to borrow her for a few minutes."

Then she led Lou over to an empty booth. As they each slid in on their respective sides, Lou said, "I can't wait to hear. Tell me everything."

"Well, to start with, Bobby almost blew it. He came home before I expected and almost killed JC."

"I told you he was trash. You wouldn't listen to me."

"I needed a place to stay. Your place wasn't exactly an option."

Lou sighed. "I need that old woman to drift on into a coma or something."

Charity shook her head. "Not before we get the money. One of us needs a job."

"You're right. The bitch needs to hang on a little longer. What happened after Bobby almost killed JC?"

"I had to call the cops. They arrested Bobby."

"That was convenient," Lou said.

"It played out perfectly. JC invited me back to her hotel, the Periwinkle. I didn't even have to ask."

"Oh, my God. What's it like inside?"

"Gorgeous. Three pools. I ordered a couple drinks and charged them to her room. That was fun."

"Now what?"

Charity leaned back and closed her eyes. "I'm going to enjoy it for a couple days," she said.

"You'll be able to pay for your own stay at the Periwinkle if this works out," Lou said, frowning at her. "We talked about this. Get the money and we run."

"We will. All I want is a couple days. It's fun doing it on her dime, without her having any idea what's coming."

"What's she like?" Lou asked, draining her drink.

Charity hesitated. JC was nicer than she'd anticipated. But people had been nice to her before and it never lasted. "She's fine. Has some nice eye candy hanging around. Some guy named Royce. He does security."

"Is he going to give us trouble?"

Charity stared at her friend. "No trouble that we can't handle. Now let's go see if we can hustle your friend at the bar for some more drinks."

After Charity left the apartment, Royce watched a little television, but it failed to hold his attention. He wondered if Jules would emerge from her bedroom, but as the hours passed, he figured that wasn't going to happen.

Unable to put it off any longer, he turned on his computer, typing names of people into the search field that he'd sworn to never think about again.

Bryson Wagoner. Royce had never met the man. Had known about his existence from the beginning of his relationship with Jules but had believed her when she'd said it was over. Believed it until that fateful last meeting with Jules and her dad. He'd been less skilled at keeping his feelings under wraps in those days, and Joel Cambridge had been an expert at casually firing the verbal kill shot.

Everyone pretty much assumes that he and Jules will be married by Christmas.

Ugly damn words. Hurtful. Frightening to a young man who'd stumbled upon the best thing in his life and knew that there was very little chance he was going to be able to hang on to it.

Royce had left the Fifth Avenue condo, his head whirling. He'd looked up information on Bryson Wagoner that night. Of course, he hadn't had the resources available to him then that he did now. But still, the rudimentary search had told him just about everything he needed to know.

Bryson had passed the bar five years earlier and was gainfully employed at one of the largest law firms in Manhattan. His father was a judge, his grandfather a noted physician and his great-grandfather had made his fortune in steel during World War II.

Bryson had been a star on the Princeton fencing team.

He was everything that Royce wasn't.

He was everything that Jules should have.

And when he'd seen their wedding announcement online just months later, he'd sworn never to look again. But tonight, here he was, breaking that promise. He clicked Enter and waited. As the sites popped up, he realized much of it was what he'd seen before. But now, in the public records, was information about the marriage dissolution.

And then, two years later, Bryson's second marriage to Ann Kennedy. There had been plenty of social media coverage of their wedding in the Hamptons. They now had two small children and were living in New Jersey. He was still working at the same law firm.

Next he searched Lara Cambridge. Her obituary was the first thing that popped up. She'd been thirty-eight years old when she'd died in a one-car accident. Her contributions to many philanthropic institutions in New York City and beyond were mentioned. She was survived by her "loving husband and daughter."

His damn hands shook when he'd typed in *Joel Cambridge*. Numerous mentions of him in the society pages. Sometimes alone. More times with a woman on his arm. Many, many different women. Joel Cambridge was rich, sophisticated and good-looking, with his thick silver hair and piercing dark eyes.

A real catch.

A real bastard.

He flipped through various sites, stopping suddenly when he came to one that mentioned the possibility of Joel's candidacy for the United States Senate. Holy hell. A reputable news source was quoted as saying that he was "seriously considering the possibility."

Royce moved quickly to other more recent sites. It became clear that it wasn't simply speculation. Joel Cambridge was running for the Senate. The election was less than a year away and the campaign was in full swing.

Jules had not mentioned this. Did she know? Of course she did. It was public record. Were the threats against her in some way connected to her father's candidacy? It was a long shot, but one that sure as hell should have been considered.

He should not have been blindsided.

Before he could talk himself out of it, he set his laptop aside and walked down the hallway. He knocked sharply at her door. "Jules," he said. "I need to talk to you."

He heard rustling from inside. The door whipped open. "What is it?" she asked. She was pulling on a robe.

But she wasn't quite fast enough. He caught a glimpse of her bare skin and the tops of her pretty breasts in the short silk nightgown that she'd worn to bed.

"I…" He stopped. His legs felt weak.

The pink robe was belted now and she was fingering the edge that hit her midthigh.

"What's wrong?" she said. "Is it Charity?"

He shook his head. "She went out. To meet a friend."

She frowned. "Not Bobby."

Royce shook his head. "He's still in jail. I'll know when he's released."

"I didn't know she had other friends here," Jules said, her tone thoughtful.

"I think there may be a lot that you don't know about her."

Jules licked her upper lip. "Is that what you pounded on my door to tell me?"

She was very sensitive about Charity. "I saw online that your father is running for the Senate."

"Yes."

Her pretty eyes told him nothing. "I would have thought that might have been worthy of a mention."

"The threats were directed at me. They have nothing to do with my father."

"Does he know about them?"

"I don't think so. I specifically asked Barry not to say anything. I think that in his capacity as chairman of the board of Miatroth he would comply with that request. However, he's been my father's good friend for years. I suppose it is possible that Barry went behind my back and advised my father. In any event, the two of us haven't discussed it."

He recalled Jules and Joel Cambridge as being very close. "That surprises me," he said.

She said nothing.

That unnerved him. That and her standing there, so absolutely perfect in her pink silk and pretty pale skin.

"Don't keep secrets from me," he said. Probably more harshly than he needed to.

She narrowed her eyes at him. "Don't bother me with nonsense again, then. I'm working."

She was trying to put him in his place. But when he looked over her shoulder, there *were* piles of paper on her bed and her laptop computer was open and on.

He probably should have held his question until morning. "I'm sorry," he said.

She gave him a quick nod, then ran a hand through her hair. "I wish I knew where Charity had gone," she said.

"I can let you know if she doesn't come home," he said. "You'll be up?"

"Sure." Nobody was getting in the hotel room without his knowledge.

"Thank you," she said.

The air was very still as the two of them stared at each other. "Well, good night," she said finally. Then stepped back to close the door.

He stood outside her room for another minute, waiting to hear the rustle of paper as she settled back in bed. But it was quiet, so quiet that he thought that she probably also hadn't moved. That they were each guarding the door.

Closed off from one another.

Shaking his head, he walked back to the living area and sank down on the couch. This was crazy. He should never have agreed to protect Jules. Too much history.

But had he not been beside her today, she might be dead.

The world without Jules Cambridge was not a better place. And he would never forgive himself if something happened to her. Yes, she'd hurt him. But he'd also loved her very much. And had known, even in the midst of the darkest hours of his despair over losing her, that she'd made the right choice. How could he be angry with her for that?

* * *

She wanted to be mad at Royce. Wanted to be angry that he'd had the nerve to interrupt her, to demand an explanation.

She had deliberately not mentioned her father's Senate run. First of all, she wasn't all that happy about it for a number of reasons. If politics had been a noble cause at one time, it had certainly lost its sheen in recent years. In her role as a CEO of one of the larger pharmaceutical companies, she knew better than most the powerful lobbying that occurred on behalf of the prescription drug industry. Knew that money made a difference to many politicians, knew that a vote could be influenced by many things.

Why her father wanted to be part of that cesspool was beyond her understanding. But the real reason she hadn't told Royce about her dad was that she didn't want to have a discussion with Royce that in any way involved her father. Royce was too perceptive of her feelings. He'd always been that way. From the first night they'd had dinner, she'd felt that he could really see her, could really know what she was thinking.

If she'd told Royce about her dad running for Senate, there might have been some discussion about his chances of winning, and she might not have been able to hide the fact that she couldn't bring herself to care about the campaign or his chances of getting elected, because everything she'd ever believed about her father might just not be true.

Since the night she'd discovered her mother's diary, crazy, ugly thoughts had swirled just below the surface. Her mom had been a nice person—everyone said so. But the thoughts she'd expressed had been so bad that it had seemed as if they must have been penned by someone else.

But she'd had the handwriting compared to that on some old birthday cards that she'd saved. It was the same.

So either her mother had been losing her mind or her father had done some very bad things. She wasn't ready to talk to Royce about either option.

Don't keep secrets from me. That's what he'd said. Well, easier said than done because all she was doing was keeping secrets from people. She hadn't told Barry the truth about why she wanted to stay in Las Vegas, hadn't told Charity the truth about their relationship and certainly hadn't told Royce the truth that simply being near him again made her remember every wonderful thing about that summer that she'd vowed to forget.

She still couldn't watch a silly fireworks show because of him.

On the third of July that summer, they'd made plans to picnic on the Fourth. Royce had wanted to buy the food at a deli but she'd insisted on cooking. Like a throwback to some primitive species, she'd wanted to cook for her man, to demonstrate with deviled eggs and fried chicken what she couldn't say out loud.

They took a blanket and a picnic basket to Prospect Park in Brooklyn and lay under a tree. It was hot and Royce had stripped down to just his cargo shorts. They drank lemonade with vodka in it and she fed him pickles and olives and he teased her with brie cheese drizzled with honey.

He raved about her chicken even though she knew that she'd cooked it too long and it was too dry.

They tossed a Frisbee and petted dogs as they walked by. By late afternoon, he sensed that a combination of ten-hour days at work, too much food and warm sunshine was catching up with her. He lay back, pulled her close, and she slept with her head on his chest for hours.

They awakened and took the train back to Manhattan, and as the sky was darkening, he grabbed her hand and led her through the city to an old warehouse in the Hell's Kitchen neighborhood.

"My friend owns the place," he said. "Swears it's the best spot to view the fireworks." He led her up to the roof, where earlier in the day he'd left an inflated air mattress.

There, they opened their cooler bag and ate the remainder of their lunch. And they made love.

As the fireworks had exploded over the city, she exploded around him, and it had seemed as if she and the blinding, blazing lights were one. And she knew it was more than sex; she knew that she loved him. Neither of them said it, but she knew that he felt the same.

And when he had held her hand as he'd walked her home, she had known that there never would be another Fourth of July that perfect.

The next year, when Bryson had suggested they watch the fireworks, she pleaded a headache and lowered all the blinds in their apartment.

Every year after that, she found some reason not to participate in the ritual.

She forced her mind back to the present but it wasn't any easier in that space. Where the heck was Charity? She was meeting a friend? Not really a comfortable thought. Charity certainly had not demonstrated the best of judgment in moving in with Bobby Boyd.

There was so much about Charity that she still didn't know. She intended to fix that the first chance she got. Tomorrow, after her panel discussion, she wasn't coming back and diving into the hundreds of emails that were accumulating in her absence. She intended to spend the day with Charity. Maybe they'd even get to the point where she'd feel comfortable telling her the truth.

One less secret to have to carry around.

They were a damn ten-pound bag around her neck, threatening to choke her. When Royce found out that she hadn't been truthful with him from the beginning, he was going to be very angry.

And more confident than ever that the very last insult he'd hurled her direction eight years ago had been true. "You're a liar."

She had not lied to Royce about her relationship with Bryson. They'd broken up months before she'd met Royce. She'd thought it was mutual. Had not expected that he'd come back at the end of summer, literally begging her to marry him.

Had not expected that it would be so important to her father, who had given up so much for her and asked so little in return.

Or so she'd thought.

She crawled back in bed and picked up her laptop. Royce had said that he would wait up until Charity came home. She would do the same. But like always, she would fill her time with work.

Royce heard the faint chime of the elevator at twenty minutes after midnight. In his mind, he counted Charity's steps, and she put her key card into the door just when he expected.

If she was surprised to see him sitting on the couch, staring at the door, she didn't show it. Her gait was not quite steady and he suspected that she'd been drinking quite a bit. Now the black eyeliner was smeared beneath her eyes and she'd pulled her long hair, which had been hanging down her back when she'd left, into a haphazard bun at the nape of her neck.

"Evening," he said.

"Hello. You didn't need to wait up, *Dad*." Her emphasis on the last word was deliberate and smug.

"I sleep better when everyone who is supposed to be here is tucked in."

"How unfortunate for you."

"Don't worry about me," he said.

"Oh, I won't," she answered, starting to walk down the hall. She stopped and looked him in the eye. "You'll learn, Mr. Security, that I really don't worry about much of anything."

Then she walked into her bedroom and shut the door behind her. She didn't slam it but neither was she very quiet, and he suspected that Jules, if she was still awake, had heard her.

If she'd heard the comment, what would she think? Would she find her mother's friend's daughter a little hard, maybe even caustic? Would she excuse her rude behavior away?

He got up, flipped the bolt lock on the door and shut off the lights. Then he returned to the couch and stretched out, determined to catch a few hours of sleep. Jules would be at the panel presentation tomorrow. For some reason, Royce had a feeling that it was very important he be sharp for that.

Ready for whatever was headed Jules's way.

Chapter 12

Royce was already awake and at the table reading the paper when JC stumbled into the kitchen, feeling as if her eyes had been rubbed with sandpaper. She hadn't slept well and it really irritated her that Royce was already showered, in clean clothes and functioning.

She still had on her robe and hadn't even brushed her teeth. "Morning," she mumbled.

"Good morning," he said. "There's coffee, pastries and fruit on the counter."

He'd already ordered from room service. And had folded up the sheets and the blanket she'd given him the night before into a neat pile.

She'd forgotten how chipper he was in the mornings. On the nights when he'd stayed over at her apartment, he'd always been up first and had always had the coffee ready.

Well, he wasn't the only one who could immediately

function. She spied Charity's beach towel that had been left in the chair. With purpose, she walked over, grabbed the towel to fold it and immediately started sneezing.

The bright morning sunlight caught the floating cat hair, making it look like a mini dust storm.

"Oh, good Lord," she said.

"It's a long-haired cat," Royce said, like it was a foregone conclusion that everything would be covered in cat hair. "Are you allergic?"

"I hope not," she said. She'd never had a cat. She dropped the beach towel and poured a cup of coffee from the silver carafe. It was too hot and it burned her tongue, but she didn't care.

"We'll leave here in an hour," she said.

He shook his head. "We'll leave here in forty-five minutes."

"Why?"

"If anybody is watching you and knows that you're in this suite, then they're going to expect you to arrive via elevator in the main lobby in about an hour. That's why we're going to take the stairs in forty-five minutes and enter through a back door to the conference room. I reviewed the schematics of the hotel last night," he added, as if daring her to challenge the decision.

She wasn't challenging anything. Even if it involved walking down fourteen flights of stairs. Yesterday's gunshot, whether directed at her or not, was still too fresh in her mind. Every time she'd rolled over, her stitches had pulled.

Almost as if he'd read her mind, he glanced at her hairline. "How's the cut?" he asked, his voice much kinder.

"Fine," she said. Kind and conciliatory could be her undoing. She refreshed her coffee, then picked up the cup. She'd drink it in her room. "I guess that since my getting-dressed window got compressed without me realizing it, I better get going. I will see you—" she squinted at the clock "—in forty-three and a half minutes."

She was pretty sure she heard him laughing as she walked out of the room.

When she got behind her bedroom door, she quickly found her cell phone and dialed Barry. His wife, who was traveling with him, answered his cell phone. "Hi, JC. Barry is in the shower. Can he call you back?"

"That's okay, Eileen. I just wanted him to know that I won't meet him outside the session room like we'd planned. I'll see him inside."

"Okay, honey. I'll give him the message. I'm going to tag along, too. Don't want to miss seeing you on the panel."

"Oh, that's sweet of you, Eileen. And it will be so good to catch up. It's been too long."

"For sure. Good luck, now."

JC tossed her phone onto the bed. Eileen Wood had been her mother's best friend. It had been Eileen who had stayed at the hospital with JC, who had made sure that all the doctors and nurses knew that the fourteen-year-old in the bed with the badly fractured leg had just lost her mother in an accident. She'd made sure that they treated JC with the kindness and consideration that her battered body and spirit had needed.

Over the years, Eileen had been a solid force in JC's life and she loved the woman, who had never had any children of her own. She'd held JC's hand after her relationship with Bryson had fizzled to a slow death and had been excited to hear that JC was dating again when she'd confided that she'd met Royce.

Eileen had said she was happy for her when JC had gone to visit after Labor Day, with news that she was marrying Bryson. Had helped her pick out a wedding dress and talk to the caterers. All the things her mom might have done. Just one time, she'd asked, *Are you sure, honey?* JC had nodded and the moment had passed.

Since Barry had retired, Eileen frequently traveled with him as he fulfilled his board responsibilities, and it wasn't unusual that Eileen and JC would find a few minutes for a cup of coffee.

JC shucked off her clothes and stepped into the shower. She was going to have to step it up because she probably only now had about forty-one minutes before Royce would be pounding on the door.

Serve him right if she opened it naked, dripping wet with water.

But she knew that would be a little like mixing gasoline and a lit match. She'd seen the look in his eyes last night when she'd opened the door before she'd had her robe tied. She'd always loved lingerie, and pretty nightgowns were an indulgence for her. She'd heard the pounding, had assumed it had something to do with Charity and hadn't taken due care to make sure she was covered.

His look had been hot, and it had reminded her of all the times in the past when he'd looked at her that way and then minutes later they'd been in bed, practically tearing each other's clothes off.

He'd been an eager lover, always wanting her, always making sure she was satisfied before taking his own pleasure. It had been a heady experience after having dated Bryson for the previous year. With Bryson, the sex had simply been fine and when she was really tired, she hadn't even felt bad about pretending to have an orgasm.

There'd been no need for pretense with Royce. She'd been all but bursting with orgasms from practically the first time he'd touched her.

So there would be no answering the door naked. She'd be fully clothed, her buttons buttoned and her zippers zipped.

JC washed her hair, being as careful as she could to keep the water away from her stitches. She'd left the bandage on, so that provided some protection. Then it was a final rinse and she was out and drying off with one of the big soft towels.

She put some lotion on and ran a comb through her hair. Then she added some styling gel and dried it. She was fortunate to have some natural curl, so she never had to mess with curling irons or hot rollers.

She used some hairspray to hold it down, then slipped into a black knit dress with a royal blue jacket. Finally, she added a scarf to hide the bruises that were showing at her neckline. She slipped her feet into black sandals, grabbed her black leather shoulder bag and was out the bedroom door.

She looked at the clock. Smiled. She had a full minute to go. Still, Royce was waiting for her. He'd changed into a gray suit with a brilliant white shirt and a navy-and-gray tie. He looked really good and she felt a physical response to his all-male presence.

"Now what?" she asked, making sure her tone was businesslike.

"Now we go down the stairs. I'll go first. When we get to the room, I need you to let me know if anything doesn't look right or feel right. Go with your gut."

Her gut was telling her that it had been a mistake to think that she could be with Royce 24/7 and not relive the memories of that summer. The best summer of her life.

"Okay," she said.

He opened the door, checked the hallway and motioned for her to come. The idea that someone could be

waiting for them on the staircase made her empty stomach feel pinched and tight.

He's just being careful, she told herself. *No need to
start seeing shadows in the corners.*

They got to the third floor and he smiled at her reassuringly, as if he'd sensed her nervousness. "So far so
good."

She swallowed hard. "Really good."

He reached out his hand, wrapped it gently around
her arm. His skin was very warm and she could feel the
transfer of heat. "It's going to be fine," he said. "I will
not let anything happen to you."

"I know." She did. But what if something happened to
him in the process of protecting her? She couldn't bear
it. "Don't be a hero," she said.

The air in the stairway became very still. Heavy. He
stared at her mouth and she got the craziest feeling that
he was about to kiss her. He leaned forward and—

A burst of laughter came from outside the door. He
straightened up. Opened the door slowly. She could see
past him. Two women, hotel workers by their dress, were
in the hallway, looking at something on a phone.

One of the women typed something and then dropped
the phone into her smock pocket. The two of them continued down the hall.

She looked at him and knew that the moment they'd
shared was gone.

"Let's go," he said. They walked down the hallway
and he pulled open a door. Just as he'd told her, they
were in the presentation space, entering just to the right
of the risers, where there was a table, three chairs and
a podium with a microphone. The front entrance to the
room had not yet been opened and they were the only
people in the big space.

"I'll stand against that wall so that I can see the entire room," he said.

He'd be off to her left, just six or seven big steps from the podium. It was crazy, because she'd been speaking to audiences, many times much larger than this, for years and she was rarely nervous. But the idea that Royce would be watching, would be judging her remarks, her performance, was making butterflies dance in her stomach.

She cared what he thought.

Still.

Had she ever stopped caring about his opinion? Was that why, after her divorce, she'd been so steadfast in her resolve that she wasn't going to find him, admit her colossal mistake and beg forgiveness?

Because she hadn't been willing to risk that she'd see the disgust in his eyes? Hadn't been willing to hear his condemnation?

She saw the doors open at the far end of the room and knew that their private time was short-lived. "Fine," she said, grateful for the interruption. She needed to focus, to think about the things she was confident about.

Attendees quickly filled the room, and within minutes, the two other speakers joined her onstage. Wayne Isman shook her hand and made small talk for a few minutes. "How's your family?" she asked.

"Good," he said. "We're going to France in April and the girls are going to be able to join us."

She shifted her attention to the other presenter, who was known as an expert on antibiotic-resistant superbugs. "Good to see you again, Lilah," JC said.

The women shook hands. "Good-sized crowd," said Lilah, not sounding too thrilled.

"Yes," JC responded. Lots of people who looked very normal, very reasonable. Most had their heads down, doing some last-minute checking of their cell phones. She saw Barry and Eileen Wood come in and take a seat toward the back. She waved to them. Eileen gave her a thumbs-up in return.

Nobody in the audience looked like a shotgun-wielding creep. She risked a glance toward Royce. He had his back against the wall, turned at just the right angle that he could see the audience and still manage to look as if he might be any other attendee who simply preferred to stand rather than sit on the hard plastic chairs.

He was doing his best to comply with her wishes that he be as inconspicuous as possible. She appreciated that.

Once the facilitator introduced the panel, the time seemed to fly by. Wayne spoke first and it made her smile when she saw many of the women sit forward on their chairs, taking every word in. They'd be disappointed with her East Coast delivery.

She looked down at her notes. Wayne's remarks were fitting in nicely with what she'd prepared. She wasn't surprised. When they'd worked together, it had seemed that they had a knack for anticipating each other's thoughts. When she looked up, she was momentarily caught off guard when she saw Charity slip into the room. She stood there a minute, then headed for a chair in the fourth row that someone had just vacated as they'd left the room, cell phone to ear.

She shouldn't be there. The conference sessions were only open to registered attendees and there were usually people at the door checking to make sure that everyone who entered had a lanyard and attendee badge hanging around their neck. However, since the session had started, those people had evidently abandoned their posts, allowing Charity to enter without notice.

How the heck had she known where the session was being held?

JC dismissed that question as inconsequential. It wouldn't have been difficult. She could have gone onto the association's website and picked up their Twitter feed, where they were doing real-time reporting on all sessions.

The more important question was why had she come? Was she interested in what JC did for a living? She hadn't expressed much interest before. But was this a sign that she was slowly opening up to the possibility that they might become friends?

JC caught Charity's eye and gave her a smile. The young woman gave her a little wave in return.

Suddenly, Wayne was sitting and Lilah was looking at her. She got up, took a deep breath and began. It was crazy but with both Royce and Charity in the audience, it seemed so much more important to do a really good job.

She was ten minutes into her presentation and it was going well. She kept her eyes moving, taking in the whole audience, making sure that she was accurately reading their faces. Did they understand? Were they interested? Had she said something that caused them to lean over and remark to their neighbor?

Mostly, everyone seemed to be listening and nodding in the right places.

Her eyes rested on Barry and Eileen Wood. Barry was smiling, probably happy that the CEO was doing fine. And Eileen... JC stumbled on her words midsentence. She looked down at her notes, found her place and resumed.

On autopilot. Having given this presentation twice before, that was easy enough to do. Thank goodness, because she was a little shaken.

Eileen Wood, who was on a different side of the room

than Charity, and at least six rows back, was staring at the young woman. And she looked...angry.

What was that about?

JC took a quick glance at Royce. Had he noticed? When she turned her head, that small motion was enough to cause his eyes to flick her direction. She could see the question in them. *Is everything okay?*

She knew that he was ready to charge the stage, ready to rescue her. He would, without a doubt, put himself in harm's way to save her.

Brave. Honorable. Maybe the exterior had changed, but he was still the same man she'd loved.

She turned back to the audience. Delivered the remainder of her remarks.

When she finished and it was time for Lilah to take the podium, she noticed that Charity stayed, although now she had her phone out and was checking it.

She looked at the Woods. Barry was listening attentively to Lilah, and Eileen was looking down, her face thoughtful.

After Lilah finished, they opened it up for questions. Hands shot into the air, making it seem as if the audience was very engaged in the talk. JC had to focus on the questions.

Finally, the facilitator was back up onstage, cutting off the questions and dismissing the audience. As inevitably happened at these kinds of conferences, once the session ended, multiple people approached the stage to continue asking questions, sometimes related to the presentation, sometimes not. Out of the corner of her eye, she saw Royce edge closer.

And she saw Charity exit the room.

She wanted to run after her, to ask her what she'd thought, but she stayed right where she was. The first woman to reach her had a question about what the drug companies were doing to curb the alarming increase in addictions to painkilling opioids. That was a complicated question and JC tried to give her a simple yet thoughtful answer. The woman left and JC moved on to the next question.

Barry came up, extended his hand. "Congratulations. Great job."

"Where's Eileen?" she asked.

"Said she wasn't feeling well. Went back to the room."

Another audience member approached. "Well, tell her that I'll call her later," JC said.

Finally, fifteen minutes later the crowd dissipated. JC gathered up her notes. "That was fun," she said to Lilah.

"Public speaking isn't my favorite thing to do," said the woman. She glanced over her shoulder, where Royce stood. Then she looked back at JC. "That man has been staring at you. Do you know him?"

"I do. He's…uh…waiting for me."

"He's very handsome," Lilah whispered. "I'd speak at more of these if somebody like that was waiting for me at the end." She picked up her briefcase. "Have a good night."

JC turned to say goodbye to Wayne but he held up a finger in her direction as he finished his conversation with the last audience member. When the young woman walked away, Wayne turned to her. "Do you have a minute, JC? I'd like to talk to you about some feedback I've gotten from our folks on the ground in Africa."

"Of course."

"Good. Let me gather up my papers and then can we walk and talk? I've got to catch a cab to an off-site meeting."

"Of course. Ready for the big awards ceremony?"

Wayne was this year's emcee. She suspected that he might have had something to do with her invitation to deliver the keynote speech, but when she'd accused him of that, he'd declined to take responsibility.

"For sure. I am glad that they're doing a practice run-through in the morning. Did you get the email about that?"

She had. She would have to share that detail with Royce since it hadn't been on the original schedule. "I know. I'm always petrified that the audio or visual won't be working right and I'll have to fill time. I can't sing and I've never been that great at telling jokes."

"I can do puppet shows with socks," he said, picking up his briefcase.

That accent and a sock could probably fill fifteen minutes. "Great. Give me just a quick second," she said. She stepped off the stage and walked toward Royce. "I'm going to walk Wayne to the cabstand. He needs to talk to me."

"Did you bring a phone book?"

She smiled. "Funny. Admit it—aren't you half enamored with him after just listening to this presentation?"

"Absolutely," he said with a straight face. "I'll try to control myself, though. Let's go."

She led the way back to Wayne. "This is Royce Morgan, an old friend. He's going to tag along with us."

"No problem," Wayne said easily, but it seemed as if his look in Royce's direction lasted just a second too long. She searched her memory for any possibility that she might have mentioned Royce to her old boss all those years ago. But came up empty. He had not been at that ill-fated awards dinner, but perhaps he'd heard something about it afterward.

They exited the room and walked down the corridor.

It wasn't jammed but there were still a number of people juggling phones and coffee cups, hurrying toward their next session. She walked with Wayne on one side, Royce on the other. Occasionally they had to veer to dodge other people and she and Wayne would separate and merge back together. Royce, however, stuck to her like glue.

They went through a set of double doors and had just stepped into the large lobby of the conference center when she heard a man shout, from the level above them, "Hey, what are you doing?"

Chapter 13

Royce grabbed Jules's arm and pulled her close.

A second later, a glass bottle landed at her feet, and glass shattered all around them. People started screaming.

If he had not pulled Jules up short, the bottle likely would have hit her in the head. From that distance, it would have had a hell of a bite to it.

When he'd heard the shout, he'd turned, looked up and scanned the upper level, looking for the threat. And he'd caught a glimpse of the man right before he'd tossed the bottle. Dark hair, dark jacket. Medium build.

He turned to Jules, gave her one more look to make sure she was okay. He wanted to grab her and hold her tight but all he said was, "Stay here."

He was going to have to trust Wayne Isman. He turned his attention to the man. "Don't leave her. Do not leave this spot."

He waited just long enough for the man to nod before starting to run toward the stairs. He took the steps two at a time, pushing his way around startled people. When he got to the second floor, he stopped and looked both directions.

"If you're looking for the guy throwing stuff, he went through there." A young man, still near the railing, pointed toward an exit sign.

It matched the voice that had called out the initial warning. Royce nodded his thanks and took off. The doors led to a second-story breezeway that crossed between the convention center and the hotel. He'd studied the schematics very carefully last night. He knew exactly where it led.

The corridor was empty. He ran down the length of it, tore open the door into the hotel and looked down another heavily carpeted corridor.

No sign of the man. Damn it. He wanted to tear the hotel apart room by room, but knew that was a stupid idea. He needed to get back to Jules, get her safely to her room.

He ran back into the conference center and then down the stairs. He saw Wayne first and realized that the two of them had moved to one of the wooden benches that lined the walls. Wayne was standing and Jules was sitting. She was composed but he could see the stiff set to her shoulders, knew that trauma was cumulative and that her shell was probably wearing thin.

"Did you catch him?" Jules asked as he approached.

He shook his head. "Are you okay?"

"Yes. I told Wayne just a bit of what's been happening," she said.

"Those letters sound damn scary," Wayne said. "I'm

glad that JC has hired security. You need to catch these bastards."

Royce nodded. "Let's get back to the room. Then I'll contact management here. There are multiple cameras in all the corridors. I'm confident they'll have picked up something helpful."

"Be safe," Wayne said, reaching for Jules's hand. "I'll see you tomorrow."

"Absolutely. Sorry for the dramatics," Jules added.

"Of course." Wayne waved her comment aside. "But I have to admit, it does seem like a rather inefficient way to hurt somebody."

The man was right. And Royce could see that Jules had already been thinking the same thing. If it was the same person as before, why not use the gun again? A shot to the back of the head would have been much more efficient.

The idea made him want to vomit, but it had to be examined. Throwing a bottle was…well, the only word he could come up with was *juvenile*. And based on his quick look at the attacker and how fast he'd escaped, he thought he was probably in his twenties or thirties but certainly not a kid.

"Nobody ever said the bad guy had to be smart," Royce said, dismissing the comment. He'd had to trust Wayne to stay with Jules when there was a chance of catching the attacker. But now, he certainly wasn't going to share his thoughts about the case. He'd save that for a discussion with his partners.

As Wayne got into a cab, Royce hurried Jules across the lobby, constantly checking their six. Nobody was following them. As they passed one of the people handing out water and dark chocolate, he held out his hand and quickly accepted two pieces of the candy.

When they were in the elevator headed toward the fourteenth floor, he stood in front of Jules. But the elevator made no other stops and soon they were standing in front of their door.

He did a quick sweep on the suite once they were inside but it seemed fine. Charity was not there.

"Did you see Charity at the session?" Jules asked, as if she'd read his mind.

"Yes." It had surprised the hell out of him. And he didn't like to be surprised. He didn't yet know what her game was, but he was determined to figure it out. If she was any kind of threat to Jules, then he didn't care how good of friends their mothers had been.

"She slipped out the back at the very end."

He'd seen that.

"I wonder where she is now," Jules added, looking around the quiet suite.

He didn't know or care. He handed her both pieces of dark chocolate.

"Don't you want one?" she asked.

She was too pale still. "Nope. Enjoy. Look, I've got to make some phone calls." He intended to contact Detective Mannis and bring him up to date. The man could request security videos.

"Will you keep me apprised?" Jules asked.

"Of course."

"Do you think this was an attack directed at me?"

"I don't know. Your old boss was right. Throwing a bottle at someone seems like a crime of opportunity versus a planned attack."

"Is it possible that my remarks might have upset someone?"

He'd already considered that. One of the reasons he wanted facility security video was that he needed to see if the bottle thrower wore a conference badge. And whether they could place him inside the session. "Your remarks weren't controversial. Hard to argue that the drug companies have a role in preventing physicians from overprescribing antibiotics."

She nodded. "Lots of crazies out there, though," she said, her tone thoughtful.

She was right about that. "Don't worry about it. You've got one more event here, right? We'll beef up the security for it. For large jobs, we've got a relationship with another agency in Vegas. I'm going to contact them and get more resources. I'd rather have my partners there, but this will work."

"Tell me about your partners," she said.

He was confident that she'd likely read the public bios on the website. The very discreet sanitized version of the group's skill sets.

"We met in basic training."

"So all four of you were in the air force?"

"Yes."

"And you became friends and ultimately business partners?"

"It could have gone another direction. I liked Trey Riker immediately, couldn't figure Rico Metez out and thought Seth Pike was a jerk."

She smiled. "And now?"

"I'd trust them with my life. Have done that on numerous occasions and I'm still here to talk about it. Trey is supersmart and mechanically inclined, so we joke that we can give him an empty tin can, a ball of string and a box of matches and he can come back with a version of a 727 that flies."

"I doubt that," she said.

"Okay. I'm exaggerating a little but he's amazing."

"And Rico, why couldn't you figure him out?"

"He was really secretive about his background. It took years for me to find out that Rico grew up in the mountains—his parents were fruit growers in Colorado. Not a lot of money in peaches. But Rico made his first million before he was twenty-two in the stock market. He actually reads all those prospectus statements that everyone else immediately throws away. Not sure when he achieved his second or third million because he's never going to say. He's got a ton of money but still fights for the underdog. Most of the pro bono work that our firm does comes through him."

"But you didn't like your fourth partner?"

"Like I said, I thought Seth Pike was a jerk. He seemed to be looking for a fight, and in the early days of boot camp, we mixed it up a few times. But he's dog-loyal on steroids. Once he decides that he likes you, you've got a friend for life and he'll take a bite out of anyone's hind end to help you."

"It will be nice to meet them," she said.

He stared at her. "When I took this job, I didn't tell Trey that I knew you, that we'd…dated."

She didn't blink. "Why not?"

"Because I was afraid that he'd tell me to turn down the job, that I shouldn't take it if I couldn't be objective."

"Can you be objective?" she asked, her voice a mere whisper.

Hell no. "I can do what needs to be done," he said. His heart was thudding in his chest.

She didn't say anything for a long minute. Finally she stood. "Of course. I have work to do." She walked out of the room.

Royce wanted to put his fist through something. He wanted to tell her the truth. That five minutes after seeing her again his objectivity had gone out the window. He could not bear it if she was hurt.

I can do what needs to be done.

She better hope that was true. The shooting had been poorly executed and the bottle-toss poorly planned. But the next time, the person could get lucky and Jules could be harmed.

And then what the hell would he do?

She wasn't sure what to do.

About the threats. About Charity. About Royce.

For a woman who made rapid-fire decisions, she was becoming amazingly indecisive. It didn't feel good.

The letters were the most tangible threats. They had come to her, with her name and address on the envelope. But the almost hit-and-run the other night, the bullet that may or may not have been aimed at her and now a bottle tossed from above were harder to get her arms around. Was someone trying to hurt her? Scare her? Drive her crazy?

Well, they were winning on the third option. For sure.

And then there was Charity. Her coming to the session had been surprising and a little disconcerting. And the fact that she'd seemed to be interested had been sort of cool. It would be neat to share her professional life with her sister.

Sister.

Her secret. She hadn't told Charity or Royce and definitely not her father. But that was going to have to change soon. Charity deserved to know the truth. Of course, there was the possibility that her mother had been wrong. Lara Cambridge believed that Joel Cambridge had slept around and fathered another child. According to her diary, she'd had good reason to. But perhaps it was all a lie, for some crazy unknown reason, and Charity was no more sister than the woman at the front desk of the hotel.

But JC didn't think so. There was something very familiar about Charity, something that told her that her mother had been right.

Was it even possible that Eileen Wood knew something about her father's affair with Linette White? Knew something about Charity? What else would have caused the woman to stare at Charity with such unmasked venom in her eyes? And was it a coincidence that Charity and Eileen had both departed rather quickly from the session? Was it as simple as Charity had gotten bored and Eileen hadn't felt well? Or was it something much more complicated?

There were too many unknowns here. She ran a company where science was the bedrock of what they did. When all else failed, she knew to trust the science.

A DNA test would confirm the suspicions. Ultimately, that would have to occur.

Then Pandora's box would be opened and the lid would likely never fit tightly again. That knowledge was causing her to have stomach pains and interrupted sleep. Her inability to leave it alone, to simply ignore what had been in her mother's diary, was the equivalent of letting the horses out of the barn.

She wasn't getting them back in again.

Her father, if her mother had been right, was going to be furious with her. Could she make him understand why she'd done this? Why it had been so important? Or would he simply be terribly angry that she'd gone behind his back rather than coming to him?

And what would Charity do with her newfound knowledge? Would she be grateful to finally know the truth or would she be so angry that her existence and birthright had been denied that she wouldn't want anything to do with JC?

And Royce? Had fate brought them together again for a reason? He was different but yet she sensed that he was still very much the man she'd fallen in love with.

She heard the suite door open and Charity greet Royce. Soon, she needed to find the right time to tell Charity the truth. And they would simply have to deal with the fallout.

She opened her door just as Charity flopped down on the couch. "Hi," said JC. "I heard the door."

"Have you had lunch?" Charity asked. She reached down to pick up Hogi, who had raced from wherever he was hiding to greet her.

"Uh…no. We haven't."

"I thought maybe we could have lunch together," Charity said. "Just the two of us."

Royce was never going to go for that. But maybe there was another way. "We can do that," she said. "But I'd like to eat here."

She turned to Royce. "You slept on the couch last night. That couldn't have been all that comfortable. Maybe you could take a nap in my room and Charity and I could have this area."

He stared at her. "That would probably work."

"Great. Thanks." She doubted Royce had any intention of napping, but she appreciated that he clearly understood that she was trying to find a compromise they could all live with. Charity wanted lunch. She wanted information. And Royce wanted to keep them all safe, behind locked doors.

She picked up the room service menu and handed it to Royce. "What would you like?"

"I'm not that hungry," he said. "Go ahead and order.

I'll get the door when they knock." He left the two women in the living area.

JC pivoted to face Charity. She handed her the menu. "How about you?"

The young woman stared at her. "I want what you had…" she said, then paused. "Yesterday," she added.

The hair on JC's arms rose. Had Charity's word choice been intentional? Did she know more than she'd been letting on? Did she mean, I want what you had and what should have been mine? "The crab cakes?" JC asked, her voice too high.

Charity nodded. "Yeah, what did you think I meant?"

"Nothing," JC said.

Charity sat on the couch and belched loudly. "Sorry," she said, looking embarrassed. "Guinness always makes me burp the next day." She started scrolling through her phone.

"Is that your drink of choice?"

Charity didn't look up. "Not really, but you know, in Rome, you do what the Romans do. You want me to order or are you going to do it?"

"I got it." JC picked up the phone and quickly gave the lunch order. Then she smiled at Charity. "I heard you come back in last night. It was late."

"I met a friend. Lou."

"I see," JC said. "Someone that you and Bobby knew?"

"Lou can't stand Bobby," Charity said, still looking at her phone. "She thinks he's stupid."

She. "So Lou is short for Louisa?"

"She's been Lou since second grade," Charity said, finally looking up.

"Does Lou live in Vegas?"

Charity didn't acknowledge the question but she did put her phone down.

"I guess I'm grateful then that you chose to stay here with me rather than crashing at her place."

"She doesn't have her own place. She lives with an old lady and takes care of her. The woman's son stops by like twice a day to check on them."

Charity and Lou had grown up together. Under different circumstances, JC would have known Lou. "Good that you've kept in contact even as adults."

"We're like sisters."

JC again felt a chill. Charity had said it innocently enough.

Was JC reading into the tea leaves too much?

"My mother never really liked her."

This was her chance. She knew the answer to the next question she was going to ask, but there was no way for Charity to know that. "How did your mom die, Charity?"

"She and her boyfriend were on his boat. They did that on the weekends. Would take it out all day and then anchor it and sleep on it at night. It caught fire. They didn't make it off."

The story had made the front page of the Charleston paper. The private investigator had produced a copy. She wondered if it was any consolation to Charity that the coroner believed the couple had been sleeping in the hull and had died of smoke inhalation before the flames had gotten to them.

The fire had occurred eight months ago, just two months after early rumors started circling that her father intended to announce his candidacy for the Senate. And regardless of the news coverage, the death of two strangers hundreds of miles away would have gone totally unnoticed by her if she hadn't found her mother's diary four months later and started looking for Linette White.

"I'm sorry," she said.

"Yeah, it sucks," Charity said. She stared off into space. "You know, I didn't like my mom all that much when I was a teenager. We fought a lot. You know, about stupid rules and other stuff. Sometimes about Lou. But the last couple years, it was better."

The young woman's dark eyes filled with tears. "We would talk and sometimes go shopping and—" she swallowed hard "—and I wish I'd told her that I loved her more. I think she knew it but I should have said it more."

JC's throat was closing up. She'd traveled much the same path after her mom had died, but she'd been processing it with the brain of a fourteen-year-old. Charity had the benefit of being ten years older.

But perhaps age was irrelevant in these circumstances.

A mother's death was hard, so hard, regardless of maturity. "I'm sure she knew how much you loved her," JC said. Others had said the same to her. It had been some comfort.

"I think so. I hope so, anyway." A tear ran down Charity's cheek. She wiped it away with the back of her hand. "You know, she loved butter pecan ice cream. I ate a half gallon of it the day we buried her."

JC smiled. "Sounds like a fitting tribute." They'd waited to have her mother's funeral until JC was out of the hospital. But she'd had very limited mobility. After the funeral, nobody had said much when she'd crawled into bed with a picture of her mother and hadn't left her room for four days. Even then, the picture had remained under her pillow for years.

"I was a little surprised to see you at the session this morning," JC said, not wanting Charity to be upset.

Charity shrugged. "I didn't know what to expect. But it was interesting. Although those stories about the superbugs are kind of gross."

JC smiled. "Agreed. Wash your hands. Often. That's my motto." She hesitated. "You know, it was good to have support in the audience. My good friends Barry and Eileen Wood also came."

She watched Charity carefully, looking for any reaction. But the girl was busy rubbing Hogi's belly.

"I spent a lot of time with Eileen after my mom died," JC said.

"Yeah," Charity said, as if she knew she was supposed to say something but didn't know what. "I've got to feed Hogi."

Twenty minutes later, there was a sharp knock on the door. Royce shot out of the bedroom. "Where's Charity?"

"In her room, feeding her cat."

"I thought she wanted to have lunch with you," he whispered, when they heard Charity's door open.

"Let's make that happen," JC said.

Like before, Royce checked the peephole first, then opened the door. A woman wearing the standard black pants, white shirt, and periwinkle blue and olive green cummerbund and bow tie pushed a cart in, with three covered dishes. It took her a few minutes to set everything up on the table. Charity picked up the remote control for the television and started flipping through channels. She had the sound all the way down so JC assumed it was more something to do rather than something she was really interested in.

Once JC had signed the slip and the attendant had left, she handed Royce a plate. "I ordered you some chicken quesadillas. Just in case."

Royce took the plate. He glanced at Charity, who still sat on the couch, her back to JC. "Everything okay here?" he asked softly.

"Fine," she said. "Really," she added when he didn't seem inclined to move.

"Let me know if you need me," he said.

"I will," she said, grateful that he wasn't pushing the issue. "Don't spill salsa on my bedspread."

Chapter 14

He'd spilled red wine on her dining room rug. It had been a week after the Fourth of July. She'd invited him over for dinner and when she'd offered him a glass of wine, he'd accepted even though he wanted a beer.

They dined in candlelight with music in the background.

The filet had been a perfect medium rare.

The art on her walls had probably cost more than his parents' house.

It was a night of disjointed thoughts and memories because halfway through dinner, about ten seconds after she asked him to pass the salad, she blurted out that she thought she might be falling in love with him.

He knocked over his wineglass in response. And she laughed and kissed him.

Prior to that night, he'd been afraid to say the words, afraid that he'd scare her away. But her admission gave him permission to tell her what was in his heart. And when he told her that he loved her, too, her eyes had filled with tears. *I thought so*, she said.

They made love, leaving the wonderful dinner cooling on the table. And hours later, when she slept and he scrubbed the beige carpet, he felt like a million bucks.

He'd been mostly successful but a small stain had remained. The carpet was perhaps not ruined but no longer what it had been. And during the few hours of sleep he got that night, his euphoria faded and he started to worry that Jules would regret more than simply offering him wine.

But the next morning, Jules had glanced at the stain and waved it away. She had left for work wearing her fancy clothes and expensive perfume, and he stayed behind. When he stared at the damage, he knew. She was too good for him. He was going to stain her life—maybe not ruin it, but certainly damage it.

He hadn't confessed his concerns. Not that morning, not that next night when they'd been back in her very comfortable bed, nor anytime over the next weeks. She'd have told him he was wrong.

But he knew he wasn't.

Now, as he returned to his leather chair in the corner of her room, there was no chance of spilling salsa on the bed. He sat down and balanced his plate on his lap.

When Jules had suggested he use her room for a nap, he'd understood that she wanted some alone time with Charity. Fine by him. He could work in her room just as well as anywhere else.

Well, that wasn't true.

She still wore the same perfume, and it was stronger in here. That interfered with his concentration, and the big bed in the center of the room didn't help. There was no way he was lying down. It was too intimate, too much, to share the same space, even if he was fully dressed and she was nowhere in sight.

There was something going on between Jules and Charity that he didn't understand. Jules was wound up tight. He'd been able to see it in the set of her jaw.

That bothered him because Jules was supersmart and very intuitive. If she was worried about Charity, or concerned about something that Charity was up to, then that put his anxiety off the charts.

His cell rang and he looked at the number. Detective Mannis. Good. Royce had left him a message fifteen minutes ago.

"Thanks for calling me back," he said.

"No problem. You mentioned an incident."

Royce told him about the bottle thrower. The man listened carefully. "Well, I'm glad Ms. Cambridge wasn't hit," he said. "Anything, even a bottle, thrown from a distance can have some stinging power."

Yeah, but generally not deadly. "Maybe he's playing with her," he said. "I wanted to know if you'd be able to get the security tapes from the hotel and the conference center. I want to see if he was wearing a conference badge and I really want to know where he went after he disappeared back into the hotel."

"I'll make some calls," he said.

"Thank you," Royce said. He ended the call. In the meantime, he had plenty to do. He clicked to see if any of the background information he'd ordered had come back. He saw that the report for Charity was available.

Charity White. Born in Brooklyn. Moved to South Carolina when she was two. Her mother was Linette White and the two of them had lived in the same house until Charity was seventeen. She'd been a solid B student through high school.

She'd been arrested the summer after she'd graduated from high school for retail theft under $300. Pled guilty and successfully completed her six months of probation. Weeks after that ended, she moved to a different address than her mother. Still in Charleston but closer to the coast.

She got a job at a discount chain where they bragged everything was a dollar but it really wasn't. Got a roommate, too. Her name was Louisa Goodall, a nursing student at the local junior college. Cable in Louisa's name, electric and gas in Charity's.

The rent on the apartment was $1,500 a month. The checks had been written by Louisa Goodall with no obvious reimbursement from Charity.

Nice friend to have.

Charity's paychecks had all been cashed at the same grocery store. No record of a checking or savings account.

Maybe she paid for all the groceries. Maybe she bought drugs with her money. Hard to know.

But he couldn't fault kids for attempting to spread their wings. After all, he'd done much the same, except that his escape had been to enlist in the air force.

She'd stayed at the job for more than four years. But then quit shortly after her mother had died eight months ago.

No record of her working after that. What the hell had she lived on? Her mother hadn't left any trust fund. There had been $1,311 in her mother's checking account the day the woman had died. No savings. No retirement accounts. No life insurance. Unpaid vet bills for her golden retriever.

It really was amazing how much information was readily available.

With a high school diploma, some work history and a relatively clean rap sheet, Charity should have been able to get a job. But unless she'd worked for cash, there was no record.

Three months ago, the lease on Louisa and Charity's apartment had ended. And based off the cell phone activity, they'd picked up stakes and moved to Las Vegas.

But there was no record of utility hookup here for either of them. He knew Charity had somehow ended up with Bobby Boyd but had no idea where her friend had landed.

He was willing to bet big money that Charity had been hanging with Louisa Goodall last night. But why so secretive? Why not just tell him that she was meeting a friend from back home?

He chewed the lunch he hadn't wanted, but it tasted pretty good. Had it been a lucky guess or had Jules remembered his penchant for ordering Mexican food? Kind of like he'd remembered her love for dark chocolate.

Kind of like he remembered where she liked to be touched. Just so. And how her tight body had felt around him when she'd—

His cell rang. He looked at the number and felt almost embarrassed. He was acting like a seventeen-year-old with raging hormones, and Detective Morris was busy trying to solve the case. "Morgan," he answered.

"I'm sending a video to your phone," the detective said. "It's actually three different videos that we spliced together. We found your bottle thrower. Have him from the minute he came into the hotel, took the escalator to the second floor, crossed over the walkway to the conference center and waited on the second floor. He was there for about ten minutes, just leaning over the railing, before he pulled the bottle out of his pocket. There's people all around him but he's not paying any attention to them and they're not really noticing him."

"Until the one guy shouted," Royce said.

"Yeah. That might have rushed him and affected his aim. All I know is that once he let go of the bottle, there's a couple-second delay before he runs."

"Probably was seeing if he'd hit his target?"

"Maybe. Although he wasn't being too careful about it. He was pretty much still hanging over the railing."

Royce knew that. In fact, that's why he'd gotten a pretty good look at the guy. "Then what do you have?"

"After he runs from the second floor, he uses the crosswalk to get back to the hotel."

Royce knew that. He'd chased him that far. "Then?"

"He takes the elevator on the second floor up to the third floor, switches elevators in the lobby, takes the second one up to the sixth floor, and then immediately accesses the stairs."

"I assume there are cameras in the stairways."

"Of course. He goes all the way to the first floor and exits via a side door of the hotel. We lose him in sidewalk traffic then. I've got a technician trying to find him again but I'm not hopeful. Easy to slip away in that many people."

Royce cursed all the people who visited Vegas. Why the hell couldn't they just stay home and lose their money?

"Is he known to the police?" Royce asked.

"Not to me. But that's why I want you to look at the video. Let me know if you recognize him."

"Okay. I will. Thank you." Royce hung up, and within seconds the video had arrived. He watched it twice. The man was white, wore a cheap-looking blue sweatshirt, blue jeans and red tennis shoes. He looked to be about thirty. His hair was brown. No visible tattoos. No jewelry, not even a wedding ring.

Royce didn't believe he'd ever seen the man. He knew he needed to show it to Jules. And almost as if there was some telepathic connection, there was a knock on the door.

"Hey, it's me," she said.

Holy hell, he thought as he almost dropped his plate. He thought of the memories he'd been indulging in before Detective Mannis had called. If she really was able to read his mind, he was in big trouble. "Yes," he said, already moving toward the door.

Once he opened it, she stared at him, then frowned. "Is everything okay? You look a little flushed."

Well, of course he did. "It's warm in here," he said.

"Is it?" she asked, a frown on her pretty face.

"I got a video from Detective Mannis," he said, hoping to divert her attention.

"And?"

He held out his phone, pressed Play. "Does this guy look familiar to you?"

She watched it once, then pressed Play to start it again. "No," she said, shaking her head. "I don't know him."

She sounded very disappointed. "It's okay. We'll figure it out," he said. "Where's Charity?" he asked.

"She went back down to the pool," Jules said. "That's why I came to get you. I wanted you to know you could come out."

He walked over and picked up his dirty plate. "How was your lunch?" he asked.

"Good," she said.

He stared at her. "I'm not sure I understand where you think this is going with you and Charity. Is this a onetime thing, or are you hoping to have a friendship with her?"

"Why is that necessary to define right now?" she asked. She walked toward the living room, giving him her back.

He stepped up his pace and got in front of her again. "Just stop it, Jules. I think it's time for you to tell me the truth about Charity and why she's so important to you."

She desperately wanted to tell Royce everything. Desperately wanted someone else to be in on the secret, to help her think it through, to help her sort fact from fiction.

But it was possible that the truth had the potential to destroy her father. And Royce might want that very much. "Royce, I think you're imagining things. I'm just trying to get to know her a little."

"Did you tell her that you almost got hit in the head with a bottle earlier?"

"No."

"Did you ask her where she was after your session?"

"No."

"So what the hell did you two talk about while I was hiding in the bedroom?"

She wanted to smile. He was exasperated and it reminded her of the Royce she'd known eight years earlier, before he'd gotten so polished and professional.

"Rémoulade sauces and white bean chili."

"Huh?"

Now he looked really confused. "Charity ordered the crab cakes. They came with a rémoulade sauce. She started talking about how she made a similar sauce. Then I told her how I make my famous white bean chicken chili."

He lowered his chin. "You're famous for your white bean chicken chili?"

Now she did laugh. "Well, maybe in my own mind. But it's really good."

"So you were talking about cooking?"

"Yes." It had been easy conversation while they'd eaten their lunches. Pleasant.

The kind of thing she expected sisters might talk about.

"I make a pretty mean pot roast," he said.

"Fine. We'll include you the next time." She sat down on the couch and leaned her head back against the cushion. "I think she's really into food. Her eyes light up when she's talking about it and it seems like she knows a lot. She said that she watches cooking shows all the time."

"Maybe she should try to get a job at a restaurant."

She heard what he wasn't saying. He'd always had a strong sense of responsibility and it likely bothered him that Charity had been so blasé about not having a job or being in school. "It takes some kids longer than others to find their way."

"At twenty-four, you were already a manager at Geneseel."

With responsibility for a staff of more than twenty associates. "I was an overachiever," she said, her tone deliberately light.

He wasn't buying it. She could tell. "I read your bio," he said. "I listened to you yesterday talking to Cole Hager. I heard this morning's session. You really know what you're talking about. You're the real deal."

She felt very, very warm. She'd always worked hard and tried to do well, but since her divorce, she'd been driven to succeed. Work was really all she had. "I appreciate you saying that," she said.

It wasn't all that she appreciated. "I…I want you to know that I'm very grateful for all your help these last two days. I really didn't know how this was going to work with the two of us being together like this but you've been so professional. It's really been amazing."

He stared at her. "I never wanted anything bad to happen to you. I still don't."

"What happened after that night at my father's condo?" she asked. "I'd really like to know how you got from there to here."

He sat down in the chair opposite of her. "I went home to Texas. Licking my wounded pride," he added with a small smile.

He was probably trying to make her feel better. But she'd seen the look on his face that night, had realized that her admission—that she planned to marry Bryson after all—had hurt him terribly. "And you went back to school?"

"Yes. And worked. Did both full-time."

"Talk about driven," she said.

He looked very serious. "I wanted to be a better man."

She looked down at her hands. "I think you'd have to look a long way to find a better man. You are kind and honorable. A very good man."

"I was uneducated and unemployed. Certainly not suited for you."

"I thought we were suited. We seemed suited."

The air in the room seemed to be tight, making it hard for her to breathe.

"But here's what I don't get," he said. "Those things were both true. But they weren't new news. I hadn't hidden anything from you. Yet something your father said that night when I stepped out made a difference."

He was getting too close to the truth. And there was no way that she could have that discussion with him. He was too smart.

"I never meant to hurt you," she said, desperate to redirect his attention from that night. "I'm grateful that you moved on," she added quickly. "That you forgot about me."

She saw a quick flare of emotion cross his eyes. "Is that what you think?" he said, practically spitting the words. "Do you think that I simply shook the Fifth Avenue dust off my boots and eased into the rest of my life?"

She didn't know what to say.

He evidently took that as permission to go on. "Did that make it easier to sleep at night?" he asked, his tone full of disgust. "Did you tell yourself that it was nothing, that it meant nothing?"

"I never thought that," she managed. She was going to cry. She did not want to do that in front of him. She stood up fast.

But he was faster. And he caught her before she rounded the edge of the couch. He crowded her, his big body walking her backward until she came up against the wall.

He was so close. His body was pulsing with energy. With one hand, he gripped her chin, not hard enough to hurt her but enough that she was forced to stare into his eyes.

"I almost lost my damn mind," he said. He was close enough that she could feel his warm breath on her face. "I didn't want to live anymore."

No, she thought. But knew that it was true because she'd felt much the same. Except she'd had the additional burden of acting like the happy bride-to-be while slowly dying inside. But she couldn't tell him that.

"I'm sorry," she said.

"You said the same thing that night. It didn't make a difference then. Do you think it makes one now?"

She'd hurt him badly. "You were right to hate me," she said.

He jerked in surprise. "Hell," he said. "I never hated you. I loved you."

He bent his head and took her lips, his kiss punishingly hard. And she felt it. All the years of pain and loss and loneliness.

And his hand was under her shirt, groping. His hips pressing into her, grinding. He was hard and her body, so starved for his touch, ignited as if a match had been lit.

She jerked his shirt from his pants, desperate to feel him. His back was taut hot skin and muscle and everything that she remembered. And she tilted her hips, rubbing herself against him.

He lifted his mouth, his lips hovering just the smallest of distances. "Jules, Jules," he murmured, before kissing her again. This time more gently.

She wasn't having any of that. Her hands still under his shirt, she moved them quickly, circling around his ribs. And she pinched his flat nipples. Hard.

And she nipped at his lower lip.

And hitched one thigh around his waist, opening herself to him.

"Take me," she said, slipping her tongue inside his mouth.

He reached both hands down, under her butt, and lifted her. Her back was against the wall, her legs around his waist, and she let her head fall back, giving him access to her neck.

"Hang on," he muttered, his voice guttural.

And he carried her back to her bedroom, closing the door with his foot. Then he dumped the two of them on the bed and they fell in a tangle of limbs.

He ripped the buttons on her blouse in his haste. She didn't care. She yanked down her skirt, squirming under him.

He tossed her underwear aside and she was naked in

his arms. And when his fingers found her, she arched in his hand, her hips inches from the bed.

Hot skin. Hot need.

He had too many clothes on. She found his belt buckle and fumbled with it. Hissed in frustration.

She heard his soft chuckle. "I got this," he said.

And he was good at getting naked fast. But then he slowed down. Took his time licking and sucking her breasts, until she was begging him. Ran his fingers gently over the scrapes on the back of her knee that she had gotten from the exterior of the Periwinkle. Gently kissed her there, then set a trail of kisses up her thigh, settling at the base of her spine.

"Now. I need you now," she said.

But still he lingered. Until finally, she heard the rip of a condom opening. She opened her eyes and watched his face as he so carefully entered her.

He was a big man in all ways and she appreciated his care. But once he was in, seated deep, the need to have him even deeper roared through her. She wrapped her legs around his waist and squeezed her inner muscles.

"Jules," he said.

She did it again. And then he was moving. Deep strokes, touching her in places that hadn't been touched for so long. Their bodies were slick with sweat and when he kissed her, she could taste salt on his skin.

Her need was spiraling out of control. She wanted, she wanted, oh my, there it was. She broke, coming in waves, her body heaving with the joy of it.

And he rode through it. And only when she was done shaking did his strokes become long and sure again. When he came, his big body jerked and a small cry escaped his mouth.

He slipped out of her and she felt the bed shift as he

rolled to his side and then up. She heard the toilet flush in the bathroom and then he was back, with a soft towel. He handed it to her.

Even with his hair all tousled like a little boy's, he looked very serious.

"Are you okay?" he asked, still sitting on the edge of the bed. "That was…pretty fast," he said.

She shook her head and smiled. "Fast would have been if you'd taken me against the living room wall. Once we got in here, you were dawdling."

"I guess I wanted to give you time to change your mind."

He said it lightly but she suspected it was the truth. If she'd have told him to stop, he would have. There was no doubt in her mind.

"I wanted you," she said.

He let out a big breath and lay back down in the bed. Then he gathered her into his arms, letting her head rest on his chest.

She closed her eyes, feeling at peace for the first time in days. The afternoon sun was shining through the partially open blinds and she felt safe. The day felt clean and pure.

When she woke, she was disoriented. The room was not dark but the bright light of the sun had slipped away. She raised her head.

He was awake. And when she moved, she saw him stretch his arm, as if it might have gone numb.

"You should have asked me to move," she said.

He just shook his head.

"What time is it? We have to get up," she said. How was she going to explain this to Charity? She threw back the sheet and hurried to sit up.

He was watching her with unabashed interest. When

he reached out, palmed her breast and lightly pinched the nipple, she felt an immediate response between her legs. They were going to be right back in bed if she didn't do something fast. She gathered up her clothes and practically sprinted to the bathroom.

She cleaned up and ran a brush through her hair. As quick as she was, by the time she finished and opened the bathroom door, she saw that the bedroom was empty, with the sheets and bedspread loosely pulled up and straightened.

When she went out to the living room, Royce was dressed and sitting at the table, his computer in front of him.

"Jules," he said. "I'm not sure—"

She held up a hand, stopping him. That made two of them. She didn't know why she'd been so out of control with need and she sure as hell had no idea what to do or say about it now. "Please," she said, "can we not talk about it just yet?"

He didn't look happy but he nodded. He closed his laptop. "Bobby Boyd is out on bond. About an hour ago."

Chapter 15

"I don't believe Charity would go back there," she said. "She's smarter than that."

He wasn't as confident of Charity's good judgment but given that his own was pretty damn awful, he shouldn't be casting stones.

He never should have kissed Jules. And he sure as hell shouldn't have had sex with her.

Because now that he had, it was going to take a damn lifetime to forget about it. He'd simply been fooling himself when he'd told himself that he was over her.

I loved you. That's what he'd confessed when he'd had her back against the wall. At least he'd had the smarts to put it in past tense.

Because there was no doubt, he wasn't over her.

She didn't want to talk about it.

Probably for the best.

He glanced at his watch. "What time did Charity say she was coming back from the pool?"

"She didn't. But yesterday, she was down there for a couple hours. She came back about five."

It was almost six o'clock. Maybe she'd fallen asleep in one of the lounge chairs. Jules had needed rest, maybe Charity felt the same way. "She has her phone, right? Why don't you call her?" he suggested.

Jules picked up her phone, pressed a couple keys. She had it on speaker. It went right to voice mail.

"Try again in a couple minutes if she doesn't call you back first," he said.

Five minutes later, they went through the same drill and got the same results.

Royce picked up the hotel phone. When his call got answered, he spoke fast. "Do you have the capabilities to page a guest in the pool area?"

"Uh…yes, we do."

"Then, I need you to page Charity White. That's Charity White. She needs to contact this number."

"Sir, we hesitate to page overhead. In deference to the guests who may be resting. I'm sure you understand."

"This is important," he said.

There was another pause. He supposed the clerk on the other end was looking at the daily bill rate of the suite Jules had rented and considering options.

"Well?" he prompted.

"We'd be happy to do that, sir. The page will go out within the next five minutes."

Fifteen minutes later, there was still no call from Charity. He could tell that Jules was very anxious as she paced around the suite. "I'm going to go look for her," she said.

He'd been expecting this. "Absolutely not." There was no way that Royce intended to let Jules go to the pool area, even if he was with her. Way too open, way too many places for somebody to hide. If something had happened to Charity at the pool, perhaps it was done in an attempt to draw out Jules.

He would go look for Charity but he wasn't leaving Jules alone. Not even if she was behind a locked door.

Trey did twelve-hour shifts for Billy-Bob Anderson, usually from 5:00 a.m. to 5:00 p.m. Billy-Bob liked to take his plane up during the day and frequently invited Trey along for the ride since Trey was one of the few security personnel whose stomach handled the dips and razor-sharp turns that Billy-Bob loved.

He should be done with work now, probably on his way back to Vegas. Royce picked up his phone.

Trey answered on the third ring. Royce could hear the faint drum of highway noise in the background. The airstrip was almost an hour west of Vegas.

"I need an assist," he said to his partner.

"Okay," Trey said, sounding much more awake. There would be no questions, no smart remarks hinting that he should have been able to handle his own case.

He knew that Royce rarely asked for help. He would know immediately that this was important.

Royce explained the situation and Trey said he'd be at the Periwinkle in fifteen minutes. Royce hung up. "My partner Trey Riker is on his way. He'll be here while I go to the pool and look for Charity."

To her credit, she didn't argue. That, more than anything, told him that she was finally taking the threats against her seriously.

She swallowed hard. "Do you think something has happened to her?"

"I don't know," he said. "I think there's a good chance I'll find her at the tiki bar, having drinks with some guy she's just met."

"I hope you're right," Jules said.

Royce slipped on his sports coat so that his gun was out of sight. He put his cell phone into one pocket and the key card into the other. He paced around the room, silently cursing Charity. "What was she wearing?"

"What she had on this morning. Blue jeans. A white T-shirt and a pink hoodie. She mentioned something about getting really cold at the pool yesterday."

"Did she take a bag with her when she left?"

"An off-white beach bag," Jules said. "I don't know what was in it."

"I'm going to check her room." He walked down the hallway, aware that Jules was following him. The room had been cleaned by the maid that morning. But there was a comb on the sink and her open suitcase in the closet.

It did not appear as if the girl had intended to leave. Maybe she was simply just not watching the time. But when he found her, he was going to read her the riot act for making Jules worry.

He heard a knock on the door. He smiled. Trey, always prompt, had made it in twelve minutes. He walked back to the living room, checked the peephole and opened the door.

When Trey came in, Royce saw him take everything in. The suite. Jules.

And he felt the first stirrings of jealousy in his gut when Jules smiled at the man. Trey was a good-looking guy and never had any trouble finding female companionship.

And he knew his partner well enough to know that the man liked what he was seeing.

"Trey Riker, this is Juliana Cambridge," he said.

When Trey glanced at him again, a question in his eyes, Royce knew that he'd done a poor job of tamping down his emotions. His tone had been sharp, too sharp.

Jules stepped forward. "Please, call me JC," she said, extending her hand.

Trey shook it, smiling. "Nice to meet you," he said.

Damn. Maybe he should send Trey looking for Charity versus asking the man to keep watch over Jules. But he knew that didn't make sense. He'd never met Charity; he couldn't pick her out of a crowd at the pool.

"Jules has a friend staying with her who has not returned from the pool as expected," he said. "I want to go look for her but I can't leave Jules alone."

"Okay," Trey said. He looked around. "Nobody else here?"

Royce shook his head.

"Expecting anybody else?"

Both Royce and Jules shook their heads.

Trey took off his jacket and slung it over the back of the dining room chair. "I brought some cards, JC. You up for a game? I play a mean hand of poker."

JC dealt the cards, her mind whirling. She was very worried about Charity. It made her crazy that she didn't know her own sister's habits well enough to know if this was usual or very unusual behavior. Charity had not seemed upset when she'd left the suite. There was no reason to think that she hadn't planned on returning.

But Bobby Boyd was out of jail. Was it even possible that Charity had gotten a call from the man and had jumped at the chance to get back together?

She couldn't be that dumb. JC just couldn't accept that.

But was she malicious? Was she deliberately staying away, knowing that it would make JC worry? Did she want to cause trouble for JC?

"I'll take two," Trey said, setting aside two cards.

She smiled at the man who was Royce's partner. He

was an inch or two shorter, and maybe a few pounds lighter than Royce, but that still made him a very imposing figure. He wore jeans, a black T-shirt and black boots—definitely had a more casual style than Royce, who'd yet worn anything but carefully tailored dress clothes.

She was generally good at assessing people, and she'd come to a very rapid conclusion that Royce and Trey were not just partners but very good friends. She suspected Trey knew a great deal about Royce.

She gave Trey two cards and took three for herself. "So, you and Royce were in the military together?" She tried for nonchalant and thought she'd succeeded.

He smiled, showing white even teeth. "That's right." He slid a dime into the center of the table.

They were bidding with change she'd found in the bottom of her purse. She matched the bid.

He flipped over his cards. "Two pair. Jacks and threes."

She showed her cards. "Three nines."

He pushed the twenty cents her direction. "Why does Royce call you Jules when you seem to prefer JC?"

Royce had told her that he hadn't been forthcoming about their prior relationship. Well, she didn't intend to give Trey the nitty-gritty details, but she'd say enough to satisfy him. "Royce and I knew each other years ago. When we both lived in New York. I didn't use JC as much then."

He dealt the cards. "Sounds as if the two of you might have lost touch since he left New York."

"I got married," she said.

He picked up his hand, seemed to study it. Then lifted his eyes. "I always suspected there was someone who had stomped on his heart and broken it."

His voice was cold. It had been a bold jump in logic but so close to the truth that she could feel the muscles in her hands jerk as she gripped her cards. "I never expected to see him again," she said.

"Are you still married, JC?" he asked.

"No. I've been divorced for more than six years." She stared at her cards, but it was hard to see them through the tears that were filling her eyes. She pushed a nickel into the middle of the table.

He stared at her. "Tell me that you didn't set this up. That you didn't orchestrate an elaborate scheme to get his attention."

Anger flared in her stomach. "Of course not," she said. "I would never do something like that."

Trey put his cards facedown on the table. He leaned forward. "Royce Morgan is one of the most decent men I've ever met. I wouldn't like to see him used by somebody he cares about."

"He…he doesn't care about me," she said, swiping at a tear that spilled over and ran down her cheek.

He picked up his hand again, then carefully discarded three cards. He waited for her to make her discard. She threw four in. He dealt. Picked up his cards. Casually bid a quarter.

"You've got a big job at a big company," he said easily. "I wouldn't expect that you'd be a fool."

"I'm not sure if that's a backhanded compliment or an insult."

"Just an observation," he said. "Royce is an onion. Lots of layers. Protective armor, I always thought. I think now I'm starting to understand things a little better."

"I…care for him," she admitted.

"Maybe even love him?" he asked.

"You make some bold assumptions, Mr. Riker."

He showed his cards. Four kings. She had nothing, not

even a pair. She pushed the two quarters in the middle of the table toward him.

"Please, just Trey," he said, smiling. "I have a feeling that we're going to be friends, JC. That's assuming, of course, that you don't screw over Royce."

Royce was overdressed at the pool. His suit jacket felt heavy and tight across his shoulders and he had an itch in the middle of his back that he couldn't reach.

Face it. He was jumpy.

He wanted to think that Charity was pulling a stunt, either because she wanted to worry Jules or because she simply didn't care. But his gut told him that he might be wrong, and if he was, it might be bad.

The lights were on—both the low-level lighting in the green spaces that surrounded the kidney-shaped pool and overhead. Even though the sun had set forty-five minutes earlier, it was a nice winter evening in Vegas, probably at least fifty degrees.

There was nobody in the pool, but in the Jacuzzi there was an elderly couple, probably in their seventies, hanging on to each other like they were teenagers. The man was cupping water in his hand and tossing it on the woman. She was laughing and he caught the sparkle of a big diamond ring on her finger as she skimmed her hand across the water to splash the man.

He liked thinking that they'd been married for fifty years. That love endured.

At least for some.

There were two other women at a table off to the side, both with cigarettes and cocktails. They gave him a look as he went past. He ignored them.

He walked the length of the pool and then made the return trip on the other side. Deck chairs were three-deep and probably a third of them were still full. It was too cold for swimsuits but there were people in shorts and other casual clothing. Many people were reading or sleeping, some chatting with friends.

No sign of Charity. He crossed over to the tiki bar in the corner of the pool area. A young man wearing a Hawaiian shirt and white shorts put a napkin in front of him.

"What can I get you?" he asked.

"I'll take a beer," he said, pointing to one of his old favorites. He rarely drank beer anymore, but right now it sounded really good. And he suspected that he might get more information if he ordered something and left a big tip. He pulled cash out of his pocket and pushed a twenty across the counter. "I'm looking for a friend," he said. "I think she was at the pool this afternoon. Early twenties. Very dark hair. Has her eyebrow pierced and her nose, too."

The bartender gave him eleven dollars in change but Royce left it there. "Drinks vodka on the rocks?" the young man said.

Royce had no idea. "Always has," he said easily.

"She was here for a couple hours. Sat in that cabana right over there," he said, pointing off to his left, maybe forty feet away. The two lounge chairs were both empty. "She left maybe forty-five minutes ago. Something like that."

"Alone?" Royce asked.

He could see the sympathy in the man's eyes. The guy probably thought he'd been dumped. "I'm not sure about that. I was pretty busy here at the bar."

"I think she was hoping that her brother would meet her here."

The guy picked up a bar towel. "Now that you mention

it, I think a couple guys did join her. They left shortly after that."

A couple? Had Bobby Boyd brought a friend with him, just to make sure that he could *convince* Charity to come back? To run interference if Royce or Jules decided to challenge him? "They go back into the hotel?" Royce asked.

The bartender shook his head. "I don't know. Only two ways to get out of the pool area. Either back through the hotel or out that way." He pointed toward a wooden gate that was in the middle of a fence that Royce suspected ran across the back of the hotel property.

He took another sip. Pulled his phone and found one of the pictures of Bobby Boyd from the background check he'd done on him. "This is her brother. One of the guys look like that?"

The bartender considered the picture. The sympathetic look was back in his eyes. "Hey, I'm not sure, but you know, I don't think so." He dipped his towel into what had to be bleach water given the smell and started earnestly wiping off the counters. "All I know is that she left in a hurry. Had ordered a drink and before one of our pool servers could carry it out, she was gone."

She'd left in a hurry. But not with Bobby. Who the hell had the two men been? And did it have anything to do with Jules?

He slid off the stool to take a closer look at the cabana where Charity had been sitting. It was then that he realized that there was an off-white beach bag underneath one of the lounge chairs. It almost blended in with the cement.

He squatted down, carefully opened the bag. Inside was a hairbrush, a paperback book and a half-eaten bag of pretzels. He had no way of knowing if it was Charity's but he wasn't leaving it. He tucked it under his arm and stood up. Then quickly walked the remaining distance to the gate at the rear of the property.

He pushed it open and walked through. There was foliage, a mixture of large flowering shrubs and palm trees, about four feet deep. Beyond that was a sidewalk, not smooth poured concrete but rather a collection of large flat stones nestled in thick brown mulch, creating what might have been a visually pleasing border for guests to stroll on, but Royce wasn't there to enjoy the experience.

He wanted a quick look before anybody else trampled the scene. Because he was going to need help. He pulled his phone and dialed the number for Detective Mannis. He needed information from the hotel and it was unlikely he could get it on his own. But if the request came from the Vegas police, his chances were a lot better.

The phone was answered. "This is Mannis."

"Detective Mannis, it's Royce Morgan. I need your help. Charity White is missing. I think it's possible that she was taken against her will."

"And you think this has something to do with what's been happening with Ms. Cambridge?"

"I have no idea. But I'm certainly not discounting the connection."

"Where are you?"

"At the Periwinkle. Meet me in the lobby."

"I'm fifteen minutes out."

It would take him that long to finish his walk around the exterior and report back to Jules. "Fine."

He hung up and continued his inspection. He saw no signs of struggle, no dropped items, nothing to give him any leads as to where Charity and the men she'd left with might have gone. But as he walked, he made a mental note of the cameras he could see and suspected there were some that were not quite so visible.

If she'd been coerced by the men, they'd been bold to do it in the daylight. It did not appear as if she'd yelled or tried to attract attention. Why not? Had the men threatened her, threatened someone that she cared about?

Threatened Jules? His foot slipped on one of the uneven stones but he managed to catch himself before he went down on one knee.

He rounded the edge of the hotel and was immediately swallowed up in the sea of people who constantly walked the strip. It was at night that the crowd increased as people went to dinner and shows and, of course, casinos.

He went into the front door of the hotel and took the elevator up to the third-floor lobby, then a second elevator to the fourteenth floor. He walked down the hallway, and while he was a man who didn't normally like looking like a fool, he was really hoping that Charity was inside the suite. He'd gladly admit to being wrong. But he knew there was little chance of that. He'd have gotten a text from Trey or from Jules.

He knocked and stepped back, making sure that he was visible through the peephole. Still, when Trey opened the door, Royce saw that the man had his gun pulled. He appreciated the care his friend and partner was taking.

Jules was at the table, a deck of cards in front of her. "Did you find her?" she asked, her voice full of hope.

He shook his head. "I found this. Is it hers?"

Jules reached out her hand, took the bag and looked inside. "That's the hairbrush she was using yesterday."

Royce told her and Trey everything that had transpired since he'd left the hotel room. "I'm on my way back to meet Detective Mannis," he finished. "I'm going to have him request the security tapes. Maybe we can get a better idea of who the men are that she left with."

"We need to find her friend Lou," Jules said.

That surprised Royce. He knew about Lou because of the background information that he'd gathered on Charity. How did Jules know about her? And what else did Jules know that she wasn't telling? "Who is Lou?" he asked, deciding to play dumb.

"She's a friend of Charity's. Today, at lunch, Charity was telling me about her, that she had met her last night for a drink. Maybe the two men are friends. Of Lou's. Of Charity's. Maybe both. My gut is telling me that Lou is a part of this."

"So what do we know about Lou?" he asked.

"She and Charity have been friends since they were kids. Lou works as some kind of in-home health-care provider."

That made some sense. If she was staying in someone's home, she wouldn't have made any paper trail renting an apartment or getting utilities hooked up.

"You didn't happen to get the address where she works?" Trey asked.

Jules shook her head. "I…I didn't think it would be important." Her voice broke.

Royce crossed the room in three strides. Knelt down at her side, looked her in the eye. "This is not your fault, Jules. No way, no how. Don't take it on. Keep your head straight."

He wanted desperately to take her into his arms, to kiss her, but mindful that his partner was in the room, he kept his hands to himself. Yet, when she looked at him, her pretty violet-blue eyes troubled, he knew that he was probably the one who would need comforting later.

He was going down for the count. And there was no

reason for this to end differently than the last time. He stood up fast. "I've got to go."

She pushed her chair back. "I'm going with you."

"No," he barked. She was safer in this room.

"Royce," she said, her tone pleading. "I have to do something. I can't just stay here. I can't."

Damn. "Fine."

She practically ran to her bedroom. "Give me two minutes," she said over her shoulder.

When the room was empty, he turned to face his partner.

The man looked relaxed, just leaning against the wall. "I hope you know what the hell you're doing," Trey said conversationally.

"I'm going to talk to the manager and—"

"Not that," his partner snapped, straightening up. "I know you can work a case, Royce. You're one of the best. But you've never been in love with the client before."

In love? What the hell had Jules said to Trey?

"I have to tell you," Trey went on. "She's not a great poker player. Lousy bluffer."

"But?" Royce prompted, knowing his partner well enough to know this was leading up to more.

Trey smiled. "She is gorgeous and seems very nice and gets a real dreamy look in her eyes when she says your name."

Dreamy was not a word that he'd ever expected to hear Trey utter. "We have history," Royce said.

"Well, I imagine the question of the hour is whether you can put history aside. If you can, great. If you can't, don't fall into the abyss, man. Let this one go. I'll take the case. You take my place on the Anderson project."

"Billy-Bob only trusts you."

"The assignment is almost over. It will be fine."

If only it were that easy. Trey could step in and he could walk away before Jules hurt him again. His partner was truly excellent at what he did. Jules would be in good hands.

But not his hands. "No," he said. "She hired me to provide security. That's what I'm going to do."

They heard a door close. "Who's going to protect you?" Trey hissed.

"I'm not a twenty-five-year-old kid anymore. I know what I'm doing."

"I sure as hell hope so," Trey said. "Because you know what they say—history has a way of repeating itself."

Chapter 16

JC's head was whirling as she, Royce and Trey took the elevator down to the lobby. They were going to meet Detective Mannis and then talk to the manager. Royce believed there was a good likelihood that Charity's departure had been captured on film.

Once they stepped off the elevator, Royce led them to one side of the lobby. With their backs against the wall, he and Trey, without a word or a look, each took a position on the side of her.

They were her fortress.

She was putting them at risk. Hadn't thought about that when she'd demanded to come along. Had only been thinking that she needed to do something. "Maybe I…"

Detective Mannis entered the lobby at the far end. Saw them and headed their direction.

Royce extended his hand. "Thank you for coming so quickly. This is my partner Trey Riker."

Trey and Detective Mannis shook hands. The detective nodded at her. "Ms. Cambridge."

"JC, please," she said, doubting it would do any good. The detective was a formal kind of guy.

"Anything change since we talked?" he asked.

Royce shook his head.

Detective Mannis motioned them toward the elevator. "I connected with the manager on my way over, thought it might save us some time. Her office is on the sixth floor. She's expecting us."

Royce motioned for her to follow Detective Mannis and then he and Trey fell into step, one on each side. They were a walking triangle, with her in the middle. "She's probably thinking we're more trouble than we're worth," Royce said. "After all, this is the second time today that we've needed them to pull security tapes."

"She did seem a little surprised," Detective Mannis admitted. "But when I told her it was a possible abduction, I had her full attention. Not good for a hotel's reputation, you know."

No one answered.

When they got to the executive offices, there was a woman at a desk in the lobby. "Detective Mannis for Sonya Tribee," the detective said, handing the woman his card.

"Of course," she said. "Please follow me."

Sonya Tribee had a corner office with two walls of windows. She wore a red suit, a silky white blouse and three-inch black heels. Her very blond hair was pulled back in a tight chignon and she had diamond studs in her ears.

Her desk was immaculate, with just an empty inbox and a computer on it.

She was maybe thirty, and as professional as she probably was, her mouth literally fell open with she looked at Trey and Royce. Her office was likely rarely filled with that much raw masculinity.

If either man noticed, they ignored it. Detective Mannis introduced himself, then JC, Royce and Trey in turn.

Royce motioned for Detective Mannis and her to take the two chairs in front of the manager's desk, and he and Trey stood behind them.

"I'm very concerned with what you told me, Detective Mannis," she said. "I was just on my way out for the day and I'm very glad you caught me."

"We appreciate you staying," Royce said, jumping in. "We're looking for a young woman, age twenty-four, about five-three and maybe a hundred and five pounds. She was in the pool area today, in one of the cabanas near the tiki bar. Your bartender remembers her. He also thinks that she was approached by two men at some point and left the area."

"And this was unexpected?" the manager asked.

"Yes," JC said. "She's…a friend and has been staying in my suite. I expected her to return from the pool."

"I hope you know, Ms. Cambridge, that these things don't happen at the Periwinkle. I'm just terribly sorry."

"I have the highest regard for the Periwinkle," JC said. She did not want the manager to cover up important information just because it might look bad for the Periwinkle.

Detective Mannis cleared his throat. "If we could just look at that video footage."

Sonya motioned for them to come behind her desk. She clicked a few buttons and suddenly there was the pool area in all its opulent glory. "I want to see the cabana to the left of the tiki bar about five this afternoon," Royce said.

She clicked a few buttons and the video was in a fast rewind. JC had to look away because the fast jerky movement made her sick to her stomach.

Or maybe it was the very horrible realization that something had happened to Charity and she was never going to get to know her only sister.

"There," Royce said.

Sonya stopped the rewind and JC saw Charity lounging back in the chair. Her eyes were closed. There was a partially empty glass on the small table next to her.

JC wondered if she was sleeping, but within minutes, Charity stretched an arm out for the glass and finished her drink. And five minutes went by before the pool server stopped by to ask if she wanted a refill.

"This has to be it," Royce said. "The bartender said that she ordered a drink but left before the server could deliver it."

JC wanted to scream at the computer. *Open your eyes. Be careful.*

It was like waiting for the train wreck that you knew was coming. And sure enough, a minute or two later, two men, both wearing dark slacks and long-sleeved white shirts, entered the shot. They both had on straw hats, pulled low. "We're going to need to know how they got in," Detective Mannis said.

"We'll have that," Sonya said.

"Stay here," Royce said, his attention laser-focused on the screen. "We'll get that later."

The two men squatted down next to Charity's chair. She sat up fast, as if they'd startled her. She opened her mouth but closed it fast.

The angle was wrong. They couldn't see the men's mouths. Had one of them said something that made her suddenly decide not to scream, not to create a disturbance? The one on the right reached into his pants pocket. Royce thought maybe he was pulling a gun. But it wasn't that. It was something flat and he extended his hand, letting Charity see it.

Charity stood. Leaned in the direction of her beach bag but then straightened up fast before reaching for the item. The men each took a side, with the man on the right grabbing her arm. They vanished from the shot.

Sonya pushed some buttons, probably going to another camera, and sure enough, there they were. Walking out the back gate.

"How far can you follow them?" Trey asked.

"Almost to the street," Sonya said, clicking keys. JC wanted to close her eyes, to not watch, but she kept them wide-open. Saw the men hurry Charity down the sidewalk, saw them looking left, and then maybe thirty seconds later, a black late-model sedan drove up to the curb. One of the men got in the front passenger side, the other man and Charity piled into the back.

The car sped away.

The room was absolutely silent.

"Can you back that up and slow it down?" Royce asked. "Can we catch a plate number, maybe a view of the driver?"

Sonya gave it a try but the angles weren't right.

"Don't worry about it," Detective Mannis said. "There are cameras all along the strip. We'll be able to find them. Give me an exact time," he said to Sonya.

She leaned forward, closer to the screen. "Five sixteen," she said.

JC felt her face heat up. All this was starting to happen while she was sleeping in Royce's arms.

She felt sick. But they couldn't stop now. "Let's go

back to how those men got to her. Did they come through the back gate or through the hotel?"

Royce nodded, as if he'd been about to ask the same question.

It took Sonya just minutes to find it. A young couple, holding hands, left the pool area by the back gate. As they did so, the men had entered. In fact, the woman held the door open for them, smiling.

Oldest game in the book. Wait for somebody to open the door and come in. It was a security risk that most employers were constantly addressing. At Miatroth, where drug tampering in the manufacturing process was always a concern, associates were shown videos on how not to fall for the same scam.

Royce ran his hand across his head, ruffling up his short hair. "The two of them must have been waiting outside for some time. Can you back that video up? I want to take a better look at their faces."

The men had waited for eleven minutes before somebody had left by the back gate. But it was almost as if they suspected that there were cameras. They kept their faces down.

Sonya shut off her computer. "I'm sorry," she said, looking at JC.

"Thank you," JC said. Her throat felt tight. Charity could be in terrible danger.

They all shook hands with Sonya and left her office. Once they were back in the hallway leading to the lobby, she looked at Royce. "Do you think Bobby is behind this?"

He shook his head. "Doesn't feel right," he said. "Bobby would come himself, make a scene in the hotel. This looked…"

She waited. But Royce didn't look as if he intended to finish the sentence.

"This looked pretty well orchestrated," Trey said, finishing the thought. "They got in and out fast and it was less than a minute before that car pulled up."

"I'm still not confident that she didn't go willingly with those men," Detective Mannis said.

They hadn't been dragging her to the car. Yes, one had his hand cupped around her elbow, but maybe he was just being a gentleman, trying to make sure she didn't trip on the uneven stones.

But if she'd gone willingly, why hadn't she called? It was now almost seven o'clock. Certainly past the time when Charity should have returned from the pool. JC wanted to rail at the detective, to tell him how terribly wrong he was. But she knew that she was influenced by her deep desire that Charity be the kind of woman who did the right thing, hung out with the right kind of people.

Be a sister she could be proud of.

What could Charity possibly be involved in that would have two men—no, make that three, because somebody had to be driving that car—gang up and kidnap her?

"Now what?" she asked, because her head really was spinning.

"Let's go back upstairs," Royce said.

"I'll contact you once I've gotten a chance to look at the street video. If I know anything more, I'll share it," Detective Mannis said. "We'll also check Bobby Boyd's apartment again. Just in case."

"There is one thing you should be aware of," Royce said. "Charity shared with Jules that she was out with a friend last night. They were drinking at a bar."

The detective pulled out his little notebook. "Name?"

"Louisa Goodall."

JC didn't even blink. But her brain, already scattered, started smoldering.

She'd never mentioned Louisa's last name. She hadn't known it.

Trey looked at Royce. "What else can I do for you?"

"I've got this," Royce said. "Get some sleep. But in case we need you later, take this extra room key." He tossed it at Trey.

Trey caught it, then turned to smile at her. "Nice to meet you, JC. Difficult circumstances and all that, but still my pleasure."

"Thank you," she said.

Trey and Detective Mannis walked out of the lobby together. And Royce didn't waste any time hustling her into the elevator. "You should eat something," he said.

"You have to be hungry, too," she said, feeling suddenly quarrelsome.

"I'm okay," he said, his voice tentative. "Jules, you know that this isn't your fault, right?"

She shook her head. "How do I know that?" she asked. "How do I know that this isn't one hundred percent connected to me?"

She was practically yelling now, and within the tight confines of the elevator, her words seemed to bounce off the walls. The bell dinged, announcing their arrival at the fourteenth floor.

Royce held up a finger, then stepped in front of her. He motioned for her to follow. Once they were inside her suite, as usual he checked the rooms before allowing her to leave the entryway.

He'd no more finished doing that before she confronted him. "When I mentioned Lou, you acted as if you'd never heard of her. Yet you told Detective Mannis that Charity had a friend named Louisa Goodall. I never told you

Lou's last name. I didn't know it." She took a breath. "Royce, I want to know how you know that and what else there is that you're hiding from me."

Chapter 17

In all the time he'd known Jules, he didn't think he'd ever seen her angry. But she was steaming right now.

She was so damn smart that he wasn't at all surprised that she'd picked up on his slip, all without even missing a beat.

"Can we sit down?" he suggested, his tone even.

"No."

Her back was rigid and her chin was slightly lifted, as if she was awaiting a physical blow.

"I did a background check on Charity. Louisa Goodall's name came up a few times because they were roommates, apparently for a few years after high school." He pulled his cell from his belt. Thumbed through the emails and found the one he needed. "Here's a couple pictures of her. I've got some of Charity, too."

Jules reached for the phone and stared at the pictures for several minutes. "What else did you find out about Charity?" she asked.

There was something in her tone, something that didn't sound exactly right, but he couldn't put his finger on it. She was angry, sure, but there was something else. "What you'd told me. Raised by a single mom who died about eight months ago. High school graduate. No college. Entry-level retail job. Moved to Vegas a few months ago."

"That's it?" she asked.

Had she expected something more? "Yeah."

"Fine. We need to find Louisa Goodall. They were drinking last night. We need to find the bar where they were drinking."

"Jules, this is Vegas. That's a whole lot of bars."

"She said it was a ten-minute cab ride home. I think it was an Irish bar because she was drinking Guinness and said something about when in Rome, do what the Romans do. We need to figure out what Irish bars are a ten-minute cab ride at two in the morning."

"You know, she might not have been keeping exact time. She'd been drinking," he said. "Maybe her ten minutes was really seven or maybe even fourteen."

"We have to start somewhere," she said. "I'm not staying here. I'll go crazy."

"Have you forgotten that somebody is threatening you? That they have tried to harm you?"

"I'll wear a disguise. Something that nobody will recognize me in."

Royce debated his options. He was fairly confident that if he shut Jules down, she was determined enough that she'd attempt to sneak out of the hotel later. He'd be able to stop her but the whole thing might come off the rails. She'd been very compliant with her security precautions up to this point. He didn't suddenly want her to rebel and make protecting her so much more difficult.

"I suppose, if I wore one, too," he said. "I'm not letting you go by yourself."

"Fine. Whatever." She picked up her smartphone. "Let me see if there are costume shops close—"

"No," he interrupted her. "If we're going to do this, we do it right." He picked up his own cell phone.

"Hey, I know I told you to get some sleep," he said, once his partner had answered, "but I need a favor first."

Once he was confident his partner understood exactly what he wanted, he ended the conversation. "He'll be here as soon as he can. And he's getting us a different car."

"Wow," she said. "I guess you've done this before."

Providing security was their main focus, but on occasion, that required some surveillance work, too. Changing up cars was common practice, especially if it was long-term. They also had an arsenal of high-quality disguises—hairpieces, mustaches, clothing and the like—that could be used to alter their appearance.

They didn't have much for women, however, so Trey was going to need to get inventive.

Jules picked up her laptop. "I'm going to answer some emails," she said.

He gave her credit. She had to be worried sick about Charity but she also knew that she had a responsibility to lead her organization and couldn't just suddenly be AWOL. He liked the fact that she was able to do that. He had not discounted the fact that someone internal to her organization was behind the threats. If they saw evidence of her working, they would assume that everything was status quo.

They'd have no idea she was about to blend into the Vegas nightlife.

Twenty-four minutes later, Royce got a text from Trey. Coming up the back stairs. He knocked on Jules's bedroom door. He expected to see her sitting on the bed, where she'd worked before, but she'd chosen the chair, the same chair that he'd been sitting in.

Did the bed feel differently to her now that they'd made love there? He stared at her. Her face was giving nothing away.

"Trey is on his way."

She set her laptop aside. "I'm sorry I was…difficult… earlier. I want you to know that I appreciate this. Appreciate everything you're doing to find Charity," she said.

"We're going to find her," he promised. He wasn't sure what else he could tell her that might make it better.

By the time he got back to the living room, Trey was using his key to come in the door. "You do all fourteen floors?" Royce asked, ushering him into the suite.

"Yeah. Came in through a side entrance at ground level. Didn't meet anybody."

People didn't do stairs in these buildings. Most of the guests probably hadn't even noticed the signage pointing them out as an emergency exit.

Jules came out of the bedroom. "Hi, Trey. Sorry we keep interrupting your nap."

"No problem. I hope you like red."

"Huh?"

Trey pulled a dress out of the bag that he carried. It was red with silver sequins and skinny silver straps. It looked vaguely familiar.

"I got it from the boutique across the street from us."

That's where he'd seen it. There was a woman's boutique directly across from Wingman Security. The mannequin in the window had worn this.

Next, he pulled a blond wig from the bag. "We had this."

Royce recognized it and remembered when his partner

Seth Pike had purchased it. He'd disguised himself as a woman sitting in a car, believing it made the neighbors in the gated community less nervous to see a woman in a car versus a man.

Trey handed both items to Jules. She made no comment.

"What do you got for me?" Royce asked.

"You're just another slick cowboy with too much money and too little good judgment." Trey proceeded to pull out dark blue jeans, a silky white shirt that snapped instead of buttoned, a belt with a buckle the size of his fist and a hat that had a band of silver sequins that came close to matching Jules's dress. The last item was a pair of heavy-framed glasses.

They might just pull this off. He grabbed up his items and went into the bathroom to change. When he came out, Jules was already back in the living room with Trey.

She looked…amazing. The dress fit her like it had been made for her, and the blond wig altered her appearance so significantly that had he not expected it, even he might have been momentarily fooled.

Trey was smiling at him, looking amused. "She cleans up well," he said.

Indeed. He would speak if his mouth didn't feel as if it was stuffed with cotton.

"Put your hat on," she said.

He did, pulling the brim low on his forehead.

"Wow. You look totally different," Jules said.

That was the plan.

"I put sensible shoes on," she said, pointing to her feet. "You know, in case we have to run. They don't really go with the dress."

They were black wedges, with just a small heel. "Don't

worry," he said honestly. "In that dress, nobody is going to be looking at your feet."

She blushed, her cheeks turning almost as red as her outfit.

The air buzzed with tension.

Trey cleared his throat. "Well, kids, what's the plan?"

Royce picked up his cell phone. "Charity mentioned to Jules that it was a ten-minute cab ride back to the hotel from the bar. At two in the morning. She also said that she was drinking Guinness, so we're focusing on Irish bars or pubs. I've plotted four Irish bars that are approximately the right distance."

"Will I be a little overdressed?" Jules asked.

"Anywhere but in Vegas," Trey said. "Here, the flashier the better. The strip is filled with designer merchandise and buyers flaunt it. Think of it as hiding in plain sight. You're dressed to get attention so nobody gives you a second thought."

Trey was right and he was wrong. Jules could wear a brown paper bag and she'd still grab a man's attention. But she quite frankly didn't look anything like a consummate CEO.

His cell phone dinged and he looked at the incoming text. He read it twice. Looked up. "It's Mannis," he said. "They were able to get plates off the black 2015 Lexus but they belong to a 2011 Grand Prix that was parked on a residential street about ten miles from here. So that's not too helpful. And he has been to Bobby Boyd's apartment. The loser was there. Alone. And Mannis believed him when he said he didn't know or care where Charity was."

"If the men were driving a car with fake plates, that has to prove that they were up to no good," Jules said.

"I don't think Mannis was doubting that they were

bad guys. I think he simply isn't convinced that Charity was taken against her will."

"I know she was," Jules said. "On the tape, it's clear to me that she starts to grab for her bag that's under her chair but then she stops, as if she rethinks the action. I think she wanted it found, wanted somebody to know that she'd left without her stuff."

"Or," Trey said, "she didn't think she was going to be gone for long, so perhaps no reason to take it."

Royce appreciated the fact that Jules didn't try to immediately rebuke Trey's statement. She simply nodded, as if she accepted that there were other plausible explanations.

"I guess we won't know for sure," she said, "until we find her. We should go."

Trey put his hand on the door, to open it for them. "Have fun," he said. He looked at Royce. "Be safe."

"No worries," Royce said. He turned to Jules. "I got a hankering for bangers and mash, darlin'," he said, his voice deeper and the Texas twang much heavier.

She was grateful for her sensible shoes as they quickly went down fourteen flights of stairs and out the side exit. Royce led the way to the hotel parking lot, where he seemed to easily find the brand-new Ford F-150 pickup truck that Trey had left for them. It was a shiny red.

Just what a flashy cowboy with too much money might drive. They were definitely hiding in plain sight.

"Where to?" she asked as they got belted in.

He pulled out his phone and handed it to her. "These are the most logical places," he said. "We'll start at the first one."

"Have you been to any of these before?"

"Yeah, two of the four. The one we're headed to now has some decent food if you feel up to eating."

She should eat. It seemed like forever since she'd had lunch with Charity. "I'll get something."

"Once we're inside," he said, "you should limit your talking as much as possible. Hair, makeup and clothes are easy disguises. It's much harder to change your voice, both the general tone and speech patterns."

"You did a pretty good job back there in the hotel."

"I've had more practice," he said. "If you need to use my name for any reason, call me Tex. What do you want me to call you?"

"Chambri," she said.

He frowned at her.

"It will be easy to remember. It was my nickname in college."

He smiled. "I don't think I ever heard this story."

Probably not. "I was seventeen when I started college. I went to my first party and when somebody asked me what I wanted to drink, I said champagne. It was what I remembered my mother drinking. Well, you can imagine how that went. They combined *champagne* with *Cambridge* and from that day on, I was Chambri."

"Did they have champagne at the party?"

She could tell he was amused. "Beer in red cups that cost five dollars."

"Well, tonight, you can have a beer in a glass for ten bucks," he said.

"Lovely."

They were silent the rest of the ride. When he pulled into the lot, she looked at the clock. "Fifteen minutes."

"I know. Traffic is heavier now than at two in the morning."

"How do we play this?" she asked.

"We're on a date. We'll scope out the place, looking for Charity or Lou. If we don't see them, once we've had a drink and left the bartender a really good tip, I'll ask if he or she knows Charity or Lou or has seen them recently."

She pasted a bright smile on her face. "Let's go, Tex." She opened her door and got out. He was already around the vehicle. He slung a casual arm around her shoulder.

She was amazed. His whole persona had changed. It was more than the clothes. He walked differently and held his head differently. She was going to have to up her game.

She leaned into him and they entered the combination bar/restaurant. It was dark and noisy and the waitresses wore short black skirts, white shirts and little green hats. One breezed by them. "Two for dinner?" the young woman asked.

She simply nodded, remembering his advice not to talk too much. They were led to a corner booth and he surprised her when he slid in after her on the same side.

"Never have your back to the room, darlin'," he whispered, his lips close to her ear.

"See if they have Guinness on their drink menu," she said.

"It's an Irish bar. I'm pretty sure they do."

"If they don't, we're leaving."

The server walked up to the table. "Evening. My name is Maddie. Can I start you out with a cocktail?"

"You have Guinness?" Royce asked, easily slipping into Tex's persona.

"Of course."

Royce settled back into the booth.

"Chardonnay, please," she said. JC preferred a pinot noir but tonight she was Chambri and that woman drank white wine.

Regardless of color, the drink would likely do her good; her nerves were on edge. On the way to the bar, she'd been looking at her cell phone every five minutes, as if looking at it would make Charity call. She had not been able to ignore the looks of sympathy Royce was sending in her direction.

"Great," Maddie said. "Here's some menus." She walked away.

JC didn't even open hers. How could she eat?

"How about a nice fillet?" Royce asked, "maybe with some mushrooms?"

"We don't have time for that," she said. "We need to get in, ask our questions and get out."

He sighed. "Here's the thing. It's likely to be a long night. I'd prefer that you don't fall over halfway through it. Can we compromise?"

She nodded.

"When Maddie comes back with the drinks, how about we order a Reuben sandwich? That should be pretty quick. Then I'll ask her?"

He was true to his word. After the young woman set down their drinks, he ordered the sandwiches and said, "We're looking for a couple friends of ours. Charity White and Louisa Goodall. I think they were here last night."

Maddie shook her head. "I don't think I know them," she said.

Royce pulled out his cell phone and showed Maddie Lou's picture. The waitress shook her head. He thumbed through to Charity's photo and got the same response.

"You might want to talk to the bartender," Maddie said. "He was here last night."

She left the table. Royce leaned close. "Don't move. Please."

She nodded and watched him amble toward the bar. Saw the women in the room take notice of the flashy cowboy. He leaned across the bar in a familiar manner that was so at odds with his very formal behavior that it was shocking. She watched him talk to the bartender, show his pictures, and she knew by the body posture that it was a bust.

He came back to the table and sipped his beer. She had yet to touch her wine and she took a big drink, and coughed when the alcohol hit the back of her throat. "Careful," he said. "Didn't you learn anything at those college parties?"

She'd been way too focused on excelling to go to many parties. "Can you eat and drive?"

"What?"

"We should take our food to go. Save some time."

He took one more sip of beer. "Fine. I'll let the waitress know."

Within five minutes, they were back in the truck, two foam containers on her lap. She opened one and handed him his sandwich.

"I'm really grateful that we didn't go for the steak. Hell of a lot harder to eat on the move."

She laughed. And it felt good. "This is a real shot in the dark, isn't it?" she said, staring out her window.

"Yeah, maybe. But what's the alternative?"

"Trey tried to distract me with poker."

Royce took a bite of his sandwich, chewed. "He's a better card player than me," he said.

"He really cares about you," she said. "He wasn't all that friendly when he put two and two together and decided that I'd been the one to break your heart."

"He wasn't rude?" Royce asked, sounding upset.

"No. Protective." She closed the lid on her sandwich. She really could not eat. "With good reason."

"I told him that I had a handle on it."

Now he was staring straight ahead. The lights from the oncoming cars were bouncing off the hard planes of his face.

Neither of them had a handle on it. She knew that. He knew it, too. "This afternoon was probably a mistake."

He didn't answer. Instead he looked at his GPS, where he'd programmed the next address, and quickly turned the corner. The buildings were less well-kept, the streets were narrower and the electric sign in the window said PEN.

"They need an *O*," she said—somewhat inanely, she realized as soon as it was out of her mouth.

"They need more than that."

She was sorry they had reached their destination. There was so much left unsaid. "When I said it was a mistake, I didn't mean that I... I was sorry about what happened today," she said.

"I'm not sorry, either," he said.

But he wasn't happy. "We should go inside," she said.

"Yeah. Let's go."

Chapter 18

He wanted to pound something. And the kid behind the bar, who barely looked old enough to drink let alone to pour them for others, was a good enough target.

If he could get him to stop flirting with the two women at the end of the badly scratched wooden bar. This place was a dump. And the garland sagging from the ceiling tiles gave the place a morose feeling.

Royce scraped the bar stool against the wood floor as he moved it out of the way.

The young man gave him a look but finished his conversation with the two women. Finally, he sauntered over.

"What can I get you?" the young man asked.

"Guinness," Royce said.

The bartender switched his gaze to Jules.

"Orange juice," she said.

Royce pulled a fifty out of his pocket. The bartender

brought their drinks and looked at the money. He picked it up, made change and left it on the bar.

Royce didn't pick it up.

Took a sip of his beer.

Besides the two young ladies at the end of the bar, there was one man in the middle of the bar. Early forties. Shirt cuffs were starting to fray, as if the garment had been washed often. Brown shoes needed shining.

Royce watched the bartender get the guy another drink. Watched as the guy motioned the man close before speaking. The bartender snuck a quick look at the women then shook his head.

Royce caught the bartender's eye.

"Need another?" he asked.

Royce shook his head. "We're supposed to meet two of our friends here. Charity White and Louisa Goodall."

The bartender shook his head.

Royce pulled his phone. Showed the pictures. Sensed that the man was looking just a second too long. Pushed the forty bucks and change in the bartender's direction. The man stopped looking at the pictures and was now sneaking glances at the man in the brown shoes.

"I think they were here last night," he said. "With him."

Bingo.

Royce nodded his thanks, motioned for Jules to follow him and quickly moved toward Brown Shoes. "Hey," he said, sliding onto the stool next to him. "I hear we have friends in common."

The man turned, raised an eyebrow. "Who?"

"Louisa Goodall and Charity White."

The man's face was blank. Damn. Had the bartender been wrong?

Royce pulled his phone, showed it to the man. Immediately, his expression changed. "What did you say their names were?" he asked.

"Louisa Goodall and Charity White."

"That's not what they told me. But—" he shook his head in disgust "—given that they snuck out when I went to the john, after I'd bought them both several drinks, I'm not surprised that they didn't use their real names."

Royce decided to take a chance. He reached into his pocket and pulled out a business card. "My name is Royce Morgan from Wingman Security. These two women are not my friends but my client is interested in finding them." No need to tell him that Jules was the client.

"Probably 'cause they screwed him, too," Brown Shoes said.

"No doubt," Royce murmured. "Did either one of them say anything that might give you a clue as to where they lived or worked?"

"The blonde said something to the dark-haired one about the old lady going to sleep at eight o'clock, that everybody at Everpark went to sleep at eight."

"Everpark?" Royce repeated.

"It's senior citizen housing," Brown Shoes said. "North a couple miles, not too far off Interstate 15."

Royce remembered he had heard of the place. Supposed to be pretty pricey. His partner Seth's mother was living there and he was pretty confident that Seth was picking up the tab. Never complained about it but in the early days of starting the company, Seth had worked a second job as a bartender, and Royce was pretty confident that had been the reason why.

He made eye contact with Jules and nodded. He thought she got the message because she picked up her orange juice and drained it. She had to be running on fumes and he hoped the sugar jolt did the trick.

He pulled a fifty from his pocket and placed it on the bar. "For some of their drinks," he said.

The man picked up the money. "Sure. No problem. They weren't the worst way to spend a few hours, you know."

Jules practically ran to the truck. He caught up and slid into the driver's seat. He hated to disappoint her but he was going to have to give her the bad news. "This is good," he said, "but I don't think there's much we can do with it tonight."

"But..."

"It's a retirement village. They'll have a main office but they sure as heck aren't going to be open tonight."

"Can't we just drive around, look...do something?" she finished up weakly.

"We'll start early tomorrow," he promised. "After we get some sleep. And who knows, maybe we'll hear from her before that. Maybe she'll be back at the hotel."

"You don't really think that," she said.

He didn't know what to think. "It's okay to be hopeful," he said.

She didn't respond. He took his eyes off the traffic just long enough to give her a look. She was staring at him.

"Jules?" he asked.

"Sometimes hope makes it hurt worse in the end."

Huh? "What are you talking about, Jules?"

Now she was looking straight ahead, into the dark night. "Never mind," she said.

He wanted to push her, to demand an answer, but in his gut, he knew that she was hanging on by a thread. So he simply drove back to the Periwinkle and made sure the valet knew where he wanted the truck parked. They would resume their disguises tomorrow, just in case.

And they would hopefully find Lou, who would lead

them to Charity, and then Jules's eyes would no longer look bleak.

They went through the side door and walked all fourteen floors. He opened the stairway door, checked the corridor to make sure it was empty, and then they walked quickly to her suite. He unlocked the door, pushed it open and entered.

And immediately saw the mailing envelope that was on the floor, just inside the door. Scrawled across the front in blue ink was JC Cambridge, CEO.

He heard the breath leave Jules's body and knew that she'd seen it. "Don't touch it," he whispered.

Then he pulled his gun and motioned for her to stay by the door while he did a quick sweep through the suite. Nothing was out of place.

When he got back, Jules was standing where he'd left her, simply staring at the envelope. He expected her to look terrified, and there was some of that, sure, but she mostly looked very angry.

"Whoever is sending these was here," she said. "They put it under the door."

He was pretty sure she was right. The other envelopes had been addressed to JC Cambridge, CEO, and they'd had the street address for her office and a postmark.

This one didn't have either because it hadn't come through the mail. He bent down and touched it with the tip of his finger. It was almost flat, likely with just one sheet of paper inside.

He opened it, being very careful to touch only the edges. Pulled out the sheet. Read it quickly and felt a hot ball of fury ignite in his gut.

Smarty, in your blue suit
You're top drawer.

But talk is cheap
Actions mean more.

All of you liars and cheaters
Know that the truth will be heard.
Written by my hand, in your blood
Not a single word blurred.

I am almost ready
So filled with joy.
For I am the hunter cat
And you are the little mouse toy.

Royce pulled his phone off his belt, punched in Detective Mannis's number. "Sit down," he said to her as
he waited for the man to answer. She had absolutely no
color in her face.

"Mannis."

"It's Royce Morgan. Jules got another letter. We think
it was slipped under her suite door while we were out."

"Did you open it?"

"Yeah. Carefully. The idiot's poetry isn't getting any
better," Royce said. Damn it. Who was this guy? "In it he
mentions a blue suit. That's what Jules was wearing this
morning when she did her panel presentation."

"Was there news coverage?"

"Not that I saw. But anybody with a cell phone is a
newsmaker these days. Social media is the biggest network out there."

"You're right. I'm on my way. I'd like to get it into our
lab, see if we can get some prints, or maybe there's some
residue on the paper that will give us a lead. I'll call the
hotel manager, too, to have them pull video of that hallway. It was gutsy to shove it under the door."

Nothing more dangerous than a bad guy who thought he was invincible. They did stupid things and innocent people got hurt.

Royce put down his phone. "Detective Mannis is on his way."

"I don't think it's that big of a deal that the person figured out I was staying at the Periwinkle. After all, it is the conference hotel. It's the most likely place for a presenter to stay."

"But to know which one is your room, that takes inside information. Like somebody who has access to registration data. Who made your reservation?"

"My administrative assistant. She made my reservation and Barry's. She got suites for both of us. When we arrived together, I picked the fourteenth floor so he took the twelfth."

"Okay." He looked at his watch. "I'd like it if you could get packed before Detective Mannis gets here."

"Packed?" she repeated. "What are you talking about?"

"You're not staying here. Not now that we know that whoever is behind this knows the location of your room."

"I can't go to another hotel. What if Charity comes back? I need to be here."

He didn't think Charity was coming back. But he didn't want to tell her that. "We'll leave contact information for Wingman Security with the hotel manager."

"Where will I go?" she asked.

Home. He wanted to say it. If there was danger here, he wanted her as far away from it as possible. But what he didn't know was whether home was safe for her. Would the danger simply follow and he wouldn't be there?

The idea of that was simply not acceptable.

He had evidently been quiet for too long because she

put her hands on her hips. "I'm not leaving Vegas. Not until I find Charity."

"Well, the only way you're staying is if you relocate to my house," he said, the words falling out of his mouth.

"What?" She looked appropriately shocked.

"My house. I've taken certain…precautions, let's say, to ensure that it is very secure."

"What? You say that like it's some fortress."

No. A respectable brick ranch with steel entry doors, bulletproof glass in the windows and a safe room that they could live in for several weeks without much trouble. "Please, just get packed. Take off your disguise but make sure you put it in your suitcase because you'll need it tomorrow. I'd like to get out of here as quickly as possible."

"I need to call Barry and let him know what's going on."

"No," Royce said.

"What?"

"Once we're out of here, you can tell him that you've changed hotels but that's it."

"Are you suggesting that Barry has something to do with this?" she asked, pointing at the letter.

"As far as I'm concerned, nobody gets a free pass. And nobody gets to know any more than we tell them."

"Don't you think Barry will simply look you up? You're not the only one who has resources."

"He won't find me," Royce said. He was very careful. Used the office address for all his bills. His house had been purchased by a Nevada corporation, the same one that paid the real estate taxes.

"Why are you doing this, Royce? Why are you making this your problem?"

Because I never stopped loving you. "Because you hired me to provide security. Money was exchanged.

Commitments were made. I take those things seriously. Now, you've probably only got a few minutes before Detective Mannis arrives. Maybe you want to make good use of it, because when he leaves, we do, too."

She was hauling her suitcase out of her bedroom when she heard a sharp knock on the suite door. She saw that Royce had changed back into his suit and his suitcase was also in the kitchen. He motioned for her to stand back before he looked through the peephole.

Then he opened the door and ushered Detective Mannis inside. "Ms. Cambridge," the man said.

"Thank you for coming, Detective Mannis. Here's the letter," she said, pointing at where Royce had dropped it on the table.

The detective did not touch it. Read it, then used an ink pen to flip it over. There was nothing on the back. Then he inspected the envelope. "It's three stanzas," he said.

It gave her some comfort that the detective was smart enough that he'd quickly identified the difference between this letter and the others. They had only had one stanza each.

"I'm not sure what that means," Royce said.

"Maybe it means the sender is getting more intense, feels the need to express himself more fully," Detective Mannis said.

"Or maybe," JC said, "he thinks this is going to be his last letter and he just wants to get it all out."

Her words hung in the air, little bits of flotsam, like the cat hair when she'd shaken Charity's beach towel. If she was right, then it meant that the sender thought things were coming to an end.

Which likely wasn't good for her, JC thought. She

didn't say it, however. Both Royce and Detective Mannis looked as if they were chewing on nails already.

There was a knock on the door. "That should be the manager," the detective said. "She was going to pull the tape of all activity in this hallway since you left here approximately two hours ago."

Royce answered the door and Sonya Tribee entered. Her face was pale. JC expected her to hand over the information and leave. Instead, the woman said, "I've copied all the activity onto this DVD. If you don't mind, I'd like to stay while you view it."

"Are we going to see something on this?" Detective Mannis asked.

Sonya licked her lips. "I pulled it immediately after you called. And I only had a chance to look at it once but... I would just feel better if I'm here when you see it."

The two men exchanged glances. JC could practically read their minds. There was no real harm in allowing her to stay. After all, she was the one who'd pulled the data. She knew what was on the DVD.

"Fine," Detective Mannis said. He opened the cabinet that housed the television and DVD player. He inserted the disk, and in seconds they were looking at the hallway. It was a clear image, better quality than the pool.

Like they were reading each other's minds, Sonya said, "We upgraded our internal video about a year ago. We use it," she added, somewhat apologetically it seemed, "to monitor associate productivity. You know, how long a housekeeper is in the room. How many trips they have to make back to the cart. Whether they spend too much time chatting with other staff."

Detective Morris operated the controls. There was a clock in the upper right-hand corner. It said 20:20. They watched as the video captured Royce and JC leaving the suite and using the stairwell. Neither he nor Sonya showed any reaction to the fact that she and Royce looked very different. Trey had been right. In Vegas, nothing was out of place.

Detective Mannis fast-forwarded until there was activity in the hallway. Then he quickly stopped the speed so that they could easily see what happened. Clock in the corner said 20:44. The suite door past JC's had opened and a middle-aged couple came into the frame. They walked past JC's door without pausing. They got into the elevator.

There was no other activity on the floor for another forty minutes, which took them six minutes to view. But then at 21:29, or almost 9:30 p.m., a housekeeper pushed a cart off the elevator. The video slowed. They watched as she went directly to suite 1402. Then she reached into her pocket and pulled out a white envelope. Then bent and slipped it under the door.

After that, she pushed her cart back to the elevator and disappeared from sight.

"I want to talk to that housekeeper," Royce said. "Now."

Sonya Tribee looked him squarely in the eye. "I'd very much like to do that same thing. Unfortunately, she doesn't work here. I'm afraid someone was impersonating a Periwinkle associate. I'm very, very sorry."

"What?" JC asked. "How can you be so sure? There have to be hundreds of associates employed by this hotel. You probably don't know them all. Maybe it's somebody who was recently hired."

Sonya shook her head. "As I mentioned, we use video for productivity tracking. To ensure that we know exactly which associate is demonstrating which behaviors, as part of the hiring process, we scan their faces. It's entered into facial recognition software to ensure that our productivity statistics are one hundred percent accurate. The woman who slid that envelope under your door matches no one in our database." She paused, looking at each person in the room. "I do not know how this has happened. And it is certainly inexcusable. But it appears that someone successfully infiltrated our hotel and was able to pose as one of our employees."

JC gave her props for not trying to make excuses.

Detective Mannis cleared his throat. "I'm going to assume that neither of you recognize the woman in the video?"

Royce shook his head. JC did the same even though something nagged at her. She was confident that she'd never seen the woman before and yet, there was something oddly familiar about her. She'd been overweight, at least thirty to forty pounds, mostly carried around her middle. She had coarse dark brown hair that hit her shoulders.

"We need to track her movements out of the hotel," Royce said.

"I was able to do that," Sonya said. "She got out of the elevator on the second floor, left her cart in the hallway and took the stairs. She exited out a side door. From there, our cameras lost her when she melded into the heavy nighttime pedestrian traffic."

Royce looked at Detective Mannis. "Will you be able to pick her up?"

"We'll give it our best shot."

Sonya stood. "If you have any other questions for me, do not hesitate to call. Again, I'm sorry."

Royce shook his head. "No. That's not good enough."

Sonya didn't look as if many people ever told her that. "I beg your pardon."

"The cummerbund and the bow tie that the woman wore are very distinctive. You can't simply pick those up at a department store."

"We special order them," Sonya said.

"Exactly. I'm willing to bet that our impersonator got them from somebody who works here. I want to talk to your employees."

"We have hundreds of associates. And with all due respect, I couldn't possibly authorize you talking to them. That might be very upsetting for them."

"Ms. Tribee, I'll tell you what's upsetting for me is that somehow in the span of a couple hours, a twenty-four-year-old woman goes missing from your pool area and you allow a stranger to successfully impersonate hotel staff."

Sonya Tribee no longer looked so confident.

"I want every employee questioned," Royce said. "We need to know if they know this woman."

Sonya probably realized that arguing about it wasn't going to make a difference. "Fine. I'll start an internal investigation tomorrow. But I want the human resources staff here at the hotel to do it."

"Tell them to work fast," Royce said.

Sonya gave him a tight smile and walked away.

"I'll report back when I've had a chance to check our other cameras," Detective Mannis said, rising from his chair.

"Call my cell," Royce said. "We won't be here."

"Where will you be?" the detective asked.

"Someplace safe," Royce said.

She could almost see Detective Mannis's internal struggle. The question: Should he attempt to force the location from Royce? And then the decision: No, it wouldn't be worth the effort. Royce Morgan was not a man easily forced to do anything.

And it hit JC like the proverbial ton of bricks. That's what had been bothering her for eight years. Royce Morgan had simply gone away.

So easily. Too easily.

Because he hadn't loved her enough.

When this was over, he was going to run again.

She was sure of it. That's why he'd thought this afternoon was a mistake.

"I go first," he said. He knew Jules wasn't crazy about relocating, but she'd stopped protesting.

He led her down the stairs and out the side door. Then he flagged down a cab and they were off. "Why aren't we taking your car or the truck?" she asked.

"We have to assume that the vehicles may have been compromised."

"So we cab it from now on."

"I have another vehicle at my house." He had two more. In addition to the BMW, he had a Jeep and a Volvo station wagon. The Jeep was especially helpful when they used a particular safe house that was fifteen miles out of town, in the desert. The Volvo was more practical when he was trying to blend into an upper-crust neighborhood.

She didn't answer and he thought she was perhaps trying to reconcile the man he was now with the poor ex-airman he'd been just eight years earlier. He directed the cab to the intersection of Flamingo Road and Las Vegas Boulevard, one of the busiest on the strip. They got out and quickly crossed the street, using the overhead sidewalk. On the other side, he picked up another cab.

"What are we doing?" she asked.

"Just making sure nobody is following," he said. He

was watching the traffic all around them and it didn't appear as if anybody had any interest in them. But still, when they got close to his house, he had the cab stop a block away. He waited until it drove off and was out of sight before directing her to his house.

It irritated him that he was so damn needy that he wanted to see her reaction to the place he lived. Why should he care? She was certainly used to something much grander, although he was proud of his place. In Vegas, to have a yard meant to have a commitment to watering every day. That wasn't practical with his travel schedule and not eco-friendly. Instead, he'd gone for plants native to the desert climate, big rocks and substantial pieces of outdoor sculpture.

It suited him. And at night, with the low-level lighting that he'd installed, he thought it was especially cool.

Who cared if she liked it?

"Interesting," she said as she looked at the yard, after he pointed out his door.

What the hell did she mean by that?

"Did you do this yourself?" she asked.

"Yes."

She turned to him. "It's really lovely."

The compliment floated on the night air, warming his heart. Threatening to make him be a fool and admit that her approval was indeed important. "Why don't we just get inside," he said, his tone impatient.

He opened the door, heard the beeping of his security system that assured him that no systems had been breached and ushered her inside. The design was a split ranch, with the master bedroom and bath on one side of the house and the guest bedrooms and baths on the other side. In the middle was a great room filled with comfortable leather furniture and a fireplace that took up one wall, a dining room that could seat eight but never had and a kitchen that looked like something out of a magazine, or so his partner Seth had said, not making it sound like a compliment.

But now that they were inside, in the well-lit living space, he could tell that Jules did like what she saw.

"Where should I put my things?" she asked.

He directed her to the first guest bedroom. He'd had it professionally decorated in blues and greens. "Lovely," she said again. She looked up at the skylight where just a hint of moonlight slipped in. Most anyone would think it was merely a nice design element, never realizing that it had been installed to provide another means of egress from the structure.

"I'll be right next door," he said. Normally he slept in the master bedroom, but he didn't want to be that far away from her if he needed to get to her quickly. Sometimes, seconds mattered. They should be very safe in his house, but he wasn't taking any chances.

She sat down on the bed. He looked away. Thinking about Jules and a bed in the same sentence was a dangerous thing. "Do you want anything?" he asked. "Water? Glass of warm milk?"

She smiled. "No, thank you. I…uh…guess I'll see you in the morning."

He shifted his weight from one leg to the other. "Yeah. In the morning. Good night."

He left her room, but before going to his own, he prowled the dark house. Checking doors that he knew were locked, windows that were undoubtedly secure, weapons that were always loaded.

When he finally went to lie down, he stretched out in his clothes, on top of the bedspread. This room had been done in bronze and gold—relaxing colors, his decorator had said. But it did nothing to relax him tonight. He was wound tight. He forced himself to close his eyes. To inhale deeply, making his diaphragm work. To let it out slowly, to the count of six.

To see sheep. With dirty-white bodies and bland faces. Vaulting effortlessly, yet so very slowly, over a gray picket fence.

And at some point, it must have worked. Because he was sound asleep when he was jerked awake by Jules's bloodcurdling scream.

Chapter 19

"Don't shoot," she said.

She could see just enough to know that Royce was in the doorway, his arm extended, his gun pointed at her.

"Jules?" he said, his gun still at the ready.

"I'm fine," she said. "I...I think I had a nightmare."

She saw movement near the door and suddenly soft light filled the room. Royce was staring at her, bright spots of color on his cheeks, breathing through his mouth. "I'm going to check the house," he said.

She wasn't sure if he was trying to give her time to get her wits about her or if he was calming himself. Either way, she appreciated the effort. Her heart was racing in her chest.

It had been so real. So very real.

"Everything is secure," he said, once again in the doorway. He was holding a glass of water and he brought it to her. She reached out a shaky arm.

"Jules," he said, sinking down onto the bed. "You're okay. Just calm down."

"I'm so sorry," she said. "I had a horrible dream. Like before. After the accident."

"The accident where your mom died?" he asked, his voice gentle.

She had told him the story eight years ago. The sanitized version. He'd seen the scar on her knee and asked. She'd told him that she and her mom were in a car accident and that she'd been badly injured and her mother had been killed.

But she hadn't told him about the nightmares. They'd been over for years by the time they met and she'd seen no need to bring up such horrible memories. "Did I scream?" she asked.

He nodded. "Your lungs are healthy," he said drily.

She managed a smile. "I really am sorry."

"Tell me about it," he said.

She closed her eyes. She had never told anyone the truth about the nightmare. But maybe it was time. First, he needed to understand more about the night of the accident. "We lived in New Jersey. That night my mom and I had gone into the city for dinner and the theatre. It had been so much fun. But by the time we left, it was raining. And it was a very dark night. But we were doing okay. We were going slow because the roads were slick and there were lots of hills and trees near our house. We were close. So close."

She closed her eyes. Swallowed hard.

"Jules, it's okay if you can't," he said.

"My mom was laughing and talking about the play and then suddenly she got quiet and said, 'that idiot.' A car had come up behind us and they were way too close. It went on for maybe a mile, them riding our bumper and

I could tell that my mom was worried. She reached over, checked to make sure I had my seat belt on. I couldn't drive yet but I knew that something was wrong. Finally the car decided to go around us. But then it came over into our lane, pushing us off the road. My mom did her best but the shoulder was soft, that's what people said later on, and when her wheels hit it, it was enough to flip the car."

Her leg, the injured one, started involuntarily twitching, as if it could remember the pain. He gently put the palm of his hand on it. "It's okay."

"I was unconscious when they airlifted me from the scene, with a serious concussion and a compound fracture of my right leg. I…I didn't realize that my mom was dead until I awoke in the hospital after surgery with my dad at my side and he told me that we were going to have to go on without her."

Now the tears came.

"I'm so sorry that happened to you." He scooted closer and wrapped an arm around her shoulder.

"I always feel cheated when I have the dream. Because it never starts in the beginning. It never starts with us at dinner, or the play, or with my mom laughing and talking. It always starts with the lights of the car coming around the back end of our car and me thinking that he's going to pass. And then he doesn't. And it's slow motion, as he crowds us off the road. And then we're rolling and rolling and it hurts."

"Don't think of it," he said, leaning back against the headboard. She allowed herself to be pulled close. She had to tell him all of it.

"I can hear my mother screaming. The noise, it just stays in my head. And then the car stops and there's no more screaming. And I look down, and my mother's head, it's been severed from her body, and it's in my lap.

Her eyes are open. Wide-open. And then I start scream-ing. I think that's when I usually wake up."

"That's what you dreamed tonight?" he asked softly.

She nodded. "Intellectually, I know that my mother was not decapitated. That never happened. We struck a tree on her side of the vehicle. She died of blunt-force trauma to her head. But tonight, like before, I'm holding her head in my lap and…blood and brains and all kinds of things, start to pour from her eyes and her ears."

"I don't think anybody understands how or why our brains process things the way they do. Did you ever talk to anyone about the nightmare?"

She shook her head. "I couldn't tell my father. He'd lost his wife. He didn't need to worry that his only child was going crazy."

"It had to have been an incredible strain on you. That's probably why you had the dream tonight. Because you're under strain again, with the attacks, this new letter, and Charity being MIA and maybe in trouble."

She closed her eyes and leaned her head back. "That's not why," she said. God, she was pathetic. "I had the nightmare tonight because of what I was intending to do."

He frowned at her. "Not following."

She rubbed her forehead where a hell of a headache was gathering. "After the accident, I had the night-mare. Multiple times. And then after a few months, it went away. But then every time I either did something I shouldn't have or even thought about doing it, it would come back. It got to the point that I started thinking that my mom was watching out for me, that she was stepping in to guide me using the only tricks she had."

He was silent for a long moment. "You don't really think that's the case, do you?"

"I don't know. All I know is that I intended to do something tonight that, with the perspective that comes from—" she paused and squinted at the bedside clock "—three twenty-three in the morning, I'm not too proud of. I think the nightmare was payback. You know, I wasn't paying attention to my moral compass and it jumped up and bit me in the butt."

He smiled. "Now you've lost me."

"I wanted to give you a reason to stay."

He sat up, his back ramrod straight. "Uh…"

She'd made him speechless. "I was going to wait until you'd fallen asleep and then I was going to crawl into your bed naked. I figured it might be hard to resist the temptation if I was right there."

"Try impossible," he said.

"I was being selfish. I know that after this is over, you will walk away. The same way you walked away eight years ago."

He removed his arm from around her shoulders. "I didn't *walk* away eight years ago. I was practically bagged up and put on the sidewalk, like kitchen garbage."

She'd made him angry. Well, fine. She was a little angry, too. "I caught you by surprise that night. I know that. But…" She had to tell him. She had to say what had been bothering her for eight years. "But you didn't fight for me. It was so easy for you to simply move on."

Simply move on. Nothing about that time had been simple and he sure has hell hadn't moved on. That implied that he'd put a line through an item on a list. Juliana Cambridge. Check. What's next?

"How was I supposed to stay and fight for you?" he asked. "You made it clear that you were accepting Bryson Wagoner's proposal. I believed you when you said that you were done with the guy." He'd been a sap.

"I was," she said. She pushed her hands through her short hair. "It all happened so fast. I hadn't heard from Bryson for over six months. And then right before the Labor Day weekend, he contacted me, said he couldn't live without me and begged me to marry him."

"And that was all it took?" Royce said sarcastically. "He wagged his finger at you and you came running."

Her pretty blue eyes filled with tears. "It wasn't like that at all," she said, her voice soft.

He was not going to let her off the hook. Maybe he hadn't realized it, but he'd been waiting eight years to have this conversation. "Then what was it? What did he say that convinced you? I mean, I get that his offer was a lot more attractive than any I could have made."

Her eyes narrowed. "What does that mean?"

"It means that you've always been a smart woman. I think it was pretty clear that your life was going to be better with Bryson than with me. I didn't have a job, an education or a family fortune."

"How could you say something like that? How could you even think something like that? You don't know me at all. I would never have married Bryson for those reasons," she said, her voice cold.

That didn't make it better. His chest hurt. "Then you must have really loved him," he accused.

She shook her head, looking sad. "No. And that was unfair to him. I believed I could love him. I was confident that I could make it work. I'd been making situations work for a very long time."

His head was spinning. If she hadn't loved him and she hadn't married him for his money, then why the hell had she changed her mind? "There's something that you're not telling me," he said.

She sank down on the end of the bed. As if all the life had gone out of her. "No. Nothing."

She was lying. That left an awful taste in his mouth. "Listen, Jules, you have to know that nothing you could ever say changes the commitment that I've made to you. I'm not leaving you alone to deal with this crap."

She waved a hand. "Is that what you think I'm concerned about?"

"Then what is it?"

"It's…it's nothing," she said. "Look, I'm tired."

She probably was. But there was one more thing he had to say. "Listen, you did the right thing."

"Marrying Bryson was the right thing?" She sounded incredulous. "We were divorced within eighteen months."

What could he say to that? "Still," he said.

"Still what?" she snapped. "How could it have been the right thing?"

"Because I was the wrong thing. Wrong background, wrong education, wrong job prospects, wrong social skills. I'd have embarrassed you. Held you back."

She looked at him as if he was crazy. "What are you talking about?"

"I didn't know anything about your world. Hadn't gone to college. Hadn't spent a year in Europe. Had never sat at a table where there was more than one fork. Didn't know anything about wine or art or music. Had never had more than a couple hundred bucks to my name. And had no prospects of changing any of that."

She opened her mouth, then shut it. "I have no words," she said finally.

What else needed to be said? He'd named the elephant in the room. "I hope you'll be able to get back to sleep," he said, his words sounding stiff and formal.

He got to the doorway.

"Wait," she said. "Actually, I do have something to say."

Neither of them had had enough sleep. Now probably wasn't the time to have more conversation. "Let's just leave it, okay? And try to get some sleep."

"No," she said sharply. "How damn shallow do you think I am?"

Huh? "I've never thought that about you."

"Mean-spirited, then?"

"No."

"Then I'm lost," she said. "Why do you think I cared about any of that?"

"Because you'd have been a fool not to. I didn't even have a damn job."

"You were transitioning back after military service. I thought you deserved a little down time."

"I was drinking too much."

"You were," she said. "But you never drank too much when you were driving or when you were in any way responsible for my well-being. You didn't even drink too much if you knew we'd be out late, walking home. You wanted to stay sharp. For me."

What could he say? It was true. "I embarrassed you when you got your award."

"That guy was a jerk. Who monopolizes a woman's time when she's there with a date? I was just being polite because my work friends were at the table."

"I could have handled it better."

"Probably. Who hasn't done something and later thought, *wow, I wasn't at my best with that*?"

She was going to argue every damn point. He'd known he wasn't good enough. She had, too. "Leave it, Jules. It's the past. Concentrate on the now. Staying safe and finding Charity."

"I can't," she said. "Not until you know the truth."

He didn't know how much more he could take.

"I married Bryson—" her voice was very soft "—because my father told me that he was sick. Very, very sick. And he wanted to see me married to Bryson before he died."

What? Her father had looked as healthy as a horse that night. "I don't understand," he said.

"When you stepped out of the room, my father told me that he was dying and that his last wish was for me to marry Bryson."

He had the crazy urge to laugh. "And you believed him?"

She pressed her lips together. "He showed me the test results, showed me the referral he'd gotten to see an oncologist at NYU medical center. He said there was a strong likelihood he wouldn't survive it."

None of this was making any sense. "But he's alive and well today?"

"I know."

"Why didn't you tell me?" he asked. "Why the hell didn't you tell me the truth?"

"He asked me not to. The banks, they were in such an uproar at the time. Senior executives were losing their jobs every day. He said he was afraid that if it got out that he was sick, that he'd be an easy cut for them to make. He was really scared about that. His work meant a great deal to him. Plus, I couldn't do that to Bryson. If I was going to marry him, I certainly wasn't going to take a chance that he'd ever discover the reason that I'd said yes."

Would he have been the type to throw it in the other man's face? He didn't think so but he could understand her concern. And he knew Jules. She would have wanted her marriage to have the best chance of success. "But your dad made it," he said, stating the obvious.

"He went through treatment and responded much better than anyone anticipated. Of course, I'm grateful for that."

There was something else. "But…"

"But I recently learned that he was never sick at all."

"No way." Who lied about something like that?

"You know, political candidates are vetted very carefully by their own parties before there is any public support."

"Right." He was trying to track with her.

"Part of the vetting is a medical questionnaire."

He had a crazy idea of where this was going. "You saw it?"

"I was…looking at some things in the condo. Something I found made me start to look in places that I would normally have stayed out of. My father's office. His files. When I found it, it became readily apparent to me that he had either lied to me eight years earlier or he'd lied on the questionnaire."

"Did you ask him?"

"No. For several reasons, I wasn't ready to talk to him. I left the apartment before he came home and I left the questionnaire on the dining room table, knowing that he would see it."

"What happened?"

"He came to see me. Two days later. Told me that he'd lied to me and begged my forgiveness. Said that he'd done it because he was confident that I'd be happy with Bryson. Said that he couldn't bear it if I didn't forgive him."

"Did you? Did you forgive him?" Royce could not believe this. Joel Cambridge had screwed with their lives.

"I told him that I loved him but I wasn't sure if I could forgive him. We haven't talked for months."

Her eyes were steady on his face. "I gave up so much. *We* gave up so much." She reached for the wall switch and shut off the light. The room was lit only by the moonlight coming in the skylight.

He, who had with an abundance of caution but very little real fear faced roadside bombs and indiscriminate snipers, felt a shiver of unease run up his spine. "And now?" he asked, his voice breaking.

She relaxed one shoulder and the strap of her nightgown slipped down. Then the other shoulder. Same result. She'd said earlier that she'd planned to seduce him. This wasn't a seduction. It was more of an attack.

"And now, I'm taking," she said. She pulled down her nightgown and let it fall in a puddle around her feet. She stood before him, wearing only the skimpiest of silk panties. Her breasts, so pretty, so perfect. The nipples, dark, round, delicious. The sweet triangle of hair, barely hidden.

"Jules," he said.

"Please don't tell me no," she said. "Not tonight."

Damn his needy self for wanting her so. "I…"

"I want you. That's all I need you to say," she said, advancing toward him.

That was easy. He'd always wanted her. Probably always would. "I want you," he whispered.

She pressed the palm of her hand flat on his chest and pushed. He let himself fall backward onto the bed. "Lie back," she said.

He would do anything she asked. His head hit the cushion and he could smell her scent, the perfume that had been driving him crazy all damn day.

She straddled him, her strong legs on either side of his hips. He was about to burst out of his pants he was so damn hard. And when she settled herself on him, it didn't matter that layers of fabric separated them. He reared his hips up, desperate to be closer.

"Not yet," she murmured.

And then she bent down to kiss him. She gripped his jaw with her hand and held him secure. Not that he ever wanted to tear himself away. Her mouth was warm and sweet and when she leaned down to kiss him, her pretty breasts were there for the taking.

He raised his hand to touch her. She lifted her lips and shook her head. "I'll tell you when you can do that."

Oh, God. "Uncle Sam taught me how to follow orders," he said.

"Never like this," she responded, sounding amused, before her lips settled upon him again.

She kissed him for a good long time. And then worked her way down his body. When her hands fumbled with his shirt buttons, he wanted to rip the thing off, but instead he grabbed the sheets with his fingers.

And held on tight.

Finally, the buttons were undone. And then her hot hands were under his T-shirt, her nails were raking over his nipples, and an electric current charged through him and he desperately wanted to grind against her.

But it was her show.

"Good job," she murmured, leaning over him, her breast dangerously close to his mouth. He didn't say a word. Couldn't. Her hands were now on his belt buckle.

And on it went. Until he was fully naked. "Jules," he said. He was willing to beg.

"Shush," she said, and moved so that she could take him in her mouth. He closed his eyes and saw stars.

It felt so damn good. But too soon, there came a point when he didn't think he could hold on to it anymore. "I'm going to come," he said. He could almost feel her smiling against him.

"Not yet," she said, lifting her mouth.

Then she was straddling him again, this time her panties gone. She sank down on him and the damn stars exploded, a virtual light storm. Up and down she rode him, and he let her take him until finally, with a hitch of her breath, she came hard.

And he had had enough.

He let go of the damn sheet and grabbed her hips. Pumped into her. Once, twice, and came with such force the third time that he thought the top of his head was blowing off.

And he somehow floated back to earth in one piece.

He was still inside her. She was lying on him, her breasts pressed flat against his chest. It was perfect.

"I can't sleep on top of you," she mumbled.

He had no intention of sleeping. He flipped her over onto her back. "Your turn, sweetheart."

JC woke up in the daylight. It was streaming in through the skylight. She was on her side and Royce was spooned around her, one hand on her hip, the other cupping her breast.

She turned her head. He was awake. By the looks of it, had been for some time. His eyes were focused, his gaze intent. "Hi," she whispered.

"Doing okay?" he asked.

She nodded. "What time is it?"

"I imagine it's about eight."

"We have to get up. Get to Everpark." She rolled to her back. Sat up. Winced.

"What's wrong?" he asked, ever vigilant.

"Nothing that a hot shower won't fix," she said. There

had been no end to the inventive positions that Royce had thought of once he'd gotten the upper hand. It had been exhausting and absolutely wonderful. She swung her legs over the edge of the bed. "I'll be ready in twenty minutes."

He had nice soap in the shower and expensive shampoo. His towels were thick and soft. She had packed her own toothpaste and toothbrush.

Seventeen minutes later, she was getting dressed. She remembered that Royce had said that they would visit Everpark in costume but she could not bring herself to put on the red sequined dress this early in the morning. Instead, she pulled on gray wool pants and a pink sweater with a gray-and-pink-checked scarf around her neck. She added the blond wig and her sensible shoes.

She walked into the kitchen. He was not there yet. Feeling a little cocky, like she might perhaps lord it over him that she'd been ready first, she crossed the living room and entered the master bedroom. The bathroom door was closed and she could hear the shower running.

While she had her chance, she took a look in his closet. It was filled with dress slacks, long-sleeved dress shirts, leather shoes and cashmere sweaters. On the top shelf, there was a stack of CDs. She took a peek. *Learning Conversational French*. She looked at the next one. Same thing but this time Spanish. Next one was for Italian.

The door of the bathroom opened, startling her. In a fog of steam, Royce emerged, a towel wrapped low around his hips. She felt the rapid rush of lust gather between her legs.

"What's going on, blondie?" he said easily.

"Are you planning a big trip?" she asked.

He shook his head.

She pointed to the CDs. "French. Spanish. Italian." She walked over and sat at the end of the king-size bed. "Your clothes. This house and everything in it." She was trying so hard to get her head around what was troubling her. "You're so different. And I wonder, is the old you gone?"

There was a long pause. Rivulets of water ran down his torso, getting absorbed by his towel. He looked around the room, as if the answer was somewhere in the corners.

Finally, he made eye contact with her. "I did it for you," he said.

"What?"

He sat next to her on the bed. "I was born in Texas. My mother was a waitress at the local diner and my dad packed boxes at the freight company on the edge of town. They probably drank too much on Friday nights and didn't think about saving for retirement. But they had a good time. I think I knew we were poor but most of my friends were living exactly the same way."

"Eight years ago, you told me your parents were dead."

"And they are. I was guarding a military base in Afghanistan when I got word that they'd tried to beat a train on the tracks just two blocks from our house. Their luck ran out."

"I'm sorry," she murmured.

"I was okay with my life. Served my country with a lot of guys who weren't that different than me. Came home and met you." He paused. "And everything changed for me. I knew you were different. So much better. That you deserved better."

Her empty stomach felt sick. "That's why you didn't fight for me."

He didn't answer.

She turned to look at him. "And you changed everything about yourself?"

"I…I knew I'd lost you," he said. "But I wanted to be the kind of man that you'd have been proud of. I have worked very hard these last eight years, trying to make every day count, trying to be better every day."

The enormity of his words hit her. Settled on her, like a heavy weight, making it feel as if her lungs could not expand.

"I feel awful," she admitted. "Awful that I somehow made you feel that you weren't good enough."

He reached for her hand. "You didn't. Ever. But I knew. Everyone knew. They'd have been blind not to see it. Your father knew."

Her father. She looked at him sharply. "What about my father?"

"Nothing," he said. "It's not important."

"It is to me," she said. "He said something to you that last night, didn't he?" She'd asked her father about it afterward but he'd denied it. But since he'd lied about something even more important, why was she surprised?

"Water under the bridge, Jules."

Not to her. It was part of a rushing river that was picking up steam and about to sweep her away. "I want to know what he said."

"He said that you were too good for me, that I'd be an albatross around your neck and that I needed to hit the road."

Her father had lied to her. If her mother was right, he'd lied about a great many things. This was the man she believed had devoted his life to raising her following his wife's death. Was that a lie, too?

"I need to tell you something," she said. "Something important."

"Okay."

She shook her head "Not here. Not with you in a towel. Get dressed. I'll make us some toast. Because I've got a hell of a story for you."

Chapter 20

Royce dressed fast. He was still tucking in his shirt and zipping his pants when he entered the kitchen. He saw Jules and stopped short, feeling heat flood his face.

It was crazy given the things they'd done to each other's body the night before to be embarrassed by being caught zipping his pants. But it was the familiarity of walking into his kitchen, of having her sitting in a chair, of just being there with him, that made him smolder.

She'd poured two cups of coffee and made two pieces of toast for each of them. She was sitting so he sat, too.

She looked nervous or agitated, he wasn't sure which. Wasn't sure it mattered. Whatever she was about to say was going to be important.

"My mother died when I was fourteen."

He nodded. He'd known that. She knew that. But he wasn't hurrying her.

"It was a devastating blow. My father became my rock."

She paused. Royce waited.

"As you know, my father has his condo on Fifth Avenue. When he decided to run for the Senate, it was suggested that he might want to change his residence. Buy something a little less showy."

She drummed her index finger on the kitchen table. Neither of them had yet to take a bite of their toast.

"He asked me if I would remove my things from the condo. Most of it was in boxes that he'd packed up while I was in college."

He took a sip of coffee. It was too weak for him but when he'd set it up the night before, it had been the most natural thing in the world to make it the way she liked it.

"I put it off for at least a month but finally, one Saturday morning I went there. He was out, at a meeting somewhere. Instead of just loading the boxes in my trunk, I started going through them. It was kind of fun, especially when I found some of my old diaries that I'd had when I was eleven or twelve."

He smiled. He bet she'd been a cute kid.

"Then I opened one and…realized that it wasn't my handwriting. It was one of my diaries, I'm almost sure of it. But I had several extra—you know. My mom knew I liked to write and she would pick one up for me if she happened to see one that she liked. So I ended up with a few extra."

Made sense but that wasn't the important question. "Who wrote in your diary?" he asked.

"It was my mother's handwriting. She'd dated the pages. It was written just a month before the accident."

He was getting a bad feeling. It wasn't anything that Jules had specifically said. It was just the overwhelming sense of grief that she emanated.

"She was angry when she wrote it," Jules said. "Angry with my father."

That wasn't so hard to believe. After what he'd learned last night, Royce was more confident than ever that the man was an ass.

"She'd discovered that my father had had a relationship with a woman and that they'd had a child together. That woman was Linette White."

"Charity," he whispered.

"Is my half sister."

And he'd thought things were complicated before. "I thought that Linette White was your mother's friend." The minute he said it, he knew it was stupid. Friendship was rarely an impediment in these situations.

She nodded. "They were. It was all true. Linette White came to our house to wash windows. She and my mom hit it off. Ultimately, my mom asked my dad to help Linette out by giving her a job at his bank. He did. Linette worked at the bank for several years, all the while staying friends with my mom."

"I think I'm starting to get your mom's anger."

"According to the diary, Linette had told my mom that her baby's father was a one-night stand. When Charity was two, Linette left New York and didn't respond to my mom's efforts to reach out to her."

"I need to do the math," he said. "Charity is roughly ten years younger than you. That means that you were twelve or so when she moved. Your mom wrote this diary entry approximately two years later."

She nodded.

"How did she find out the truth?"

"I don't know. I read the diary three times and there is absolutely nothing in there that gives any clue."

"Do you think she said something to your dad about her suspicions?"

"I don't know. All I can be confident of is that my dad never took the time to read the diary. If he had, I'd have never seen it."

All this time, this damning evidence had been sitting in a box in his condo. "Is that when you started looking at the other paperwork in the condo and found the medical questionnaire?"

"Yes."

Amazing. Everything had unraveled. "So then you decided to contact Charity."

"First, I hired a private investigator to do some research on her. That's when I discovered that Linette White had died recently. I wasn't sure what to do and stewed over the information for at least six weeks. And then I realized that my coming to this conference and Charity living in Vegas—that those two things could only mean that I was meant to connect with her. That's when I called her and arranged for us to meet. You know the rest."

"What do you think? Is she your half sister? Was your mom right?"

"She has my father's eyes."

He hadn't really looked at her eyes, didn't like looking at the ring in her eyebrow. Plus, he'd only met Jules's father once. "Is it possible, Jules," he said gently, "that you're seeing something that isn't there just because you want to see it?"

She didn't seem to take offense. "I don't know what I want. I am an only child so the idea of having a sibling is exciting, I guess. But under these circumstances? It's really horrible. My mother had to be so hurt and it pains me to know that this is how she spent the last month of her life. And I don't even know what to think of my father if it's true. How could he have done that to my mother? And if he knows about Charity, how could he ignore his child, never publicly acknowledge her?"

Royce let out a breath. "Is it possible that Charity knows the truth?"

Jules shrugged. "I've recently had those same thoughts. I don't think so but I'm beginning to realize that I don't know her and she's probably capable of things that I haven't even contemplated."

Royce got up and poured himself a hot cup of coffee. He held the pot in Jules's direction but she shook her head. He sipped, needing time to think. "Maybe you should ask your dad?"

"I don't want to, not yet."

"What are you hoping for here, Jules? What's the best outcome of all of this?"

"Well, I suppose the best option is that it's all a terrible mistake. Charity's dad really was a one-night stand and not my father. That makes it simple. I guess the next best option is that Charity is my half sister but that my father didn't realize it. That would mean that he was duped, too."

He'd disliked Joel Cambridge but he certainly hadn't considered him to be stupid or easily duped.

"Is it possible that your mom just got it wrong?" he asked.

"Of course," she said. "But my mom…well, you know, when you lose someone, you have a tendency to put them on a pedestal. But I'm trying not to do that here. My mom was smart, always positive, said nice things about other people. She just wasn't the type to come to some crazy misguided conclusion about her husband."

"You were fourteen when she died," he said. "You

didn't have the opportunity to see her through an adult lens. Maybe you'd feel differently now."

"Maybe. But that's not an option," she said, pushing back her chair. "The only real option I have right now is finding Charity and asking her to submit to a DNA analysis. Then I'll do the same. If we have the same father, we'll know."

She was right. Charity was the key to many things. "We need to find her friend Lou," he said, setting down his coffee cup.

They were at the door of his house when she turned to him. "I want you to know, Royce, that I'm sorry I didn't tell you the whole truth before. I guess I keep giving you reasons not to trust me, to think that I'm a liar."

She was standing close and he could smell her perfume, could see the worry in her pretty blue eyes, could feel the tightly-coiled tension in her body. "Jules, make no mistake about this. I don't think you're a liar and I would trust you with my life. Now let's go."

I don't think you're a liar and I would trust you with my life.

He had no idea how much those words meant to her. For eight years, she'd shouldered the burden of him saying that she was a liar. It had angered her and saddened her, in that order. It had also tormented her in way too many dreams. The accident nightmare wasn't the only one she suffered. Sometimes it was Royce standing at the edge of some unknown precipice, about to step to his death—which she somehow interpreted to mean him being gone from her life—screaming *liar, liar, liar.*

It was also a substantial relief to have told Royce the truth. It was the first time she'd been able to articulate her thoughts to anyone, and to have someone react in a calm, rational manner affirmed that she wasn't a crazy person.

Now that there was no need for any more subterfuge, she could be absolutely forthcoming.

They left the house in the pickup truck. It took about ten minutes to drive to Everpark. It was a huge facility. There was a main building that had two wings, both as long as a football field. Then there were twenty or more condo-type dwellings. "My guess is that those are the assisted-living spaces," she said, pointing to the smaller buildings. "You live there if you're still mostly independent."

"But you might need somebody to provide a little care," Royce said.

"Somebody like Louisa Goodall," JC agreed.

Once they were inside, they had to wait ten minutes for an administrator to see them. The waiting area was directly across from a large room that seemed like some kind of activity center. Seniors—some with walkers, some in wheelchairs and others more mobile—were playing cards and dominoes, or watching a game show on the television that was way too loud.

"That's your future," he said, teasing her.

"I was kind of hoping that I'd spend my golden years on a beach with a pool boy who had an affinity for wrinkles."

He was prevented from answering by the arrival of the VP of Administration, or so her badge said. Marjory Bender looked about forty-five, and was dressed in black slacks and a blue sweater, and wore even more sensible shoes than JC.

"How may I help you?" she asked.

"My name is Tex and this is Chambri. We're in a little bit of a pickle. Chambri's younger sister has gotten herself into a jam and we need to talk to her friend. Her name is Louisa Goodall."

The woman shook her head. "There's no Louisa Goodall employed by Everpark."

Royce showed no reaction to the news, just pulled his cell phone and flashed a picture of Lou. Marjory studied it.

"It's possible that's the young woman helping Agnes Lowry. Our residents who live in their own condos are able to hire help either directly or many use the same agency. It looks a bit like her but the last time I saw her, her hair had blue-and-pink stripes."

"I'll need Agnes Lowry's address," Royce said.

"I'm afraid I couldn't provide that," she said. "You know, resident privacy and all."

She expected Royce to push but he simply gave her a big smile, thanked her effusively, like Tex would, and motioned for JC to precede him out the door. Once they were in the truck, he had his smartphone out.

"We need that address," she said.

"Piece of cake, now that we have a name." He pushed a few buttons. "1730 Hollyberry."

There were parked across from Agnes Lowry's driveway in less than a minute. "I'm nervous," she admitted.

"Chambri doesn't get nervous," he said. "She's too dumb," he said. "Act sweet and empty-headed. I've seen people get pretty far with that approach. Just ring the bell and ask for Louisa."

"What are you going to be doing?"

"Watching the back door. Give me your cell phone."

"Why?"

"We're going to do this the low-tech way. I'm going to use your cell phone to dial my phone. Keep it in your hand, on speaker, with the line open. I should be able to hear you just fine and will know if you're running into any trouble."

Her palm felt sweaty as she clenched the phone. Once he'd rounded the corner of the brick condo, she counted to ten, walked up the sidewalk and rang the bell. It seemed to take a long time for the door to be answered. When it was, it was by an old woman with white hair, wearing baby blue sweatpants and a sweatshirt with kittens on it. There was a man wearing a suit standing ten feet behind her. He was holding a cup of coffee.

"Mrs. Lowry?" she said. "My name is Chambri and I'm looking for Louisa Goodall. I understand she works for you."

"Your friend is tardy."

Huh? "I'm sorry. I don't understand," she said.

"I was a schoolteacher for forty-three years. Tardiness is something that I can't abide."

"Is Louisa here?"

The woman looked as if she wanted to smack her knuckles with a ruler. "Are you listening to me? She's late. My son is not happy about this, either." She pointed her thumb over her right shoulder.

JC smiled at the man. "What time was Louisa supposed to be here?"

"Stop calling her Louisa. Her name is Lou. She lives here. Of course, she gets time off in the evenings but she's supposed to be available to me from seven to five every day."

"When's the last time you saw Lou, Mrs. Lowry?"

"She left here in a hurry just before six o'clock last night. I've told her not to drive fast on this street but she pays me no attention."

Six o'clock. About the same time that Charity had gone missing. "You're sure. About six?"

"I'm an old lady but I can still tell time. Since she's your friend and all, if you see her, you better tell her to call my son."

"Yes, I will," JC managed. She turned to walk back to her truck but only got halfway before the man caught up with her.

"Can I have a minute?" he said. "I'm Martin Lowry."

She was so disappointed it was hard to summon up her manners. But she did, extending her hand. "Chambri," she said, keeping in character.

"I just want to be clear here. If you find Lou, please make sure she understands that she's not welcome back here."

"Mr. Lowry," she said. "I'm not a friend of Lou's. I know your mother made that assumption and I didn't correct her. But it is very important for me to find her."

The man shook his head. "I used to visit every other day. I could tell my mother was struggling a little and I wanted her to move into the main center where she'd have 24/7 care. It was her idea to hire Lou. And they seemed to get along pretty well. But now, I have to come twice a day because I don't trust Lou. My mother is suddenly purchasing items online. When I ask her about them, she says they are for her. But I know they are for Lou. You can tell, my mother has a strong personality but she's no match for Lou. That woman has one of those personalities that just makes people want to go along with her. You might even say captivating."

Had Lou convinced Charity to do something? What did it have to do with the two men who had taken her from the pool? Too many questions and almost no answers.

"Thank you, Mr. Lowry. I appreciate your time." She

walked back to the truck and got into the passenger side. Mr. Lowry went back inside. Seconds later, Royce was in the driver's seat. "You can hang up your phone now," he said gently.

She pushed the button. "What do you think?"

"Remember when I said that coincidences happen infrequently in real life?"

"Do you think they're both in trouble?" she asked.

"It's possible. Or maybe Lou was already in the car when those two men got Charity. Maybe it wasn't an abduction at all. Maybe they all went out and got drunk last night."

She sighed. "I need to get back to the hotel. With everything that's been going on, I forgot to tell you that they added a rehearsal for tonight's awards dinner."

He nodded. Drove for another minute. "You're still determined to do the awards dinner?" he asked. "After the fourth letter?"

Truth be told, the letter had done her a favor. It had gotten her to Royce's house and then into his bed. "It goes against my grain to let a bully win. And that's what I'd be doing if I pulled out at the last minute. They would have to scramble to find someone to take my place. And why? Because somebody with really rotten poetry skills wants me to be scared. It's a little bit like terrorism, isn't it? The terrorist wins when we're afraid to leave our houses, go to a college football game, shop at the mall. Afraid to live our lives."

"If it keeps you safe, I'm willing to capitulate to the bully."

She shook her head. "You don't really think that's the right answer. And you said that you'd have plenty of resources there."

He nodded. "I actually verified that this morning before I took my shower. That's the only reason you got ahead of me," he added, smiling.

"Sure, sure." She leaned her head back against the seat. "Let's go back to the hotel. I need to retire Chambri and resurrect JC."

Chapter 21

When they arrived at the Periwinkle, they went directly to the ballroom. Wayne Isman was already there and Royce remembered Jules telling him that the man was tonight's emcee. There was also a woman who was the special events manager for the hotel. Royce shook Wayne's hand.

Jules introduced herself to the woman and then turned to Royce. "This is my...friend Royce Morgan. I told him he could hang out and watch the rehearsal."

Friend. Had she almost said boyfriend?

There was no easy way to describe or define their relationship. Lovers. That seemed tawdry and trite. Their reunion had been so unexpected and then so quickly complicated by Charity's appearance and disappearance that they likely missed some important steps.

The sex had been amazing.

No surprise there. Always had been.

The events manager pointed to the table where Jules would be seated. "There's a seat for your guest, of course," she said, looking at Royce.

"When it's time for you to present, Ms. Cambridge," the woman said, "Mr. Isman will introduce you. You'll use those steps at the side of the riser to get to the podium. Your microphone will already be live. All you have to do is deliver your fifteen-minute presentation. I understand that there is a short video clip in it and that will be cued up and ready to go. We'll test that this morning."

Wayne and Jules both nodded.

"Great. Now let's run through the program from the top."

Royce motioned to Jules that he'd be in the back of the room. First, he called Detective Mannis and reported Jules's conversation with Mrs. Lowry. He could tell by the man's quietness on the telephone that he wasn't happy that now he potentially had two young women who were missing.

Bad for tourism, for sure. Legalized prostitution was one thing. Women suddenly missing was a whole level of something else.

The detective advised that he'd circulate pictures of both Charity and Louisa Goodall to all Vegas police. Royce was happy to hear that. The more eyes looking for them, the better. He had to believe that they'd catch a break soon. There had still been no ransom demand.

"I've got some information on Cole Hager," Mannis said. "He's hanging on to his job by a thread."

"Because of his drinking problem?" Royce asked.

"Oh, I don't think investment companies care about that," Mannis scoffed. "Rumors are circulating that he might be using his early access to financial information to benefit himself."

"Insider trading?"

"He's got a couple high-profile clients who have realized substantial gains in the past few months and…" Mannis's voice trailed off.

"What?" Royce demanded.

"And one of his high-profile clients is Joel Cambridge."

Royce almost dropped his phone. "Is Hager being investigated by the SEC?"

"Sadly, the Securities and Exchange Commission probably has bigger fish to fry. But I got it from a reliable source that his boss got wind of this and he's the skittish type with strong risk-avoidance tendencies. Wants to distance himself from anything that might harm the firm. Hager would have probably already lost his job if his mother didn't work in the governor's office."

Royce was confident that Jules was not aware that Cole Hager and her father were acquainted. She would have mentioned something when she and Royce had been initially discussing the meeting. Or said something to Hager during the meeting.

"Can you find out for me whether Hager is still in Vegas?" Royce asked.

"Already checked," Mannis said. "He's staying at the Wallington. Pretended that I was calling from a delivery company and that I had an expensive gift for him. Front desk person said his expected checkout date is tomorrow."

Hager was not getting out of Vegas until Royce had a chance to talk to him. But first, he simply needed to verify that Hager had nothing to do with Charity's or Louisa's absence. "I think we need to get up close and personal with Mr. Hager."

"Worried that he might have your two young women chained to the bed?" Mannis asked.

"I think it's a good idea to verify that he doesn't," Royce said.

"I've already dispatched a unit. I'll be in touch." Mannis disconnected.

Royce glanced up front. The three were still in discussion about something. He had time to see where Sonya was in her internal investigation. He dialed the manager's number and her assistant answered. When he gave his name, she asked him to hold.

"Mr. Morgan, I was just about to call you," Sonya said when she came on the phone.

"Good news?"

"Depends on your definition of *good*. We've talked to over fifty employees, starting with associates in guest dining, since I figured they would have the best access to a uniform. Of course, other associates also wear our standard uniform. Housekeeping, our valets. You know."

He didn't and he didn't really care. "What did you find?"

"My team talked to a woman who seems highly agitated about the questions that were asked. They thought she might know more than what she was letting on. This morning, I said something to her supervisor and he said that this particular woman had started acting oddly on the job, sort of jumpy and testy to the other associates, about two weeks ago. Given that, I've asked to speak to her. She's in my waiting room right now."

Right now. Sonya hadn't offered but he desperately wanted to talk to the associate, force her to share what she knew. He glanced at the front of the room. Jules was in deep discussion with Wayne and the woman.

He didn't want to leave her here alone. But this could be the big break they needed. And Wayne was with her.

Wayne, who had been very trustworthy when he'd stayed with Jules yesterday morning while Royce chased the bottle thrower. Wayne, who had worked with Jules for years and continued to work on humanitarian projects.

"Sonya, I'll be in your office in five minutes. I want to talk to that woman."

"That's not necessary. I've done my share of internal investigations, Mr. Morgan. I know what I'm doing."

He didn't care if she could stand on her head, rub her stomach and chew gum at the same time while she talked to these people. This was Jules's life. Nothing was more important.

"I need to talk to that woman. Five minutes." He hung up before she could protest.

He walked to the front of the room. Jules looked up from the program that both she and Wayne were looking at. She smiled and it hit him like a punch in the gut how wonderful it would be to come home every night to that smile.

"I need to go see Sonya Tribee," he said.

"Is there news?" Her eyes lit up.

"Nothing for sure but enough that I'm going to talk with somebody," he said, conscious of the fact that Wayne and the other woman were in the room. "I need to know that you're going to stay in this room until I get back."

"Of course."

He looked at Wayne. "And you'll stay with her?"

"Absolutely," Wayne said. "Good luck."

When he opened the door to Sonya Tribee's office, her assistant looked up. "Sonya said you were on your way. Wait here please," she said.

He didn't bother to sit. Because if he wasn't escorted back within thirty seconds, he was going on his own.

He didn't intend to be away from Jules any longer than absolutely necessary.

He started counting. She was back in twenty-three seconds. "Follow me, please," she said.

Sonya Tribee was sitting behind her desk and a short, middle-aged white woman sat in one of the chairs in front of the desk. He took the chair next to her.

"Mr. Morgan," Sonya said, her voice pleasant, "this is Annie Slip. She works in guest services, usually taking room service orders. I have been explaining to Annie that it is critically important that we obtain information on the woman in this photo, who we believe was impersonating a hotel associate. The safety of our guests and all our associates is at stake."

Annie said nothing.

The hell with that. Royce leaned a couple inches in her direction. When he spoke, he kept his voice low. "Ms. Slip, the woman in this photo slipped an envelope under the doorway of suite 1402. In that envelope was a correspondence that the authorities are construing as a death threat. If something were to happen to the occupant of suite 1402, and you know something about this woman, then you face the very real possibility of being considered an accessory to murder. And if you don't cooperate immediately, you can rest assured that I will do everything in my power to make sure that happens." He was going to make sure nothing bad happened to Jules, but his intent was not to paint a pretty picture. He wanted to scare the hell out of her.

Annie Slip's lower lip was trembling. "I don't know anything," she whispered.

She wasn't going to break. Damn it.

He'd been separated from Jules for five minutes and as far as he was concerned, that was five minutes too long.

He stared at the woman. "When you get a chance to do the right thing, you should take it."

And then he started running back to Jules.

Royce had been gone for just a minute when the event planner's cell phone buzzed. She picked it up and frowned. "That's odd," she said, still looking down.

Wayne looked at JC, a question in his eyes.

The events manager looked up. "I'm sorry, but I need to step out. I just got a code on my phone that every available resource needs to report to the lobby."

That didn't sound good. "Should we be nervous?" JC asked, thinking immediately that there might be some significant threat.

The woman must have understood. "Crazy, right— terrorism is the first thing we think of. But there's a different code for that." She smiled. "This might be as simple as all the leaders need to throw available resources at a specific issue. I'll be back as soon as I can."

She'd been gone for less than a minute when the door opened again. In walked another hotel employee pushing a cart. As she advanced from the rear of the room, JC got a tingle up her spine.

It was…oh, God, it was the woman with the coarse hair who'd slipped the letter under her door. The woman that the hotel said was impersonating one of their associates.

They needed to get out, get out now.

"Hello, JC," the woman said. "Hello, Wayne."

JC felt as if her legs were jelly. This woman knew not just her, but Wayne, too. She glanced at her friend and his face had turned to stone and his breathing was shallow.

JC looked closer at the woman. Discounted the coarse hair that, at close range, was obviously a wig. She felt exactly the same thing that she'd felt when she'd seen the video of this woman outside her door. She'd seen the woman before. There was something familiar about her but she just couldn't pin it down.

"What can we help you with?" she asked, trying to keep her voice warm. Something was very wrong here.

The woman ignored her, instead smiled at her phone. "So convenient to have the hotel codes, don't you think. But now, we don't have much time, Wayne."

Why was she acting like she knew both of them?

The woman reached under the towel that was on her cart and pulled out a gun. Pointed it at JC. "Here's what's going to happen. Wayne, you're going to sit in that chair and JC is going to tie up your wrists and ankles."

JC edged a step back. This woman was crazy.

"Stop that, JC. I'll shoot you here if I have to." Again she reached under the towel and pulled out a roll of duct tape. "Get busy and I'll reward your efforts. You can see your sister. Yes, that's right, Charity."

How did this woman know about Charity? JC realized quickly it didn't matter. She turned to Wayne. Together, they could overpower the woman. "Wayne," she said.

"Shut up," the woman yelled. "Sit down, Wayne."

The man did.

JC's brain was rapidly clicking through options. "I want to talk to her. If you've got Charity, I want to talk to her before I do anything." She needed to stall long enough for Royce to return to the ballroom. Plus, every crime show she'd ever watched on television always said to ask for proof of life.

The woman pushed a button on her cell. The phone was answered. "Put the girl on the phone," she said, then handed it to JC, who looked at the number but didn't recognize it.

"Hello," she heard.

Oh, God. "Charity?" she said.

"JC, help me. Please help me."

Her words faded at the end as she was likely pulled away from the phone. The woman snatched her own phone back. She spoke into it. "Stay on the line. If she tries anything funny on our way out of the hotel and I'm not here, kill the girl." She looked at JC. "Start wrapping. You've got one minute before I shoot you. And then I call my friend and tell them to shoot Charity."

Her hands were shaking but she moved as quickly as she could. Two revolutions of tape around his wrists, two around his ankles. "Now wrap him to the chair," the woman said.

She did it.

"Over his mouth. I know it will hurt when they take it off," she said, irrationally sounding concerned, "but it really is necessary. And you know, I always do what's necessary."

Chapter 22

Royce threw open the door of the ballroom and ran inside. There, in a chair, was Wayne.

No Jules.

He ripped the tape off the man's mouth. "Where's Jules?"

"A woman, somebody who works for the hotel, took her. I tried to stop her, I did. But she had a gun. Said that she'd kill both of us."

God, no. He wanted to pound the man's face, to tell him that he should have taken the damn bullet to keep Jules safe. Instead, he pulled his pocket knife from his pocket and sliced through the duct tape on Wayne's wrists and ankles. "What else did the woman say?"

"Nothing. That was it."

"Did…Jules say anything?"

Wayne shook his head. "It all happened so fast. I'm so sorry, Royce."

Stay focused. Ask the right questions. Think. Hard to do when his head was about to explode. It didn't make sense. One woman. Even if she'd had a gun, there had been two of them. Jules would have known that her greatest risk came from leaving the hotel with someone.

"Describe the woman," he said.

"She was just a woman, you know. White. Middle-aged. It all happened so fast," he added, repeating his earlier comment.

It didn't matter. They'd be able to pick her up on hotel video. "What door did they leave from?"

"That one."

Royce took off running. On the way back to Sonya Tribee's office, he called Detective Mannis and filled him in. When he arrived, he didn't stop to speak to the receptionist. He burst into the manager's office. She was at her desk.

"Jules Cambridge was just abducted from the ballroom of this hotel, taken out the west door, by the same woman who slipped the envelope under her door, in the same hotel uniform."

To her credit, Sonya didn't ask any questions. Simply put her hands on her keyboard and started pulling the surveillance video.

"I need hallways on that floor and activity at every door. Everything for the last five minutes."

As she hit the keys, he thought of options. It took just minutes for Sonya to isolate the video that he needed. There they were. Jules and the woman. Leaving the hotel. Jules in front, the woman close behind her. Her arm was extended, with a towel over it.

There was no doubt that she was holding a gun on Jules. She had a cell phone in her other hand.

Jules was smart. Even with a gun on her, he'd expect

that she'd somehow tried to avoid being taken. But the woman had her under control.

He was willing to bet his last nickel that it had something to do with the cell phone that she had in her other hand.

He shouldn't have left her, not even for a minute. He'd been crazy to think that she'd be safe with Wayne.

This was his fault. He'd been so focused on the news he'd gotten about Cole Hager that he'd closed his mind to other possibilities.

And he was going to have to admit that when he called Joel Cambridge and told him that his daughter was missing.

"I want to talk to that woman again," he said. "To Annie Slip."

Sonya looked at him, her eyes sad. "We've talked to her twice…"

"I don't care," he roared. "She knows something. Get her back up here."

Sonya picked up the phone. Spoke quietly. Put the receiver down. "She's already left the building. Guess she got the hell out of here after our conversation. Anyway, her supervisor is calling her and telling her to come back. I'm not sure how long it will take."

Likely enough time for him to go see Barry Wood. The man deserved to know what was going on.

"Send me a text when she's back," he said. This time he was getting the truth.

JC recognized the man who was driving the car. He was one of the ones who had approached Charity at the pool and taken her.

The woman had pushed her into the back seat of a small red SUV. Nobody had said a word. They had driven down the strip for about a mile and then taken a right, heading out of town. They were making no effort to keep her from seeing where she was going.

That meant just one thing. They intended to kill her. She thought of Royce and the guilt he'd feel for having failed her. It would kill him. A sob escaped.

"Stop whining. This is your fault," the woman said. "You just couldn't leave well enough alone."

What the hell was she talking about?

"And that little sister of yours. Every bit as much trouble. And her friend, she's got a mouth on her. I'll be glad to be rid of the bunch of you."

She had to think, had to figure this out. "How do you know that Charity is my sister?"

"I've known since before she was born." The woman shook her head. "That was before I realized that if you wanted something done, you might as well just take care of it yourself."

"They have you on video, you know," JC said. "A very clear picture of you slipping the envelope under my door."

The woman laughed. "I know all about their stupid technology. Have been hearing about it for years, how they use it rather than have supervisors on the floor, doing some actual work. But that's why I wore the wig and the makeup and this god-awful fat suit." She pulled up her shirt and JC could see it. "If I gained this much weight in real life, I would kill myself." She laughed as if she was really funny.

This was a sick, sick woman.

She wasn't going to be able to reason with her. She was simply going to have to figure out a way to get herself and Charity, and by the sounds of it, Lou, too, away from there.

They drove until they were well into the desert, where

the houses were literally miles apart. She tried to keep track of the time and the turns in her head, regretting that she'd stopped wearing a watch years ago in favor of seeing the time on her phone. She thought they'd been in the car for about forty-five minutes. It had been a right, right, left and a right. But now the ride seemed over. They were pulling into the gravel driveway of a small house in general disrepair. The paint, which might have been a mint green, was faded from the hot sun and there were sections of shingles on the roof that were missing.

"Welcome to my little retirement home," the woman said. Then she giggled before she clamped her hand around JC's arm and pulled her from the car. Then it was into the house, which was dark and stuffy. The woman put her hand on JC's back, shoving her down the short hallway.

"This is your room," she said, stopping in front of the last doorway. She reached in front of JC to open the door.

Charity. Her friend Lou. Both girls were sitting on the floor, on opposite sides of the small room. They were staring at the door.

Charity had been crying. Streaks ran down her dirty face.

There was no furniture in the room, not one stick. Just a dirty, matted gray carpet.

She saw the ropes dangling from big metal hooks that had been drilled into the wall, close to the ceiling. Realized that the other end of the rope was tied around each girl's ankle, effectively securing them in place. They could sit or stand but not do much else. Their wrists were secured with duct tape in front of their bodies.

"All ready to join the party?" the woman asked, her voice cheerful.

That was when JC saw the third hook.

The man who had been driving had followed them down the hall. Now he had a gun in his right hand.

"Shoot her if she tries anything," the woman said, tightening her grip on JC's arm. She started to drag her across the room.

"I have to use the bathroom," she said. Anything to buy time, buy opportunity.

The woman shook her head. "You're going to have to hold it. It won't be long. Striker is out with his tractor, digging your hole right now. Once he gets back, Shane and I will be rid of the three of you forever."

"You won't get away with this," JC said.

The woman looked surprised. "Of course I will. The only one who knows anything for sure is Wayne. And he's kept his mouth shut before. He can certainly do it again."

Royce knocked on the Woods' door. Barry Wood opened it.

"Royce?" he said. "I wasn't expecting…" The man stopped. "Oh, no. Something has happened."

"Jules has been taken," Royce said, his tongue feeling too big for his mouth. Hateful, ugly words.

He heard a gasp and looked up to see Barry's wife at the edge of the room. He remembered seeing her at the panel presentation although she hadn't stayed around afterward.

"I'm Eileen Wood," she said.

"Royce Morgan," he said.

"I know who you are. I knew about you eight years ago."

Jules had never mentioned that. But this was not the time to be wandering down memory lane.

"What happened?" Barry asked. His complexion had gone gray.

He told them about leaving Jules in the room with Wayne Isman, about returning to find Wayne bound and gagged.

When he was done, he saw a look pass between the Woods. A look he didn't understand but it made the hair on the back of his neck stand up. "What?" he demanded.

"Tell him," Eileen said. "We need to tell him. This is Juliana we're talking about."

"If you know anything—"

"Understand that Wayne Isman and I are not friends," Barry said, interrupting him. "At best, we have remained acquaintances throughout the years. Our paths have crossed professionally for probably twenty years, given that we were both executives at drug companies. For several years, we were both employed by Geneseel."

"That's when Jules worked at Geneseel."

"Yes," Barry said.

"You got her the job there," Royce said.

Barry shook his head. "I did not. In fact, I didn't even know that she'd applied or been hired until after she'd started."

That didn't make sense. When he'd met Jules, she was always working and had confided in him that she'd always felt that she had to work harder than everyone else because Barry had helped her get a job. "Jules thought you did," he said.

"It was Wayne," Eileen said, moving farther into the room.

Another look passed between Barry and Eileen. Barry started rubbing his hands together.

"Tell him, Barry," Eileen said, her voice hard. "Tell him the truth."

"He's my friend," Barry said.

"You said you and Isman were barely acquaintances," Royce accused. Which one was it?

"Not him," Eileen dismissed, tears in her eyes.

Barry shook his head. "Joel Cambridge. He's been my friend since we were kids."

"JC got her job at Geneseel because of Wayne Isman," Eileen said. "Her father probably told her it was Barry."

"Why would he do that?"

Barry put his palms flat on his knees and cleared his throat. "Because Joel Cambridge and Wayne Isman have been lovers for almost thirty years."

It felt as if his damn head was filled with wool. Wayne Isman and Joel Cambridge. He quite frankly didn't give two hoots about anybody's sexual preferences, but he did care that there were big secrets here.

Because sometimes people got quite crazy with their need to protect secrets.

"Who knows this?" he demanded.

Barry shrugged. "I believe it is very closely held information. Joel got drunk one night, shortly after their relationship started, and he told me. I told Eileen but neither of us ever told another living soul. Professionally, neither of them are out."

"Personally then? Family?" Royce asked.

"JC does not know. I'm confident of that," Eileen said. "And I don't think her mother ever knew. I wanted to tell her. But Barry asked me not to. Said we had to stay out of it. In deference to him, I held my tongue. I believe if she had known, she would have told me. She certainly told me other important things that were in this same vein."

"What things?" Royce said, already thinking he might know.

"That Joel had an affair with Linette White and Charity was conceived. I always believed that JC didn't know but when I saw Charity at the session yesterday, I wasn't so sure."

"How do you know Charity?" Royce asked.

"I made it my business to keep track of her, especially after Lara's death. You don't seem surprised, which makes me think I was wrong all those years, that Juliana did know."

Royce shook his head. "Lara Cambridge wrote it in her diary shortly before her accident. The diary wasn't found by Jules until a couple months ago."

"So many lies," Eileen said. "So damn unnecessary. I'm sure Joel didn't love Linette but he was so busy lying to himself."

Royce looked at Barry.

"After Lara died, Joel dated many women. To cover his tracks. But—" he paused, shaking his head "—maybe it's because he was my friend, but I always thought he loved Lara. Maybe he loved Linette White or maybe Eileen is right, she was just more of the same, an elaborate ruse. Her getting pregnant changed everything."

Indeed. "I need to tell him about Jules," Royce said. "Can you give me his number?" It was a bad conversation to have over the phone with someone he disliked, and the feeling was mutual. But that couldn't be helped. He couldn't afford the time to fly to New York.

Barry looked at his watch. "I can do better than that. Joel should be landing in about a half hour. I invited him to the awards dinner so that he could hear JC's speech."

Chapter 23

"Are the two of you alright?" JC asked, realizing immediately that it was a ridiculous question given that she, Charity and Lou had all been tied in place by a crazy woman.

"Yes," Charity said. "But we're hungry. This is Lou, the one I told you about."

"Hello, Lou. I'm JC. Has she fed you anything since yesterday?"

They shook their heads. She heard a car engine start. Were they leaving?

But then she heard the television. Somebody was still here.

"We're going to die here," Lou said.

"No, we're not," JC said, with perhaps more confidence than she had a right to feel. The woman's words were reverberating in her head.

The only one who knows anything for sure is Wayne.

And he's kept his mouth shut before. He can certainly do it again.

What did that mean? The woman had called Wayne by name when she'd come into the ballroom, like she knew him. But then, she'd also called JC by name. And there was something about her voice that felt vaguely familiar.

Wayne had simply capitulated to the woman. But that probably wasn't the important thing now.

She had no doubt that Royce would turn Vegas upside down looking for her. But would he find them in time? Before this woman could carry through on whatever crazy scheme she was cooking up in her demented little mind?

But Royce was smart. And tenacious. He would do his very best.

And he would expect her to do the same. "She called the man with the gun Shane. Who is Striker?" she asked. The woman had said he was digging a hole.

"I think he's Shane's brother," Lou said. "Nobody told us that but they look alike and I heard Striker tell Shane that he was going to *check on Mom*." She emphasized the words.

Sons doing everyday things. Checking on their mother. Kidnapping women. Digging graves.

"Were they all here last night?" JC asked.

"I don't think so," Charity said. "At first we didn't think there was anybody in the house. But then we heard the toilet flush and knew somebody was here. I think it was just her."

She liked the sound of that. Fighting one person had to be easier than fighting three.

"I should never have left the pool with them," Charity said, sounding very discouraged.

"Why did you?" JC asked.

"Because they told me that they had Lou, that if I didn't come with them, they were going to kill her. They showed me her necklace. It's very distinctive. I didn't know what to do. I panicked. And then once I was in the car, I knew that I was in terrible trouble." A fresh tear slid down her face. "They used my phone to text Lou, to lure her out of her house. Made her think she needed to meet me."

"Bastards," Lou said.

"How did they have your necklace?"

"I don't know. The old lady I take care of doesn't like it. She thinks it's vulgar. Like anybody is offended by the word *bitch* anymore. But sometimes if I want to keep her happy, I put it in my purse. Maybe it got taken from there when I was out."

It was certainly possible. Or they'd simply bought a lookalike one. She'd seen those kinds of necklaces in stores.

"That woman won't tell us anything," Charity added. "We don't know who she is or what she wants from us."

"I don't know, either," JC said. But that wasn't exactly true. She knew a little. The woman had said something along the lines of she couldn't leave well enough alone. And she had known that Charity was her sister.

This was not the way that sensitive news should be shared, but she was going to have to just say it. The three of them needed to be absolutely honest with each other if there was any hope of getting out of there alive.

"Charity," she said, keeping her voice soft, her tone even. "What I'm going to tell you is going to be a big surprise to you and this is so not the right time or place to share this information." She drew in a breath. "We're sisters, Charity. My father is your father."

JC waited for Charity's expression to change. But all

that happened was the woman lifted her eyes in Lou's direction.

It wasn't the response she'd expected. Maybe she hadn't understood. "Charity, I want—"

"I know that," Charity interrupted her. "I've known it for months, since right before my mother died. She told me."

"But…" JC's mind was scrambled. The stress of being forced at gunpoint from the hotel, the ride here, being tied to a hook in the wall. It was making it impossible to think. Charity had known. From the beginning. "When I called you, you didn't say anything."

Anger flashed in Charity's dark eyes. "Hell, no. I didn't know what to do."

"I don't understand, Charity."

"My mother told me that Joel Cambridge was my father and that she'd gotten money from him for years, since I was a baby. But that the checks had stopped when I was twenty-one. My mom and her boyfriend got into some financial trouble and they decided to contact *our daddy* for one final payment. Hush money, she called it. I don't know how much she asked for but it must have been too much because she told me that he'd refused. Had said that she could tell whoever she wanted."

"So she told you?" JC asked.

"Yes. She was very angry. It wasn't the answer she'd expected. She said she was going to tell everyone."

"What did you think of that?"

"I didn't know what to think. I'd just learned that I had a father when for my whole life, there hadn't been one."

"That screws a person up." This from Lou.

"She and her boyfriend were going to his boat for the weekend. She said they were going to use the time to plan the best way to make this bad for…him."

"For our father. For Joel Cambridge," JC clarified.

"Yeah." Charity again looked at Lou. "Their boat caught fire that weekend. They both died."

Lou, who'd been sitting on the floor, stood up, her movements awkward. "Those things don't just happen," she said.

What Lou was suggesting hit her hard, literally taking her breath away. *Don't faint now*, she told herself. "You think that my father had something to do with that fire?"

"Seems to me that he didn't like the choices he'd been given. He either needed to shell out some cash to keep his illegitimate kid a secret or the gig was up. I think he figured out a way to solve his problem."

It was a horrific suggestion. Impossible. "Why didn't you go to the police?" JC asked, her throat feeling tight.

"Because I told her," Lou said, "that having him in jail wasn't maybe the best thing that could happen to us. That maybe there was another way for us to get money from him. So we contacted him."

It was perhaps good that she was being held upright by a rope and a hook because otherwise she might have collapsed. "You contacted my father?" she repeated.

"I did," Charity said. "I told him that I knew who he was and if he didn't keep paying me what he'd paid my mother, then I was going to tell everyone that he was my father and let the police know that I suspected he'd had something to do with the fire."

She was almost overwhelmed with the sadness of the situation. Charity was Joel Cambridge's blood. And it must have hurt him so to have her call him and be so callous.

At the same time she thought this, an equally strong voice said that Charity had been hurt so much, too. To not be acknowledged by her father. It was a horrible situation.

"What did he say?" she asked.

"Not much," Charity said. "But the money started coming in. I thought it was over. And then you called, pretending that our mothers were friends and that you wanted to look me up. I didn't know what your game was but Lou and I decided that the best thing for me to do was play along until we figured it out."

And she played perfectly into their hands. It was a sobering thought that she'd been so stupid. "What were your plans?" she asked dully. This was all too much.

Charity looked at the floor. "We didn't know. Thought maybe we might be able to get you to make payments, too. After all, you're a big hotshot CEO. I figured you probably didn't want a stray sister hanging around." She lifted her head, looked at JC. "But then once I met you, you were so nice. I could tell you were a good person. I didn't know what to do. It was kind of nice thinking that I had a sister."

JC closed her eyes and swallowed hard. So many damaged relationships. So much distrust and hurt. So damn many wasted years. She drew in a deep breath, opened her eyes, and her glance took in both Charity and Lou.

"There's certainly stuff to sort out. But our first priority has to be getting out of here. So let's figure out how we're going to do that."

Royce was sitting on the Woods' couch when Joel Cambridge knocked on the door. Barry had agreed not to give the man a heads-up. He'd been reluctant to go along with the plan but Eileen had insisted. *This is Juliana*, she kept saying.

The door opened, Barry and Joel shook hands, and then Joel looked over Barry's shoulder and saw Royce. Immediate recognition flared in his eyes.

"What the hell is this?" he asked, turning to his friend.

Royce remained seated, his eyes steady on Joel Cambridge. For years he'd dreamed of seeing the man again, of throwing his success in the man's face.

But none of that seemed important now. This was Jules's father. Yes, he'd lied to her about being sick, which was horrible. But he'd probably done it with good intentions. A father desperate for his only daughter to make a good match. Jules had said that she still loved her father, even if she couldn't forgive him. She would want Royce to treat him with care when he was about to hear very difficult news.

"Mr. Cambridge," Royce said. He motioned to the chair across from him. "Would you have a seat, please?"

He could tell Joel Cambridge wanted to refuse, but then he looked at Barry, looked at Eileen, and was smart enough to realize that something was very, very wrong. "Where's my daughter?" he asked.

Which one? Royce tamped the retort down. Nothing to be gained by that.

When nobody answered, Joel Cambridge walked farther into the room and took the seat Royce had offered. Royce sat forward in his chair.

"I am a partner in the Wingman Security firm. I was hired by Barry and Jules to provide security for Jules while she was in Las Vegas."

"What does she need security for?" Cambridge demanded, again looking at Barry.

Barry declined to answer, simply turned his gaze toward Royce. The message was clear. This was Royce's show.

"Your daughter had received three anonymous threats,

in the form of four-line verses. While she was here, a fourth one was slipped underneath her hotel door."

"Where's Juliana?" Cambridge asked again, this time his eyes darting around the room as if he was a scared animal.

"She was abducted from this hotel about an hour ago, while she was with Wayne Isman."

Now Cambridge lost all color in his face and he sagged back against the pillows. "Wayne?" he asked, his voice breaking.

"Not injured," Royce said. "Our only witness." He paused. "I know about your relationship with Wayne Isman."

Cambridge's eyes flicked toward Barry and Eileen. To their credit, their faces gave nothing away. "I don't know what you're talking about."

"You do," Royce said. "We all do." His voice was quiet. "And there are two other young women who are missing. Charity White and her friend Louisa Goodall."

Cambridge said nothing.

Why the hell did the man have to make it so hard? "Charity White. Your daughter with Linette White," Royce added.

Cambridge ran his hands through his silver hair. "What a damn mess," he said.

A mess of your own making, thought Royce. "Your daughters—" he emphasized the plural "—are in jeopardy. Now you better stop hiding information and tell us anything that might be helpful."

There was silence in the room. Finally, Cambridge spoke. "Charity White contacted me shortly after her mother died. She wanted money."

"She knows that you're her father?" Royce asked.

"Yes. Her mother told her."

That meant that Charity had known all along that Jules was her half sister. But she'd pretended not to. What the hell had been her game?

"Did you tell anyone about this?"

Cambridge nodded. "I told Wayne. He's always known about Charity. Knew that I gave Linette White money so that she wouldn't disclose paternity."

"Who else knew about Charity?" Royce asked. He knew that Lara Cambridge had known. She'd written it in her diary and told her best friend, Eileen Wood.

"My wife," whispered Cambridge. He looked ten years older than he had when he'd entered the room five minutes earlier. "I wrote checks to Linette White from a separate checking account, one that only I knew about. Every two weeks, a portion of my paycheck went into that account. It went smoothly for years but then the company I worked for changed their payroll process and the direct deposit accounts got all mixed up. I was a good customer of the bank so they covered the check I'd written to Linette even though there was no money in the account. But, of course, they wanted me to make it right. They sent me emails but I didn't get them because I'd dropped that email and hadn't thought to tell the bank. When they were unsuccessful at reaching me, a bank employee decided to take the bull by the horns. She discovered I had other accounts at the bank and used that information to contact me." He stopped, took a breath. "They reached Lara. She was a very smart person. She figured out what was going on." He swallowed. "When she accused me, I didn't deny it. I'd already failed her in so many ways."

"She didn't know about you and Wayne?" Royce asked.

"I don't think so," Cambridge said. "She never said anything."

What had he done to ensure his wife's silence? "Did you run your wife off the road?" Royce asked.

Chapter 24

Now color popped on Cambridge's face and neck. Vivid blotches of red. "I loved my wife," he said, his tone defensive. "And I could have lost Juliana in that crash," he said.

And Joel Cambridge loved Jules. Royce was sure of that. He would not have risked his daughter's life to harm his wife.

But was there someone else who perhaps did not feel the same way about Lara Cambridge? "Did you tell Wayne that your wife knew?"

"Yes. But he had nothing to do with the accident. He was…with me that night."

Royce closed his eyes, tried to think. He was missing something. His cell phone buzzed and he read the text. It was from Sonya. Annie Slip had arrived back at the hotel and was available in her office for questioning.

"I have to go," he said to the group.

"What are you doing to find my daughter?" Cambridge asked, coming to his feet.

"Every damn thing I can," Royce said as he walked out the door.

He entered Sonya's office and her receptionist didn't even bother to get up, just waved him back. He knocked once on the door and opened it.

Annie Slip was in the chair, bending down to retrieve something from her purse. He caught a solid look at her profile and stopped short.

"Pull up that video again," he said to Sonya. "The one we just looked at, where Jules and the woman are leaving the hotel."

Annie was now watching him, wariness in her eyes. He ignored her and went behind Sonya's desk. "There," he said, pointing at the screen. "Zoom in," he said.

He studied the woman's profile and he knew. Knew what he'd been missing.

He came back around the desk and took the chair next to Annie Slip. "Jules Cambridge was abducted from this hotel about an hour ago by a woman. The same woman who slipped an envelope under her door. I know that you were lying when you said earlier that you didn't know this woman. I think you know her very well. You are now an accessory to kidnapping, which is a federal crime. So you better start talking or I'm going to make it my life's mission to make sure you pay for your silence."

Tears filled the woman's eyes. "She told me that nobody was going to get hurt. She promised me."

"Who?" he asked, his voice soft, controlled.

"Sadie. My sister Sadie."

"What's Sadie's last name?" Royce asked.

"Sadie Isman. She's married to Wayne Isman."

Noise roared in Royce's head. Isman had lied to protect his wife. "I need Isman's room number," he said, looking at Sonya.

She didn't offer even a token protest about guest privacy. She simply looked it up. "Room 720."

Royce called Detective Mannis and gave him the short version of events. Mannis listened, saying a quiet swear word when Royce identified the imposter as Sadie Isman.

"Wayne Isman is in room 720," Royce said.

"Royce, this is a police matter. I'm five minutes out from the hotel. Don't do anything until I get there. I don't want to have to arrest you for interfering in an investigation."

"Then you better hurry," Royce said, hanging up.

In the meantime, he wanted to know what the Woods knew about Sadie Isman. He took the elevator to the twelfth floor and rapped on their door. Eileen quickly opened it.

"Any news?" she asked. It appeared she'd shed some tears while he'd been gone.

"Yes," he said. He looked over her shoulder. It was only Barry in the room. "Where is Cambridge?" Royce asked.

"He left right after you. I think he wanted to talk to Wayne."

"I just spoke to a woman named Annie Slip. She is Sadie Isman's sister."

Something flared in Eileen's eyes and Royce was pretty sure it was fear.

"She has admitted loaning her sister a hotel uniform. Sadie is the woman who abducted Jules." He paused. "There is no way that Wayne Isman didn't know that. And he didn't tell us."

Neither Eileen nor Barry said anything. But like before, a look passed between them.

"I swear to God if the two of you don't stop doing that,
I won't be responsible for what happens."

"I'm sorry, Royce," Eileen said. "It's just that these are
things that we've known for years but have never talked
to another person about. It's a hard habit to break. But
you're right, now's the time. I have no idea what his wife
knows. For many years, our paths have crossed socially,
more times than not at Joel's condo when he'd be host-
ing some kind of party or event. I don't care for her. She
is really quite attractive, you know, when you first meet
her, but when you get to know her, there is something
about that woman that is deeply disturbing."

"In what way?" he said.

"She's a social climber. Loves the fact that her husband is successful, that he's called upon to speak around
the world. Loves the money he earns. Loves her perfect
little family, with her perfect children. She really acts
like she's better than the rest of us."

That was the kind of woman who wouldn't be happy
when it became public knowledge that her husband had
had a male lover for the duration of their marriage.

What would she do to protect that secret? Run an innocent woman off the road? Kidnap multiple people? Kill?

But for the first time since he'd walked into the ballroom and Jules hadn't been there, he felt hope. All they
had to do was find Sadie Isman and they would find
Jules and the others.

His phone buzzed. Detective Mannis was in the hotel,
on his way to the seventh floor. Royce took off and met
the man in the lobby. "I think Joel Cambridge is in Isman's room."

"Be ready," was all Detective Mannis said.

They knocked on the door. There was no response. "Las Vegas Police Department, Mr. Isman," Detective Mannis said. "We need to talk with you. Open the door."

Royce pulled his phone to get Sonya up there with a key. But just then, the door swung open. It was Isman. The man had been crying. Inside the room, standing by the window, was Joel Cambridge. He also looked as if some tears had been shed.

There was an open suitcase on the bed. It appeared Isman was packing to leave.

"I'm Detective Mannis and I think you know Royce Morgan." The detective stepped into the room and Royce followed, closing the door behind him.

It was a regular hotel room, with one king bed and a dresser. There was a table and two chairs by the window. Nobody sat.

"Mr. Isman, we have reason to believe that the woman who abducted JC was your wife, Sadie Isman."

Royce heard a gasp come from Joel Cambridge.

Wayne said nothing but he did sink down onto the end of the bed, next to his suitcase. He looked down at his shoes. Royce told himself to count to ten before he ripped the man's face off.

Evidently, Detective Mannis felt similarly. "Mr. Isman, may I see your phone?" he asked.

"Why? Why would you want to see it?" Wayne said, looking up.

"Because I'm going to make an educated guess that you've recently attempted to contact your wife. Your phone, please." Mannis held out his hand.

Royce could tell that Isman was mentally evaluating his options. His eyes registered the knowledge that he didn't see a path out. He looked at Joel Cambridge, swallowed hard. "I'm sorry, Joel. Terribly sorry."

"You...bastard," Cambridge said, his voice raw with emotion. "I've been here for ten minutes, telling you how frightened I was about Jules and you...you *knew*."

"It will kill our girls," Isman said. "If they find out what she's done."

It seemed to be an especially cruel thing to say to a man whose own two children were at risk. And while Cambridge didn't say so, the fury in his eyes told the story.

"Give him your damn phone, Wayne," Cambridge said.

Seemingly defeated, Wayne reached into his pocket. Gave the phone to the detective.

Mannis pushed a couple buttons. "Fourteen calls to the same number during the last half hour. No answer."

"Sometimes I can reason with her," Wayne said.

Mannis used his own phone. He rattled off the number to someone along with some quiet instructions. He hung up. "We'll track the activity on this number. We might be able to get a location."

"Where would your wife have taken Jules?" Royce jumped in.

Isman shook his head.

Royce clenched his fist. He would beat it out of the man.

Detective Mannis put a hand on his arm, his attention still focused on Isman. "There were two men who appear to be accomplices of your wife. Do you know who they might be?" he asked.

"No."

"Think," Royce demanded.

Isman threw up his hands. "My wife's sister lives in Vegas. But we rarely have come to see her. We don't have any friends here. The only person I know..." Isman stopped.

Then started again. "The only person I know in Vegas is a man that my oldest daughter dated several years ago when she was in college. I thought he was trouble the first time I met him. And soon enough it fizzled out by itself."

"His name."

"Shane Cary."

Royce was already typing his name into his smartphone. Found an address, did a quick map lookup. "Got it. Lives outside of Vegas, maybe forty-five minutes."

"Let's go," Mannis said. "Come with us, Mr. Isman. I'm going to hand you off to officers who by now are in the lobby downstairs. I suggest on your ride to the police station that you start praying that JC Cambridge, Charity White and Louisa Goodall are just fine."

Chapter 25

JC heard heels clicking on the tile floor. She motioned for Charity and Lou, who had been talking in low tones, to be quiet. She figured less than an hour had gone by since the woman had left her in the room.

The door opened. The woman stood in the doorway. "It's almost time, ladies. Just heard from Shane. He's on his way back."

"Time for what?" JC asked.

"Time for you to die," the woman said. "I've got a plane to catch. The girls will be worried."

The girls.

So familiar. She'd just heard someone use that term. It was Wayne. He'd said that the girls were going to join them in Europe. He had always referred to his daughters as *the girls.*

She stared at the woman and she knew why she looked familiar. She'd only met her once but there had been pictures of Wayne's daughters in his office. She could see the resemblance. "Sadie, it's been a long time."

The woman's head jerked up. "So you finally put it all together, huh?"

Charity and Lou were looking at her, clearly confused by the conversation.

"Actually, Sadie, I've got a couple questions. Can we start with the letters?"

Sadie waved a hand. "Did they amuse you? They did me. Every time I thought about you reading them and getting wigged out, I had some happy moments. Plus, I didn't think it would hurt to have the cops think that whatever happened to you was the work of some deranged poet."

"You shot at me at the Wallington Hotel," Jules said.

"That was Shane," Sadie said. "He's much better with a gun at close range. But the three of you will get a chance to experience that firsthand soon."

"Was it Shane who threw the bottle?"

"I don't know what you're talking about," she said.

So that had been unrelated. As they'd speculated, maybe just somebody mad at a drug company. "You said earlier that Wayne knew how to keep his mouth shut. He had done it before. What did you mean?"

"I guess I can tell you. It's not like you'll have a chance to repeat it. When I forced your mother's car off the road, my car got a little damaged. He was the one who got it fixed."

JC felt all the air leave her lungs. This woman had stolen her mother's life. *Stay focused. Keep her talking.* "Did he know what you'd done?"

"He never asked. Wayne and I didn't need to discuss these things. We understand each other."

"Why? Why hurt my mother?"

"Because…" The woman stopped, her face turning red. "Because she had the potential to ruin my life. And I wasn't going to let that happen."

"That doesn't make any sense," JC said.

"Yes, it does," Sadie yelled. "It does." She stood in the doorway and slammed the palm of her hand against the door frame. "If people found out about Linette and this one here," she said, stabbing her finger in Charity's direction, "then they were going to realize that your father was a pig. A cheating pig."

"Why did that matter to you?" JC pressed. If she was going to die, she was going to understand this one last thing.

"It didn't matter to me," the woman screeched. She was practically foaming at the mouth. "It mattered to Wayne. I did it all for him."

And suddenly it made sense. After her mother had died, her father had dated sporadically but never anyone serious. She'd thought it was because he'd still been in love with her mother.

But that wasn't it. He'd been in love with Wayne. But the two of them had been trapped by the need to keep their relationship a secret.

"How long did you know?" JC asked, her voice sounding as if it was coming from someone else.

"Our youngest daughter was two."

Wayne's youngest daughter was at least twenty-five years old. It was a staggeringly long time to have hidden a relationship.

"There were unexplained absences, quiet phone calls, all the usual stuff. I thought he was having an affair. So I followed him. You can imagine my surprise when I realized that it was your father."

"But you didn't leave him."

"I had three small children. My family meant everything to me. Of course I didn't leave him. And—" she lifted her chin "—I still loved him. And I believed him when he said that he still loved me. We understand each other. We belong together. But I told him, there could be no more secrets."

Sadie turned to Charity. "That's how I knew that your mother was stirring up trouble last year. Joel told Wayne and Wayne told me. She was a greedy bitch and she and that man, who *lived in sin*, by the way, deserved to die. You know, it's easy to start a fire. So easy."

Charity's face was absolutely white. But she said nothing.

"It should have ended there. But you couldn't let it go, could you?" Sadie asked, continuing to stare at Charity. Her voice was thick with scorn. "You were going to bleed Joel Cambridge dry and he was going to crack. I couldn't have that. I figured you'd told your BFF." Sadie's gaze flickered to Lou.

JC heard a car engine. Evidently so did Sadie. The woman smiled. "And that's why all of you have to die. You know secrets. Secrets that need to finally be put to rest so that I can stop worrying about them. I'm so tired. So very tired."

She was insane. So very insane. No doubt about it.

JC heard a car door, the house door and footsteps coming down the hall. It was the man who'd driven JC to the house. The man Sadie called Shane.

He looked only at Sadie. "The hole is ready. Striker and I want our money."

"You'll get your money," she said.

He shook his head. "Now."

JC saw her chance. "She probably intends to have you do all the work and then she's going to find a way to kill you, too. Maybe shoot you and your brother and leave you in the hole with us."

"Shut up," Sadie screamed.

But she'd gotten Shane's attention. "I don't like this," the man said.

"I've got five thousand in my purse," she said. "You can have it all. As a down payment."

"The price was thirty thousand," Shane said.

"You'll get your money."

Shane fingered his scraggly mustache. And JC allowed herself to hope.

But then he pulled his gun from his waistband and pointed it at them. "Let's go, then. I want these women out of this house."

Detective Mannis drove his SUV with lights and sirens on, keeping the speed up near one hundred on the interstate. There were three more police SUVs all doing exactly the same thing behind them. They were still five miles from Shane Cary's house when Royce's cell buzzed.

He answered his phone. "Morgan."

"They're moving. Red SUV going north on Furlough Road. You're going to want to hurry."

"Stay on the line," Royce said. "Turn," he yelled at Mannis.

The man looked at him as if he was crazy but he did it. As did the vehicles behind him. "What the hell?" he asked.

"My partner Trey Riker, he's in the air." Once Royce had looked at the map of where Shane Cary's home was located, he'd called Trey while Mannis had been busy organizing backup. On the way here, he'd gotten a text that Billy-Bob Anderson and Trey were in the air, en route to Cary's house.

"Jules?" Royce asked his partner.

"Yeah. Four women and a man left the house. She looked okay."

But now she was being taken somewhere. It could not be good.

"We're going to back off a little," his partner said. "We don't want to spook them."

"Do you see us?" Royce asked, craning his neck to see out the window, to see if he could spot the plane.

"Got you," Trey said. "You're two miles behind."

"Faster," Royce said to Mannis. He was not going to lose Jules a second time.

They were going so fast that had the three of them not been tightly packed in the back seat of the SUV, they'd have been bouncing around like Ping-Pong balls. Because nobody had taken the time to belt them in. And there was no way to brace themselves because their hands were still duct-taped in front of them.

She was in the middle with Charity on one side and Lou on the other. Shane drove and Sadie, who seemed almost manic now, would look forward, then whip her head in their direction as if to make sure they were still there.

"What's that? What's that plane?" she demanded, craning her neck to try to see out her closed window.

"Don't worry about it. He's been flying around all week," Shane said.

Then she looked at her watch. "I have got to make my flight. I need to be back in New York tomorrow. I'm on the hospital foundation board," she said brightly, looking at JC, "and we're planning our spring event."

She was crazy. There was no other explanation.

Lou leaned forward to get in her line of vision. "Well, when they ask you what you did in Vegas, make sure you tell them that you killed three innocent people."

Sadie's jaw tightened and her nostrils flared. "Shut up," she yelled, turning to face the front again. "Hurry," she said to Shane.

JC tapped Lou with her right knee and Charity with her left. Both girls gave her an imperceptible nod in response. They had a plan. They had agreed that their best window of escape would come when they were transported to the hole.

Once they were out of the vehicle, they were going to make it impossible for their captors to focus on all three of them at once. They were going to split up and then run, roll, crawl, whatever it took to try to get away. Shane had a gun but he'd already proved that he wasn't a great shot. They had to count on his poor aim.

Lou, who had danced from the time she was in kindergarten to high school, had said she intended to kick in Sadie's face. She'd said it calmly, like she didn't expect it to be any big deal.

You go, girl had been Charity's response.

All of them getting away successfully was a long shot, JC knew, but she wasn't going to make it easy for Sadie and her hired thugs. The girls had agreed that if any one of them could get away, they should take the chance and not worry about the others.

The vehicle crested the hill and slowed. "We're here," Shane said.

JC looked out the window. Here was the middle of the desert. The only thing besides sand and scraggly desert plants was a yellow tractor-like thing with a big bucket on the front next to a five-foot-high pile of dirt.

"Damn. A skid loader," she heard Lou whisper.

Striker, she assumed, was the man inside the cab. He was just waiting, with the bucket of his skid loader poised to push the pile of dirt and sand back into the hole.

The hole where they were going to be buried.

"They've stopped," Trey said. "Oh, holy hell," he said.

"What?" Royce yelled.

"There's a hole, man. A big hole."

"How far are we out?" Royce asked.

"I see them and I see you. You're a minute back. Tops."

He was not going to be sixty seconds too late. "Buzz them," he said.

He heard Trey say something in the background to Billy-Bob before he came back on the line. "Happy to oblige."

Shane opened the door on Charity's side; Sadie opened the one on Lou's side. JC had more confidence in Lou's ability to take care of Sadie than Charity's ability to take care of Shane. She slid out after her sister, who, God bless her, had put one foot on the ground while bringing her other knee up, headed in the direction of Shane's crotch.

She connected with a satisfying crunch. JC used the thirty pounds she had on Charity to propel her body out of the way. Then she brought her bound hands up, catching the stunned Shane, who was holding himself with one hand, in the nose with her clenched fist.

He let out a howl that almost drowned out the scuffle she heard on the other side of the vehicle. But then he swung the gun that he'd managed to keep hold of and pointed it in her face.

"Damn you," he yelled.

And she was sure he was going to shoot. "Run, Charity," she yelled.

The words were no more out of her mouth when the plane that had been in the air swooped down, coming dangerously low. It was enough to distract Shane for the second she needed. She bent low and tackled him, her shoulder into his middle. And then they were rolling in the rocky sand.

And she realized that she wasn't in the fight alone. Charity was there, kicking at Shane's head and face. She'd had the chance to run but she'd come back to help.

Energy roared through JC's body, giving her strength.

And then a gunshot, so close that it hurt her ears, boomed across the desert. But she didn't stop. She kept twisting and kicking and doing everything she could to keep Shane from containing her.

Until suddenly, it was over. And he was no longer there.

"Jules, honey. I've got you. It's okay."

She flopped onto her back. Royce was kneeling in the sand, pulling her into his arms, holding her tight.

"I've got you," he said again, crushing her against his chest. "It's over. You're okay."

She wasn't sure whether he was assuring her or himself. She blinked, trying to clear the sand and grit from her eyes.

Sadie was on the ground, blood pouring from her broken nose. Lou stood over her, a big grin on her face. Shane was standing, his hands on the roof of the SUV. Detective Mannis had his gun pointed at him.

There had to be at least six other cops, all of them with guns. One was on his phone, requesting medical assistance.

"I knew you would come," she said, her voice close to Royce's ear. "I knew you would find me."

He pulled back just a hair. "Honey, you probably didn't

need me. Remind me never to make you mad. You fight like a grizzly bear."

She saw Striker on the ground. His shirt was dark with blood. "What happened?" she asked.

Royce barely looked in the man's direction. "We arrived just as he was getting out of the skid loader cab with his rifle. So I shot him."

"From a moving vehicle?" she said, feeling very inappropriate laughter starting to build.

He stared at her, his hazel eyes intense. "I told you once. I'll do what I need to do."

She heard a noise and realized the plane that had buzzed them earlier was flying overhead. Quite deliberately, it dipped a wing.

"I need you to do one more thing, Royce Morgan," she said.

"What's that, Juliana Cambridge?" he asked.

"Marry me."

Epilogue

They were married a week later. It was a lopsided wedding party but nobody cared. Royce had three best men—Trey Riker, Rico Metez and Seth Pike. Her two attendants were Charity and Eileen Wood.

She wore her mother's wedding dress and Royce wore a black tux. The wedding and reception were both occurring at the Periwinkle, and Sonya Tribee was personally seeing to it that every detail was perfect. Charity was watching closely because she'd be starting in the Periwinkle kitchen the following week.

Barry Wood walked her down the aisle and before he handed her off to Royce, he shook Royce's hand and said, "Thank you."

"My pleasure," was Royce's response before he gently took her hand and drew her close.

Sadie Isman was in jail, likely never to be released. Wayne had his own set of legal troubles but was currently free on bond. Same for Shane and Striker Cary.

Her father had withdrawn from the Senate race. She'd invited him to the wedding but he'd declined, saying that he didn't want to intrude upon her happy day. In time, the relationship with his daughters might be healed. She and Charity were both willing to try.

She'd started the ball rolling on getting her office moved from New York to Vegas. Not everybody, just she and her assistant would work out of this location and travel to New York as necessary.

But first, there was a wedding to be had! She smiled at Royce.

"I love you," he said.

"I know," she whispered. "I love you, too."

Then they turned to face the minister.

* * * * *

Look for more books in Beverly Long's miniseries WINGMAN SECURITY, *coming soon, wherever Harlequin Romantic Suspense books are sold!*

And don't miss the books in her most recent miniseries, RETURN TO RAVESVILLE:

HIDDEN WITNESS
AGENT BRIDE
URGENT PURSUIT
DEEP SECRETS

Available now from Harlequin Intrigue!

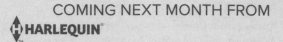

Get 2 Free Books,

Plus 2 Free Gifts—

just for trying the Reader Service!

HARLEQUIN®
ROMANTIC suspense

"Want to come in for a cup of coffee?" Jade asked.

If he went inside with her, he would have a hard time
tearing himself away and going home. "I have a meeting in
Odessa tomorrow. I have to leave early in the morning to
make it in time."

"On a weekend?" Jade asked.

"Unfortunately," Declan said.

The disappointment in her face was unmistakable.
"Another time, then."

Jade stepped out of the car and Declan followed her up
the steps to her front door. A gentleman walked his lady to
the door, a simple and kind gesture to ensure she was safe.

At the door, Jade turned.

"I'll ask again. Want to come in?" she said.

She turned and unlocked her door. Declan followed
her inside, pushing the door closed and locking it. He had
declined her offer, but he wanted to be with her. He should

keep a travel bag with him. It wasn't like the bed-and-breakfast was home. He was living on the road.

The air-conditioning cooled his skin, the humidity of the air disappearing inside the house. In a tangle of arms and legs, they stumbled to the couch. The couch was good. Better than the bedroom. Being in the bedroom would lead to one thing. As it was, this was inviting. Declan pivoted, pulling Jade on top of him.

He had several inches on her, but their bodies lined up, her softness fitting against him. The right friction and pressure made Declan want to peel her clothes away and finish this the right way. But he would wait.

She leaned over him, bracing a leg on the floor. Her hair swung to one side and he ran his fingers through it. Her blue-and-white dress was spread over them and lifting the fabric of the skirt ran through his mind.

Jade sat up. "Did you hear something?"

Declan shook his head. "Nothing." His heart was racing and his breath was fast.

"Like a creak on the porch. Like the wood shifting beneath someone's feet."

Worry speared him. Declan moved Jade off his lap and rolled to his feet. "I'll walk the perimeter and have a look."

Jade fisted his shirt in her hand, stopping him. "Maybe that's not a good idea. My mother has no compunction about killing or hurting people. I could be next. We could be next."

Don't miss
CAPTURING A COLTON by C.J. Miller,
available August 2017 wherever
Harlequin® Romantic Suspense books
and ebooks are sold.

www.Harlequin.com

LOVE
Harlequin
romance?

Join our Harlequin community to share your thoughts and connect with other romance readers!

Be the first to find out about promotions, news, and exclusive content!

Sign up for the Harlequin e-newsletter and download a free book from any series at **www.TryHarlequin.com**

CONNECT WITH US AT:

Harlequin.com/Community

Facebook.com/HarlequinBooks

Twitter.com/HarlequinBooks

Instagram.com/HarlequinBooks

Pinterest.com/HarlequinBooks

ReaderService.com

**ROMANCE WHEN
YOU NEED IT**

HSOCIAL2017

Reward the book lover in you!

Earn points from all your Harlequin book purchases from wherever you shop.

Turn your points into *FREE BOOKS* of your choice
OR
EXCLUSIVE GIFTS from your favorite authors or series.

Join for FREE today at
www.HarlequinMyRewards.com.

Harlequin My Rewards is a free program (no fees) without any commitments or obligations.

MYR17

THE WORLD IS BETTER WITH

Romance

Harlequin has everything from contemporary, passionate and heartwarming to suspenseful and inspirational stories.

Whatever your mood, we have a romance just for you!

Connect with us to find your next great read, special offers and more.

f /HarlequinBooks

@HarlequinBooks

www.HarlequinBlog.com

www.Harlequin.com/Newsletters